Praise for *Tart of Darkness*

"Once again, Denise Swanson demonstrates why her books are bestsellers. In *Tart of Darkness*, the first in her new Chef-to-Go Mysteries series, Swanson delightfully delivers murder, intrigue, and romance as she introduces us to Dani Sloan and a lively cast of supporting characters. Fast-paced and fun—as is Swanson's style—*Tart of Darkness* is utterly unput-downable. I cannot wait to revisit Dani's B&B in the next installment of what's sure to be a long-lived, well-loved series."

— Julie Hyzy, *New York Times* bestselling author

"The catering business offers plenty of opportunities for an amateur sleuth in a pleasant, if ordinary, series opener that will interest fans of the author's other works."

—*Library Journal*

"Fans of Joanne Fluke and Diane Mott Davidson will enjoy the cooking frame, the sympathetic characters, and the small-town setting."

—*Booklist*

"The first in a promising new series."

—*Kings River Life Magazine*

Praise for *Dead in the Water*

"Based on this delightful entry, this cozy series should have a long, bright future."

—*Publishers Weekly*

"It's a pleasure for Swanson's readers to welcome back her Scumble River characters, even though she throws them into danger from the first chapter to the last. A tornado, a corpse, and a kidnapping make life in Scumble River challenging for Skye Denison-Boyd as she awaits the birth of her first child, but fans of Swanson's series know she can handle it all. Swanson's strongly drawn characters and vivid descriptions make this welcome return of her Scumble River series a pleasure to read."

—Sheila Connolly, *New York Times* bestselling author of *Buried in a Bog*

"Rejoice, Scumble River fans! Skye and Wally and the whole gang are back—and Denise Swanson proves once again that she is among the top writers of the genre. With more twists and turns than a tornado—a real tornado!—*Dead in the Water* is fast-paced and fun, with a smart, savvy protagonist, some truly sinister villains, a suspenseful plot, and a delightfully satisfying ending. I can't wait to visit Scumble River again!"

—Kate Carlisle, *New York Times* bestselling author

"Denise Swanson is one of my favorite cozy mystery authors, and *Dead in the Water* is yet another hit from her. I love that Denise Swanson has remained true to the heart of the Scumble River characters and atmosphere in her reboot of the series. If you love quirky characters combined with a darned good cozy mystery, then don't hesitate to give *Dead in the Water* a try. You won't regret it!"

—*Fresh Fiction*

DIE Me a RIVER

RIVER

DENISE SWANSON

Published by Sourcebooks Landmark, an imprint of Sourcebooks, Inc.
P.O. Box 4410, Naperville, Illinois 60563-4410
(630) 961-3900
Fax: (630) 961-2168
sourcebooks.com

Printed and bound in Canada.
MBP 10 9 8 7 6 5 4 3 2 1

CHAPTER 1

Too Busy Thinking about My Baby

School psychologist Skye Denison-Boyd stopped pacing, tucked a stray curl into her messy bun, and plopped onto one of the chairs facing Homer Knapik's desk. She'd been waiting fifteen minutes, and the high school principal hadn't yet graced her with his presence.

Officially, Skye was on maternity leave for another two months, but between the frantic plea from her intern, Piper Townsend, and the incensed call from Homer, she'd agreed to come to the school for a meeting. It had taken her a couple of hours to arrange for a babysitter, pack up the twins' paraphernalia, and find something other than yoga pants that fit her post-pregnancy body.

Skye wasn't clear about the details of the actual problem—both parties had been too incoherent for her to understand their rambling—but from what she could gather, Homer was trying to slip something unethical past Piper. Doubtlessly, he was hoping that the intern's inexperience would allow him to play fast and loose with the rules and regulations governing public education.

Although Skye could have asked the co-op psychologist assigned to supervise Piper's internship during Skye's absence to handle the matter, she couldn't in good conscience turn her back on either of those women. Dealing with Homer was more of an art than a science, and expecting someone unfamiliar with his peculiarities to handle the situation would be heartless.

The Scumble River School District belonged to the Stanley County Special Education Cooperative, an entity that furnished the district with programs and personnel and managed the bureaucratic red tape of special education funding. However, the co-op's psychologist had never dealt with the likes of Homer, and Skye was afraid the woman would cut and run if the principal was his usual obnoxious self.

Then there was the poor intern who might just decide she'd chosen the wrong profession if Skye didn't help her navigate the rocky roads of Homer's fiefdom. Piper hadn't yet grasped that while the high school principal was indeed an agent of the devil, his duties were largely ceremonial.

Interrupting Skye's musings, the door banged opened and a gruff voice that scraped like a knife being sharpened at a grinding stone yelled, "It's about time you got here. Do you think I have all day to waste on this?"

Skye's skin crawled and she took a calming breath. Nothing would change Homer at this stage in his career—which, fingers crossed, was darn close to retirement. After working with him for nearly seven years, Skye's strategy was similar to the winners on her favorite reality TV show: outwit, outplay, outlast.

Pasting a cheery expression on her face, she crossed her ankles and then said, "I guess I could have brought the twins with me and breastfed them while we talked. I'm sure you wouldn't have minded helping me burp them." She gestured at his huge desk and added, "And that would probably make a pretty good changing table for their dirty diapers."

Homer glowered at Skye, stomped past her, and selected a long john from the box of doughnuts on the credenza. Next, he popped a pod into the Keurig and waited for it to brew. Once the coffee was finished, he grabbed the mug, moved to his massive leather chair, and eased his bulk onto the cushioned seat.

The principal's office was larger than many of the school's classrooms, and its furnishings were top of the line. How much of the school's budget had Homer appropriated for his grandiose display of power?

After taking a healthy gulp of the hot beverage, he said, "You wouldn't have had to come in at all if you would have just ordered Paisley to stop defying me and quit questioning my decisions."

"Piper," Skye corrected. "How many times do I have to tell you her name is Piper?"

"Who in the hell names their kid something like that?" Homer rolled his eyes. "Is her father the Pied Piper of Hamelin or something?"

"Really? At your age you've never heard of the actress Piper Laurie?" Skye raised her brows in question, but when Homer didn't respond, she said, "Whatever. It's a pretty name and it's hers, so remember it."

This was exactly why Skye and her husband, Wally, were having such a hard time selecting names for their twins. The babies were going on five weeks old, and they still hadn't agreed on what to call them—a fact that had made it very difficult to leave the hospital.

The nurses had driven Skye and Wally nuts trying to get them to choose names and fill out the paperwork. They'd practically had to sneak out of the place to take the babies home without naming them. Skye's mother, May, and Wally's father, Carson, weren't too happy with them either. But both Skye and Wally were adamant that they wouldn't rush into naming their babies. The names had to be perfect—just like the twins.

"Yeah. Right." Homer waved his hand as he reached for the phone and punched the intercom button. "Find Parker and have her report to my office PDQ."

"Piper," Skye reminded him again, her palm itching to slap him. "Or you could call her Ms. Townsend."

Homer ignored Skye as he ate his doughnut and

drank his coffee. She checked to see if she was drooling. She'd been in such a rush to get to the school she hadn't eaten lunch, and her daughter had managed to tip over Skye's bowl of cereal during breakfast.

When her stomach growled for the third time, she decided she no longer cared what Homer thought and said, "Thank you. Yes. I would like a pastry." She got to her feet and walked over to the credenza. "Coffee would be lovely, too." She sorted through the basket of pods until she found a decaf, then popped it into the machine and pushed the blinking button.

"Make yourself at home," Homer groused. "Should I get you a footstool?"

Before a snarky reply could leave Skye's lips, a petite young woman slipped into the room. Piper Townsend might have been twenty-five but she could have easily passed as a middle schooler.

Piper's youthful appearance had worried Skye when she'd originally interviewed her. She'd wondered if Piper might be intimidated by some of the larger high school boys. Now Skye realized that she should have been more concerned about the intern being bullied by the administration.

She glanced at Skye, then slid her gaze to Homer and said, "You asked for me, sir?"

"Don't act so damn coy." Homer narrowed his beady, little eyes. Considering the contrast to the size of his enormous head, they looked like raisins in a bowl of oatmeal. Or maybe poppy seeds in a block of suet.

"I'm not, sir." Piper edged toward one of the empty chairs, then sat down.

"You sure as hell weren't this sweet when you told me off in front of that parent," Homer bellowed, then turned his angry stare at Skye. "You need to teach her to be more respectful of administration."

"I'm sure Piper expressed her opinion in a courteous and professional manner." Skye took the remaining available seat and glanced at the intern. She might have been young and inexperienced, but so far, Skye had found her extremely sharp and good at her job. "Isn't that correct?"

"Absolutely." Piper nodded, her fingers nervously pleating the skirt of her gray suit. "I asked to speak to him in private, but he refused and I couldn't let him just send that poor woman away."

"It was none of your dang business," Homer sputtered. "You shouldn't have interfered. Now we'll never get rid of her or her brats."

"Brats!" Piper popped up from her chair, her ivory cheeks as pink as her ruffled blouse. She glared at Homer. "What kind of educator are you to call children that?"

"Okay, time to settle down." Skye tugged the young woman back into her seat and said, "Homer is going to tell us his perception of the incident and then you're going to tell us yours. And neither one of you is going to interrupt the other."

Skye shot them both a take-no-prisoners look,

then bit into her Bismarck and waited. When Homer remained silent, she motioned for him to begin.

"This woman comes waltzing in right when the first bell was ringing." Homer lumbered up from his desk and loomed over Skye. "She claimed her kids had gone to school here before, but I sure as hell didn't remember them, and Opal couldn't find any trace of them in our records."

Homer reminded Skye of the ogre in those animated movies. Not only because of his hulking movements or his size, but in her mind's eye, she could see his complexion turning a pale green when he was angry. His eyebrows drew a thick line across his protruding brow, random tufts poked from his ears like the cattails that grew along the ditches, and a dense pelt covered his arms and hands. Bunches even bristled from between the buttons of his shirt. If it weren't for the hair that enveloped him from head to foot, he could have played that part onstage.

Interrupting Skye's musings about Homer's appearance, Piper said, "Mrs. Brodsky explained that her oldest son was in eighth grade here in Scumble River starting in April of last year. Due to a family emergency out of state, she hadn't had a chance to register him for high school before the tornado destroyed the house she'd been renting. And since then, she's been trying to find a place to live, which is why they haven't been in school yet. But you refused to even call the junior high."

"Piper," Skye quickly interceded before Homer exploded. "Let Homer finish, then we'll hear your interpretation of the occurrence."

"As I was saying…" Homer shot a dismissive glance at the intern, then turned to Skye and continued. "I advised the woman that she should enroll her children in Brooklyn, where they are temporarily living in a motel, until their rental unit in Scumble River is repaired."

"You only told her that because she asked that her son be evaluated."

Homer swung his gigantic head in Piper's direction. "We're not paying a mint to test this kid when he doesn't even live in our district."

He leaned into the intern's space and gripped the arms of her chair, then chuckled when she shrank away from him.

Skye, her voice iced with fury, snapped, "Back off, Homer. You are dangerously close to a harassment lawsuit."

Snorting, Homer strolled back behind his desk, then, as if there had been no interruption, he said, "And the cherry on the cake is that this woman has two other children who will be sucking up our resources. And"—his mouth puckered as if he wanted to spit—"she wants us to provide transportation."

After a long beat of silence, Skye licked the sugar from her fingers and asked, "Are you finished, Homer?"

"The matter is settled." He sat down, leaned back,

and laced his fingers over his stomach. "I don't know why we're even talking about it."

"Piper?" Skye nodded at the intern, noticing that the young woman had pulled out an iPad from her bag and was tapping away on it.

Piper straightened her suit jacket and said, "Mrs. Brodsky came into the school at approximately 7:51 a.m. I was at the front desk giving Opal the passes to hand out to the students I planned to work with this morning." Piper glanced up and Skye nodded for her to continue. "Mrs. Brodsky and I began to chat, and she shared her concern about her son's lack of progress last year. I offered to review his file and talk to his previous teachers. She agreed, then requested a registration form. As she filled it out, she mentioned that due to the tornado destroying her rental, she was living in Brooklyn and asked about transportation. Mr. Knapik was summoned."

"No one summons me," Homer informed them loftily. "Opal alerted me to the situation and I came out to deal with the quagmire Pepper had stirred up."

"Her name is Piper." Skye glowered at him, then added, "Let her finish her report."

"Once Mr. Knapik informed Mrs. Brodsky that her children should enroll in the town where she was living, I attempted to speak to him in private, but he refused." Piper's description of the incident fell off her tongue in a rush of words. "I then advised him that according to the McKinney-Vento Homeless

Education Assistance Act, the Brodsky children had every right to attend Scumble River schools."

"Anything else?" Skye took a sip of her coffee and waited for the bombshell she knew was about to drop. She wouldn't have been called in if something more dramatic hadn't happened.

"Mr. Knapik stated that I didn't know what I was talking about, then told Opal not to accept the registration form and returned to his office."

"And?" Skye stifled a yawn. It wasn't that she was bored, but the twins never slept more than three or four hours at a time, and last night it had been more like two.

"Mrs. Brodsky was upset and said that she would be seeking legal counsel." Piper's professional facade slipped a tiny bit, and Skye saw a glimmer of spite in the young woman's blue eyes as she flicked a sly glance in Homer's direction. "I suggested that she check out the new law office that just opened in town."

"You mean my sister-in-law's?" Skye hid a smile. Loretta would love this case.

"Can you believe this idiot helped a parent in her quest to sue us?" Homer's face turned an alarming shade of purple and he pounded on the desktop. "I want you to get rid of her right now. She's a menace."

"No." Skye stared coolly at Homer. "Piper acted in an ethical manner." She glanced at the young woman. "Although, I suggest in the future that you not recommend specific attorneys."

"Well, I don't want this moron in my school," Homer bellowed.

Piper paled and she sat with her mouth half-open as if she were trying to respond but couldn't find the words.

Skye patted the intern's hand, then, with a chilling smile, turned to Homer and said, "In that case, you'll be out of compliance." She tapped the top of his desk. "And you'll get into trouble at your next compliance review. Should we call the superintendent and get his opinion?"

"I'll get the co-op psychologist to come in and do *your* job until you stop playing around at being a mommy and come back to work." Homer's voice oozed smugness.

Skye ignored his dig and asked calmly, "Do you have the budget to cover the cost of contracting with the co-op for additional services?"

"Fine." Homer's bottom lip pooched out as if he were going to start crying, and Skye wondered if she had one of the twin's pacifiers in her purse. "But if Peeper here screws up again, she's gone."

"Piper did not screw up." Skye turned to the intern, smiled reassuringly, and said, "Since we've settled this, why don't you get back to work, and I'll stop to say goodbye once Homer and I are through."

"Thanks." With a nervous glance toward Homer, Piper hurried from the room, her low-heeled pumps clicking on the hardwood floor.

Once the intern was gone, Homer sank back into his chair, put his arms behind his head, and gloated. "Well, that went well."

Skye blinked at him. After every meeting with Homer, when he acted like a toddler, she always wanted to ask him *Who ties your shoelaces for you?* So far, she'd resisted, but she could tell the day was coming.

Giving herself a moment to find her happy place before informing the principal that this issue needed to be resolved fully before she left, Skye got up, selected a cruller from the box, and placed it on a napkin. She'd been trying to avoid sugary treats since she'd been breastfeeding, but she was starving and Homer didn't have anything healthy to eat.

"What?" Homer's tone was belligerent, but his expression was apprehensive.

"Just because you're tired of thinking doesn't mean we've come to any workable conclusion." Cruller in hand, Skye resumed her seat. "Mrs. Brodsky isn't going to go away."

"So this McKinney-Veto thing is true?" Homer shook his head. "What next? Every brat gets his or her own personal tutor?"

"I hadn't thought about the McKinney-Vento Homeless Education Assistance Act being relevant to students who had been displaced by the tornado, but I do believe Piper is correct." Skye took a sip of coffee, then continued, "You should check with the school's lawyer, but my understanding is that the act ensures homeless children transportation to and from school free of charge and allows children to attend the last school in which they were enrolled regardless of what district the family resides in at present."

"That's a load of crap," Homer squawked. Then, with a cunning look in his eye, he said, "This Brodsky woman didn't have any records, not even immunization. Can't we deny her kids enrollment on that basis?"

"Nope." Skye was beginning to miss the twins' crying. At least when they fussed, it was usually for a good reason. They were either hungry or needed their diapers changed. She wondered if Homer had pooped his pants and that's why he was so contrary. "I'm pretty sure lack of normally required documents is covered in the act."

Homer pointed at Skye. "Why have I never heard of this before?"

"I guess Scumble River never had any homeless families before the tornado." Skye pursed her lips. "Although, now that I think of it, I doubt that's true. But we were never aware of their presence."

"Maybe this Brodsky woman will just go away." Homer tucked his chin into his chest. "Brooklyn has a perfectly good school district. Why would she want her kids to have to ride a bus over here?"

"My guess is—" Skye was momentarily distracted by the faraway wail of a siren but refocused and continued. "It's because she doesn't want them to have to change schools when she gets back into her rental."

"For crying out loud. Who writes these kinds of laws?" He huffed, "I just don't get it."

"There's nothing to get. It's the law." Skye's hold on her temper slipped. "I can explain it to you, but I can't understand it for you."

"What... You..." Homer sputtered.

Homer's dazed expression was worth the crow she'd have to eat once he had time to recover from the shock and demanded an apology. But for now, Skye finished her pastry and wiped her fingers on the napkin.

Finally, she said, "My advice to you is to contact her and make her and her children feel welcome before she gets in touch with my sister-in-law. Loretta's already bored with wills and estate planning, and she would love to handle a case like this. The district could end up building Mrs. Brodsky a home if Loretta really gets her teeth into the matter."

"Shit!" Homer's shoulders slumped. "What is it about your family that has it in for me?"

Skye tilted her head in confusion. "I have no idea what you're talking about."

"Your husband refused to do anything about that insurance idiot who is determined to rob me blind. And your mother won't put me through on the phone to him anymore," Homer snarled. "She claims he's not available."

"I'm sure that's true." Skye's husband, Wally, was the chief of police and her mother, May Denison, worked as a dispatcher for the police department.

"With the aftermath from the tornadoes, Wally is extremely busy."

"Who isn't?" Homer pasted an abused expression on his face. "You know, my property was damaged in the tornado, too."

"I hadn't heard that." Skye rose and edged toward the door. "What a shame."

She needed to get going. She had to pick up the twins from her mother's before three thirty so her mom could go to work.

"No one cares that I have problems, too," Homer whined. "How about my rights?"

"Listen, just get in touch with the school's lawyer, and if he agrees with what I've said, contact Mrs. Brodsky ASAP and enroll her son tomorrow."

"But—"

"Gotta go." Ignoring Homer's attempt to thrust those duties onto her, Skye stepped across the office threshold. She kept moving as she called over her shoulder, "See you after winter break."

As she hurried down the hall, she heard Homer yelling for Opal to get someone named Paige Myler on the phone and find out why she was late for their appointment. Skye didn't recognize that name, and normally she would have been curious since she had at least a passing familiarity with most Scumble Riverites. But not today.

Today, she was in a hurry, so without pausing to see who might be the unlucky recipient of Homer's call, Skye fled down the hallway. She was intent on finding Piper and soothing the young woman's ruffled feathers before she decided she could wait another year to complete her internship if it meant not having to work with Homer.

CHAPTER 2

Don't Worry, Baby

S KYE EXPERIENCED A WEIRD DISTORTION OF THE space-time continuum when she approached her office. Although she'd been on maternity leave for six weeks, it almost seemed as if she'd never been away, but also as if she'd been gone for years.

She inhaled deeply, taking in the familiar odors of sweat socks and heavy-duty cleansers. Blinking back a tear, she cursed her raging hormones. She was exhilarated one minute but blubbering the next. Poor Wally never knew if he would be coming home to the lady or the tiger.

With classes in session, the only sound in the hallway was the distant murmuring of a teacher's voice and the whirring of a power tool from the technology education room, or as everyone still called it, "shop."

After reaching her office, Skye tapped on the door. Knocking seemed strange, but although she'd always felt a certain possessiveness for this space, she now shared it with Piper. Her overprotectiveness was probably because there was no other area in the school for her to work, so she was always fearful of losing such valuable real estate.

She'd wrested the small office away from the boys' PE teacher/guidance counselor a few years ago after pointing out that he already had a private office in the gym complex while she had to beg, borrow, or steal a closet or cubbyhole to evaluate or counsel students. The man hadn't been happy to relinquish the space and Skye was on the alert for his counterattack.

It was downright disrespectful to her and the profession of school psychology that she'd had to battle for a ten-by-ten room with no windows. And she'd only been able to cover the ugly shade of greenish-yellow that had been on the walls for the past fifty years by buying the paint herself and sweet-talking the crews who had been repairing tornado damage at the schools into giving her office a quick once-over with their rollers.

The new, soothing blue color had helped a lot, but the uncovered fluorescent tubes in the overhead lights still cast a sallow tinge over the discarded furniture that she'd managed to forage. Scavenging a second desk and chair for Piper had been one of Skye's last acts before going on leave.

Her own old leather chair and scratched wooden desk had been discarded by someone with a budget to upgrade to nicer things. She'd scored the battered trapezoidal table, two folding chairs, wooden file cabinet, and the metal bookshelves that held her test kits from the basement's junk pile.

Still, despite their origins and less-than-pristine condition, Skye was grateful to have every piece. Even secondhand, the furnishings and office were better than anything she had at either the grade school or the junior high, where her assigned spaces were both the size of refrigerator boxes.

There had been no answer to her knock, so Skye unlocked the door and stepped inside. Piper wasn't there and Skye frowned. She'd have to hunt down the intern, but first, she'd give her mom a call and make sure her babies were okay. This was the longest she'd left them since coming home from the hospital and her arms felt empty without them.

May answered on the first ring and assured her that the twins were having a good time in their bouncy seats. She also informed Skye that she was in no hurry for them to be picked up. Just as she was saying goodbye to her mother, Piper burst through the door.

The young woman skidded to a stop when she saw Skye, put her hand to her chest, and said, "You scared me. Since I always lock the door, I wasn't expecting anyone to be in here."

"Sorry." Skye smiled. "I wanted to reiterate that you did exactly the right thing and make sure you were okay after our meeting with Homer."

"Thank you." Piper unbuttoned her suit jacket, then squeezed past Skye to her desk. She sat down, her spine as straight as a ruler. "But you were correct in saying that I shouldn't have mentioned your sister-in-law's law firm. It was just that, by then, Mr. Knapik was on my last nerve and I blurted it out."

"Homer does have a talent for that." Skye chuckled. "And swallowing all the things you want to say but shouldn't takes practice. All in all, you did really, really well holding your tongue."

"How do you manage to stay so calm when he starts ranting and raving like that?" Piper tucked a flyaway strand of hair behind her ear.

Skye chuckled. "I may look cool and collected, but in my mind, I usually have killed Homer at least three times per meeting."

Piper's jaw dropped, then she giggled. "You have to teach me that."

"My best advice is to get a mirror and practice maintaining a blank expression," Skye suggested. "It really helps when Homer is especially long winded."

"You mean abundantly verbal?" Piper's lips twitched.

"It sounds as if you've figured out the way we slip stuff like that in our reports." Skye laughed, then asked, "Other than Homer, how's it going?"

"Good." Piper picked up her iPad and swiped the screen. "I'm on schedule for the reevals and the initials." She snickered and Skye raised a brow. "The girl I was testing this morning was a hoot. After I explained why I was assessing her, she asked, 'If you're cross-eyed *and* dyslexic, does that cancel out your problem with reading?'"

When the two women stopped snickering, Skye asked, "Is the co-op psych checking on you every couple of days to answer any questions that have come up?"

"Absolutely." Piper tapped her iPad and turned it toward Skye. "I'm keeping notes on all our conversations right here."

"Great." Skye was impressed by the young woman's organizational abilities, which were an important skill in a school psych. "I'm glad you called me about the issue with Mrs. Brodsky. With something that's district specific, it's best to let me handle the matter."

"I hated to bother you, but from everything you've told me, I figured it was best." Piper grinned. "Better now than to come back to a lawsuit after your maternity leave is up."

"Exactly." Skye stood, moved toward the door, and waved goodbye. "See you in a couple of months."

Skye's next stop was the school's multimedia center, a.k.a. the library. She wanted to stop by and say hello to her friend Trixie Frayne. The dismissal bell had rung while she and Piper were talking, so she wasn't sure Trixie would be there, but it was the best place to start her search.

In addition to being the high school librarian, Trixie also cosponsored the school newspaper with Skye, coached the cheerleading squad, and had recently started a community service club to promote volunteerism among the teenagers. It exhausted Skye just to think of being responsible for all those extra-curricular duties, but Trixie thrived on the constant vortex of activities.

As Skye approached the multimedia center's entrance, an attractive woman in her mid- to late thirties brushed past her. She ignored Skye's "excuse me" and marched away as if Skye hadn't spoken.

The woman wore a blush-hued asymmetrical blazer with a plunging V-neck and perfectly tailored black wool slacks. Although Skye had drooled over that outfit in a fashion magazine, she'd known she'd never own it. The Cushnie et Ochs blazer alone had retailed at $1,700 and the largest size available was a six.

Turning to watch the woman sashay down the hall, her stilettos clicking on the worn linoleum, Skye wondered if she was a parent of one of their students. She certainly wasn't a staff member dressed like that.

Once the woman was out of sight, Skye walked into the library. The room was lined with bookshelves, and the middle of the space contained an assortment of tables, chairs, and study carrels. There was no one around, but she could hear Mark Chesnutt singing "I Want My Baby Back" from the rear.

Skye shook her head. It seemed like after giving birth every song she heard had *baby* in the lyrics. Was God trying to tell her something, like she should stay home with the twins instead of returning to work? Or was it that all she could think about was babies and only noticed songs with that word in them? Shrugging, she headed toward the workroom.

Stepping inside, the comforting smell of coffee and homemade baked goods wafted over Skye. She and Trixie had spent many afternoons working on various school projects in this little space.

When Trixie spotted Skye, she sprang from her stool and grabbed Skye for a hug. "What are you doing here? You're not coming back to work yet, are you?"

"Not a chance. I'm taking every single day they give me." Skye returned her friend's embrace and explained the mess that Homer had created.

"What a schmuck." Trixie screwed up her pixie-like features.

She punched the Off button on the MP3 player parked in the dock on the counter. Mark Chestnut's tenor was cut off mid-word as the speakers went silent.

"Don't get me started on Homer." Skye gestured to the papers spread across the worktable. "What's all this? I thought you finished your book and were sending queries to agents. You aren't tweaking it again, are you?"

Trixie had been working on a mystery novel for several years, and every time she declared it finished, the next day she started another round of revisions.

"Nope." Trixie blanched and plopped back on her stool. "Are you saying you think I should?"

"Never." Skye patted her friend's shoulder. "It's

wonderful. Certainly better than anything that author who's always on the television commercials has written in years. And he's a huge mega-bestseller."

"Yeah." Trixie's brown eyes sparkled. "It is good, isn't it?"

"Brilliant. Now start sending out queries to agents," Skye ordered as she took a seat on an empty stool and prepared for a nice chat.

"I'm working up the courage." Trixie refused to meet Skye's stare.

"Fine." Skye wasn't going to nag her friend. Instead, she asked, "How's everything with you?"

Once they'd exchanged news on their families and talked a bit about the babies, Trixie brought Skye up-to-date on what was happening with the school newspaper. "Paige has been a huge help with the newspaper."

When Frannie Ryan and her boyfriend, Justin Boward, had gone off to college, Skye had wondered if they'd ever find as good an editor as they had been. But Paige Vitale was a great writer and extremely good at encouraging the other students while improving their skills.

Skye paused. The mention of Paige Vitale reminded her of Homer bellowing for Opal to get a woman named Paige Myler on the phone. Another twinge of curiosity pinged through Skye, but she resisted. She was trying to be less nosy and keep out of trouble more.

Turning her attention back to the conversation, Skye said, "Paige is a smart girl."

"That she is." Trixie beamed. "She's also kind and thoughtful."

She smiled, thinking of the dynamic senior. Like her idol, Trixie, Paige seemed to be involved in everything and enjoyed the hectic pace.

"I'm relieved that you have such a great student editor for the paper since I sort of left you in the lurch during my maternity leave."

"I told you not to worry about that." Trixie waved off Skye's concern. "I've got everything under control, and Paige has come up with a terrific story angle. She's investigating some of the con artists who have moved into the area and are taking advantage of the tornado victims. You would not believe what's happening."

"She should talk to Homer." Skye tapped her fingers on the countertop. "He mentioned that he'd had a tornado-related problem."

"That might not be a good idea." Trixie suddenly became fascinated with the layers of her short chiffon skirt and refused to look at Skye.

"Why is that?" Skye narrowed her eyes. Her friend was up to something.

"Homer might have forbidden the newspaper from doing any stories on the tornado."

"He can't control content." Skye wrinkled her nose. "Unless it's indecent."

"Which is why I'm ignoring him." Trixie crossed

her arms. "Since he never reads the student newspaper, so far, it hasn't been a problem."

"Better you than me, girlfriend," Skye teased. "I have enough trouble with Sasquatch dealing with the special ed rules and regs without having to wrestle with him over the First Amendment."

"I don't wrestle with him." Trixie made a haughty face. "I do what I darned well please and apologize if I get caught." She shrugged. "At least that's what I do since I got tenure a couple years ago."

"Lucky you." Skye scowled. "Tenure isn't a possibility for me."

"Like you have to worry," Trixie said. "The grade school and junior high principals love you, your godfather is head of the school board, and there aren't a ton of candidates eager for your job."

"That's been true so far." Skye pursed her lips. "But Piper might decide she likes it here."

"I doubt your intern is going to try to oust you." Trixie giggled. "Not after her recent set-to with Homer. Besides..." Trixie hesitated, then said, "Are you even sure you want to come back?"

"Of course I'm coming back to work," Skye said without thinking.

Then an image of the twins flashed through her mind. It wasn't as if she and Wally needed her salary. She could be a stay-at-home mom. She did have a lot on her plate between her two babies and building a new house. Maybe she should consider at least taking an extended unpaid leave.

"What are you thinking?" Trixie demanded. "You have a funny look on your face."

"Nothing." Skye shook her head emphatically. "Just wondering if I had time to stop at the pharmacy before I pick up the twins."

"You know," Trixie continued as if reading Skye's mind, "if Piper was interested in staying on here, maybe you could work part-time."

"The district barely thinks they need one psychologist. What gives you the idea that they'd go for one and a half?" Skye scoffed.

"How do you know? They might." Trixie wagged her finger in front of Skye's face. "Until you ask for what you want, you have no idea what you can get."

"Piper would have to choose to stay here. The board would have to be willing to spend money on students' needs that don't involve sports or busing. And…" Skye squirmed on her stool, unwilling to admit that she was intrigued with the idea. "And there are too many ifs in that equation to even consider at this point."

"Fine." Trixie's smile was smug. "So what was the reaction to the *Star*'s front-page story about Wally's dad and his gazillions of dollars?"

In the years he had lived and worked in Scumble River, Wally had concealed the fact that his father, Carson Boyd, was a Texas oil billionaire. Due to

Carson's generosity in helping the community recover from the tornado, and also since it was just getting harder and harder to hide his family's wealth thanks to the internet, Wally had decided to reveal his background.

Skye had suggested the best way to tell the town was via an interview by the owner and editor of the local newspaper, Kathryn Steele. Kathryn had been thrilled and done a wonderful job on the piece. Before the article had been published, Skye and Wally told her close family members and their friends, so none of them would be blindsided. Some had taken the news better than others.

"Most folks were cool about it, at least to our faces." Skye shrugged. "Unfortunately, there were more than a few who immediately asked for 'donations' and loans. One guy wanted Wally to finance his new prosthesis, but a little investigation showed that he had two good legs. And then there are the women who proposition him."

"Yikes!" Trixie yelped. "He was already too much of a hunk for his own good."

"Yep." Skye rubbed her temples. "Of course, my uncle Dante wanted a handout."

"Seriously?" Trixie screeched. "After the dirty tricks he's pulled with the police department and then almost getting Wally killed?"

"Dante's got the long-term memory of a squirrel." Skye snickered. "He is forever forgetting which of the acorns he buried were rotten."

When Trixie finished laughing, she said, "Well, you had to let that cat out of the bag. Carson has practically bought out Babies'R'Us."

"True. We actually had to put up a temporary shed to store it all." Skye made a face. "I'm grateful for the luxury RV Carson got us to live in after the tornado blew down our house, but it is way too small for us *and* two babies *and* all their paraphernalia."

"So I saw last time I visited. I could barely get inside the door," Trixie said.

"On the bright side, now that we're not hiding his net worth anymore, I don't have to worry so much about what people will think of the house we're building." She smiled. "I was afraid they'd come to the conclusion that Wally was a corrupt cop."

"How's the house going?" Trixie asked. "Have they finished framing yet?"

"Finally." Skye blew a curl out of her eyes. "Now if Wally and I can just decide on the million details that come up every single day."

"Owen and I would never come to an agreement," Trixie said. "Thank goodness our house only lost its roof and had some siding damage." She sighed. "But Owen's truck was totaled and the barn is completely gone. A lot of trees had to be removed as well."

Skye recalled that she'd seen Owen driving Trixie's car and asked, "Are you getting a new truck for him?"

"Well..." Trixie's eyes twinkled with mischief. "That would be a good trade..."

"You are so not funny." Skye whacked her friend's arm, then glanced at the papers scattered across the counter. She'd noticed them when she first arrived, but hadn't seen what they were. Now she frowned and asked, "Are these insurance forms?"

"Yeppers." Trixie tried to sound cheerful, but Skye wasn't fooled.

"I thought you turned those in right after the tornado."

"We did." Trixie studied the buttons on her denim shirt.

"So why are you doing them again?" Skye asked, reaching for one of the pages.

"The insurance company keeps returning them marked as incomplete." Trixie growled. "In fact, the special investigator that they brought in to handle all of their rejected claims just dropped off this new set before you got here."

"That doesn't seem right. Our insurance rep practically did the paperwork for us." Skye pursed her lips again. "Who are you with?"

"Homestead." Trixie blew out a long breath. "A lot of folks in Scumble River who are insured by them are talking about suing the company. It's starting to look like we might have to do that, too. But an attorney is so expensive, and I hate the idea of getting into a long, drawn-out legal battle. Lawyers are the only ones who come out ahead on those."

"Maybe you could join together for a class action

suit," Skye suggested, making a mental note to talk to her sister-in-law about that possibility. "Suing has got to be cheaper as a group."

"What we really need is for the person who keeps denying all of the Scumble River tornado claims to disappear. And someone with a heart to take her place." Trixie bared her teeth. "She is determined to prevent every one of us from collecting any money."

CHAPTER 3

Don't Say Nothin'
(Bad about My Baby)

CHIEF OF POLICE WALLY BOYD BARELY STOPPED himself from cringing as Scumble River's mayor Dante Leofanti thumped him on the shoulder and said, "Your department has been doing an excellent job. Keep it up."

Watching Hizzoner's penguin-like bulk waddle away, Wally wasn't sure which was worse, the mayor's previous antagonistic behavior and open contempt for the police department or his new buddy-buddy attitude.

Still reeling from Dante's jovial pat on the back, Wally only half listened as Zelda Martinez gave him the highlights of her shift. She was the PD's youngest and only female officer, and by far the most enthusiastic.

Wally zoned back in as Martinez reached the end of her report and said, "I'm concerned about the new fairy godmother in town. Forget swindlers claiming to fix folk's roofs when they only slap on a few shingles.

She's taken exploiting people's gullibility to a whole new level."

"Son of a bit…biscuit!" Now that he was a father, Wally had vowed to stop swearing, but it wasn't easy to change a lifetime of behavior at his age. Especially when one of his staff obviously thought that Scumble River had somehow transformed into Once Upon a Time Land.

"Sir?" Martinez quirked a dark eyebrow, plainly confused by Wally's choice of expletive.

Once the town had settled down and began rebuilding after the tornadoes that had leveled a good part of the community last summer, Wally had known the scammers would move in. However, he had severely underestimated the sheer number of con artists and their jaw-dropping deviousness.

The police department was receiving ten or more calls a day from citizens complaining that they'd been defrauded by fake repairmen, phony debris removal companies, and double-dealing insurance appraisers.

Nonetheless, this fairy-tale thing was a new twist from the grifters, one the Scumble River PD was ill equipped to handle.

With only seven full-time officers, including Wally, it was difficult to catch the con artists in the act. And someone pretending to work magic would be even slipperier than the other kinds.

Wally had hoped that the promotion of Anthony Anserello from part-time to full-time officer would ease the burden on the rest of his team. But except for the day shift, when there was someone patrolling the streets while Wally worked in the office, there was still usually only one cop on duty at a time.

There were no two ways about it. They needed additional staff. Too bad that wouldn't happen anytime soon. It had taken a certain amount of blackmail to squeeze Anthony's increased hours out of the city council, and even now with the revelation of Carson's wealth, which had resulted in Dante becoming Wally's new best friend, the PD budget was frozen solid.

Realizing Martinez was still waiting for him to respond to her report, Wally refocused and said carefully, "So you're telling me there's a woman in town who is claiming to be a fairy godmother?"

"Yes." Martinez's voice was brisk. Glancing down at the open notebook in her hand, she stated, "Ms. Millicent Rose purchased the former Young at Heart Photography building six weeks ago. Today, she had it painted pink and hung a sign reading 'Enchanted Cottage.'"

"Okay." Wally inhaled deeply, catching the combined odors of stale coffee and disinfectant. "Has she done anything illegal?"

"Before I went out on patrol, I checked the city hall records." The young officer smoothed her dark-brown hair. She wore it in a tight bun at the nape of her neck and Wally had never seen a strand out of place. "Ms. Rose doesn't have a business license."

Martinez's face was bare of makeup and her tone clipped and professional. Wally noted that the only bit of femininity she allowed herself was her professionally manicured, bright-red fingernails. He should ask Skye if that meant anything. As a psychologist, his wife was great at helping him interpret the subtle clues that most people missed.

"What's she peddling?" Wally tapped his desktop. "Does she offer to tell your fortune? Read your palm? Perform a séance to talk to your dearly departed?"

"None of that." Martinez narrowed her dark eyes. "In fact, she maintains she isn't selling anything. And that's why she doesn't need a permit."

"So you spoke to her?" Wally quirked a brow at his employee.

"Yes. I stopped by to make sure she was aware of the police presence in town. Would you believe she wears this ridiculous blue cape with a pointy hood that she fastens with a big, pink bow?"

"After twenty plus years in law enforcement, I believe just about anything." Wally rolled his eyes.

"Right." Martinez straightened her spine and her voice sharpened to a razor's edge. "I also mentioned the PD's deep-seated interest in protecting the citizens of our small community."

"I see." Wally frowned. Martinez was eager to prove herself. He normally approved of her zeal but needed to keep an eye on her fervor. "So, what *is* it she's doing that has you wound up?"

"This Rose woman claims she can grant wishes," Martinez snorted.

"Does she charge for these wishes?" Wally kept his tone even, but blew out an exasperated breath. He hated perps who took advantage of other people's naïveté.

"She claims that she doesn't." Zelda's eyes were now so narrow Wally wondered how she could see out of them. "But you know she must. She probably just convinces her marks that they are giving her a donation or an offering."

"I assume that it's too soon for anyone to have filled out a complaint yet," Wally said, wondering if this was just a case of the rookie's eagerness to prove herself, or if she had a personal stake in the matter.

"Yep." Martinez fingered the crease in her immaculately pressed uniform pants. "But even though she just hung out her sign, she's been in business for a while and I'm hearing rumbling that odd things are happening."

"Like what?" The hair on the back of Wally's neck rose.

He quickly pulled a legal pad from his drawer and picked up a pen. Skye had bought him an iPad for his birthday, but he thought better when he wrote things down on paper.

"Someone saw Tomi Jackson go into what is now the Enchanted Cottage, and the next day, it was all over town that she'd sold the Feed Bag property."

Tomi's restaurant had been completely destroyed

in the tornado and she'd decided to retire rather than to rebuild. Although the lot where the Feed Bag had stood was in a prime commercial spot, she'd been having trouble finding a buyer, mostly because she only wanted to sell to someone who promised to open a new restaurant in the location. Since eateries were a notoriously high-risk business, no one wanted to invest in such a dicey enterprise.

"Anything else?" Wally's instincts relaxed, and he fought to keep the amusement out of his voice. Rookie officers often saw coincidences as evidence of something more.

"Belle Whitney, the school district speech therapist, was seen having coffee with Ms. Rose at Tales and Treats. Ever since Belle caught her husband cheating on her with their landscaper, she's been vowing revenge." Martinez adjusted her badge on her uniform shirt. "Last night, Mr. Whitney was pulled over by a Stanley County sheriff's deputy and found to be driving under the influence with a carload of counterfeit designer handbags."

"All that is interesting," Wally said, slowly processing the information. "But certainly nothing to do with our police department."

He was quiet for several seconds, listening to the ticking of the clock on his office wall. It was nearly five. He'd been off duty for an hour. It was time to wrap things up and get home. He and Skye had an appointment with Father Burns to talk about the babies' baptisms at seven and he'd already rescheduled it twice.

"That may be true." Martinez broke the silence, glancing at him from the corner of her eye. "However, the incident that worries me most is what happened to my friend, Farrah Miles."

"Oh?" Wally kept his response short, hoping to hurry Martinez along.

"Farrah had a baby about three months before the tornado. She isn't married to the father, and Grady pretty much walked away when she told him she was pregnant. However, the jerk's mother, Sorcha Nelson, decided she wanted to adopt her grandson and she's been making Farrah's life miserable trying to gain custody of the infant."

"And?" Wally frowned, not at all happy about where this story seemed to be going.

"After a visit to Ms. Rose by Sorcha, Farrah's baby stopped eating and became lethargic. His four-month exam was scheduled for the end of the week, and when the pediatrician couldn't find anything wrong with him, he called the Department of Children and Family Services." Martinez paused. "The doc decided that Farrah was neglecting her son."

"What happened?" Wally's gut tightened.

"Once the baby was in foster care, he started eating and recovered." Martinez shook her head. "Sorcha immediately filed for custody."

A flicker of fear swept through Wally's chest at

the thought that this so-called fairy godmother might have harmed a baby, but he pushed it away and said, "Any chance your friend really wasn't taking adequate care of her son?"

"Well, Farrah is a bit overwhelmed," Martinez admitted. "But he was fine until Grandma Dearest paid a visit to Ms. Rose."

"Unfortunately, unless you can prove either Ms. Rose or the grandmother did something to make the baby ill, it isn't a police matter." Wally paused, then added, "But keep an eye on the Enchanted Cottage."

"I plan to." Martinez gave him a sly look. "I just wanted your approval."

"Fine." Admiration at the young woman's methods forced Wally's lips to twitch.

"Anything else you want me to do before I leave?"

"Nope." Wally shook his head. "Have a good night. See you tomorrow."

"Thanks, Chief." Martinez rose and walked toward the door. "You too."

Once the young officer was gone, Wally buzzed dispatch to say that he was leaving, pushed back from his desk, and stood. It was past time to go home. If there was one thing getting married and becoming a father had taught him, it was not to confuse his career with his life.

After checking that he had his portable radio, he turned off the lights and stepped into the hallway, locking the door behind him. As he ran down the stairs, he decided to stop and pick up some flowers for his wife. He'd been putting in a lot of hours, and even though she was caring for two babies, mostly on her own, while living in the relatively small space of a motor home, Skye never complained.

Although she was employed by the police department as a part-time psychological consultant and understood the demands of the job, she still deserved a treat. And Skye adored white roses.

Heading toward the police station's attached garage, Wally remembered that he needed to talk to his mother-in-law, May Denison, who was the afternoon dispatcher. And he didn't want to telephone her from home later and have Skye overhear their conversation. Abruptly, he turned on his heel and hurried to the front of the building.

When Wally walked into the dispatch area, May looked away from the computer screen and said, "I thought you had already left."

At sixty-three, his mother-in-law had the energy of a twenty-five-year-old. She kept her house immaculate, exercised at a nearby community's fitness center three times a week, and worked the afternoon shift at the PD as a police, fire, and emergency dispatcher. May's only fault was her meddling in her children's lives.

Now that both Skye and her brother, Vince, had provided her with grandchildren, her interference had only gotten worse. And between Skye unexpectedly having twins and Loretta's unplanned second pregnancy, May was in grandmotherly heaven. Sadly, her daughter and daughter-in-law were bearing the brunt of May's intense need to nurture.

This made what Wally wanted to talk to May about a little awkward. His wife wouldn't be happy that he was siccing her mom on her, but trying to arrange the twins' christening party was overwhelming Skye and she needed help.

"I was on my way out." Wally cleared his throat. "But then I remembered that I wanted to ask you for a favor."

"Sure." May brightened. "Did you know that I got to watch the twins for a few hours today? Those babies are so cute they could do commercials."

"Not happening." Wally scowled. "And yes, Skye texted me that she had to go into work for a while."

"Have you two decided on names for my precious grandchildren yet?" May's short, salt-and-pepper hair seemed to be bristling with her displeasure. "The baptism is less than a week away."

"Almost." Wally shoved his hands in his back pockets. "And the favor is about the baptism, actually. Skye won't admit it, but she needs help with the party. With the house gone and so many people wanting to attend, she's swamped and just can't do it all on her own."

"Of course not." May scowled, yanking her uniform shirt collar away from her neck. "I've offered to help, but she said no."

"Well, I was thinking," Wally said slowly. "What

if you told her you wanted to combine the christening party with the baby shower you were planning to throw her in a couple of weeks? Make it seem as if Skye is doing you the favor. You know, use a little maternal manipulation and guilt." Wally raised a brow. "Can you do that?"

"Can a bee make honey?" May's eyes sparkled, their emerald green the same brilliant color she'd passed on to both her children. "But I'm not holding back with the shower. None of that moderation you and she always talk about regarding the twins."

"Go for it," Wally agreed. He knew Skye was afraid her mother would put on a party that would rival the royal births, but now with less than a week to plan, surely May would be limited in her extravagance.

"I'll call her right now." May snatched the receiver, tucked it between her ear and shoulder, and dialed, all the while making a shooing motion with her left hand. "By the time you get home, it will be all fixed up."

"Great." Wally's stomach knotted. Had he done the right thing in involving May?

Mentally shrugging, he headed for the police station garage, got into his personal car, the souped-up Hummer that had been a gift from his father when the tornado destroyed his Thunderbird, and settled himself in the front seat. He moved around until he was comfortable, luxuriating in the soft leather seats that were such a change from the torn upholstery and busted springs of the squad cars.

Driving out of the garage, he made two quick lefts, ending up on Basin Street. A few seconds later, as he approached the Stybr Florist shop, Wally kept an eye out for a parking place. With the dry cleaners and bowling alley on the same block as the florist, finding an empty spot was a challenge.

Spying a space, Wally pulled into it and then got out of the car. He was parked next to a matte-black SUV with fancy wheel coverings and a tiger-striped design down the center of the hood. Passing by the vehicle, Wally peered inside. It was a top-of-the-line Range Rover with all the bells and whistles. While Scumble Riverites possessed their fair share of luxury vehicles, including his own Hummer and Skye's Mercedes, the $90,000-plus car stood out.

As he pushed open the shop's door, the cool carnation-scented air washed over his face, and Wally took a minute to look around. Only one customer was present, a man that Wally didn't know. Most likely, he was the Range Rover's owner.

The guy was in his late fifties, wearing an expensive suit and tie. He seemed uncomfortable or maybe impatient, shifting from foot to foot as the florist worked on an elaborate arrangement.

She glanced up from what she was doing and said, "Just a couple of minutes and I'll be right with you, Chief."

The man turned, and in the throaty voice of a long-time smoker, said, "Sorry, but the wife is really picky."

"Sure." Wally smiled. "No problem." He jerked his chin at the vase of various purple blossoms that the florist was arranging and asked, "What kind of flowers are those?"

"Expensive," the man muttered, crossing his arms. "Very, very expensive."

"Lavender, lilacs, roses, and blue popcorn hydrangea," the woman interjected as she continued to move the stems around.

"Nice." Wally wondered if Skye would enjoy something like that.

"Yeah." The man leaned a hip against the counter and fiddled with the heavy gold nugget ring on his pinky. "My wife only wants the best. She thinks money appears by magic."

"I'm a lucky guy," Wally said. "My wife is pretty laid-back about most stuff."

"If that's true, then you sure are." The man rubbed the nape of his neck. "Mine's none too happy that she's stuck here in the sticks until I get some business settled."

"That's too bad." Wally shoved his hands in his pockets.

"It doesn't help that the only motel is straight from the 1950s and the only place to eat is McDonald's. She keeps threatening to have a meal from Katana, her favorite Chicago restaurant, delivered. Can you imagine what they'd charge for something like that?" The man rolled his eyes. "I figured flowers would cheer her up and cost less."

"So you're at the Up A Lazy River?" Wally asked, hoping the woman wasn't dumb enough to let the motor court's owner, Charlie Patukas, know what she thought of his cabins. Charlie was Skye's godfather and had his finger on the pulse of most of what happened in Scumble River. He certainly wouldn't be too happy to hear one of his guests bad-mouthing his place, outdated as it might be.

"Yeah." The guy was looking at Wally funny.

"What kind of business are you in?" Wally snuck a peek at his watch. He hoped this wouldn't take much longer. He missed his babies and wanted to spend as much time as possible with them before heading out with Skye to see the priest.

"I run a chain of video gambling cafés." The guy scratched his jaw. "I had a deal to open several in Stanley County, starting with the flagship here in Scumble River. However, now the city council is claiming that they don't have time to change the definition of what is a primary business regarding the sale of alcohol or increase the number of establishments allowed to have machines. But I think a little bird might be chirping in their ear trying to put the kibosh on my cafés."

Wally had heard that more video gambling sites were in the works, but he hadn't had time to worry about what that would mean for the community. Presently, the only machines were in the bowling alley and a couple of bars. Gambling cafés would open up a whole new can of worms. There would be more people coming into town just to gamble, which meant the likelihood of more drivers under the influence and more drunken brawls.

"Well…" Wally kept a bland look on his face. "Our town was hit by several tornadoes less than three months ago and we're still in the rebuilding process, so you can't exactly expect the city council to worry about your timeline."

"No. Of course not." The guy frowned and touched his nose. "I didn't mean any disrespect."

"Glad to hear it," Wally said, relieved to see the florist had finished the arrangement.

"Nice meeting you," the guy said. "Hope things get better for your community."

"Thanks." Wally jerked his chin, then turned to the florist and asked for a dozen white roses.

As she readied his order, the woman said, "I'm still not used to seeing so many strangers in town."

"Me either." Wally handed her his credit card. "Me either."

CHAPTER 4

Baby, It's You

S KYE HAD BEEN HOME FOR A COUPLE OF HOURS
when the twins started to fuss for their next meal.
Currently, they were on a two- to three-hour feeding
schedule during the day, and three to four hours at
night. Their grandmother had fed the babies around
two thirty with the bottles of breast milk that Skye had
pumped before leaving for her meeting with Homer,
which meant they were hungry again.

Breastfeeding was proving to be a challenge on
several levels. While Skye loved the chance to connect
with her children on such a primal level, balancing two
babies was tricky. And, unwilling to leave Wally out
of the bonding process, she had to pump milk so he
could give the twins a bedtime bottle.

Then, there was the issue of what to do when she
returned to work. Skye could just see herself leaving
meetings that had run long in order to pump. None of

her principals, even the two women, would be happy about that. They might not be able to do anything about it legally, but they sure could make her professional life hell.

The lactation consultant at the hospital had suggested pumping and freezing her milk, but she didn't seem to have enough to spare to get more than a few bottles ahead. With her workday often running eight to ten hours, that would mean there might be a shortage.

It might be better to get the twins used to formula while she was still on maternity leave rather than having a crisis her first day back at school. Another issue to put on her list to discuss at her next doctor's appointment. Now if she could just find the list.

Once the twins were full, Skye put them in their bassinets. Gazing down at her adorable babies, she smiled fondly. Her daughter had Wally's coloring—straight black hair, brown eyes, and olive skin—but her round cheeks and turned-up nose were all Skye's side of the family. While her son had inherited the Leofanti emerald eyes along with the Denison chestnut curls and pale complexion, he'd gotten his father's chiseled cheekbones and aquiline nose.

Sighing, Skye made sure they were covered and turned away. They were growing so fast. Soon they'd need cribs, and she wasn't sure where she would put the larger pieces of furniture in their small, temporary home. Did they make double-decker cribs?

When Carson had brought in the extravagant RV

for Skye and Wally to live in after the tornado, it had seemed more than adequate for their needs. However, adding two babies and the enormous amount of equipment that they required quickly became a logistical nightmare.

Who knew that the nearly forty-five-foot-long motor home that was purported to sleep five, was really too small for four humans plus one very large black cat? And the ninety-one-gallon freshwater tank should have been plenty, except that the washing machine was constantly being filled for another massive load of towels, sheets, and soiled onesies.

Thank goodness that maintaining a comfortable temperature wasn't a problem. In addition to a furnace, the RV had an air-conditioning unit that was getting a run for its money during the recent Indian summer heatwave.

Skye rarely had time to watch either of the thirty-two-inch and fifty-five-inch LED Smart HDTVs or the Blu-ray player. And they sure hadn't needed the electric fireplace yet. Too bad that the master bedroom, with its king-size bed and en suite bathroom, had become more of nursery than a place to rest or somewhere to snuggle with her husband.

Although Carson had arranged to bring in a general contractor and crew from Texas to work exclusively on their new house, it still wouldn't be finished for at least a couple more months, and the clutter inside the motor home was driving Skye crazy. While the twins slept, she tried once again to bring some kind of order to the chaos.

When she finished tidying up, she checked her watch. It was quarter to six. Where in the heck was Wally? If they had to reschedule with Father Burns one more time, Skye would never be able to look the priest in the eye again.

Deciding she'd better shower and dress now so they could eat a quick supper before leaving, Skye grabbed a pair of navy knit slacks and a sleeveless geometric-print tunic in navy, red, and white.

Twenty minutes later, Skye stepped out of the master bathroom and her heart fluttered. Her handsome husband was bending over their daughter's bassinet with a look of utter worship on his face.

Straightening, Wally turned to Skye and his warm, chocolate eyes heated. Smiling, he drawled, "You look terrific, sweetheart. It's a shame we have to waste all that beauty on a visit to the priest. I wish I could take you for a romantic dinner in Laurel instead."

"Me too." Skye walked across the bedroom, stood on tiptoe, and pressed a kiss on his tempting lips. "But we can't reschedule again. Remember, Vince and Loretta have to get a babysitter too, and we've already inconvenienced them by changing the date twice."

"They'd probably be happy to have a couple of hours to themselves too." Wally arched a dark brow. "Another week or so won't matter."

"That may have been true earlier today." Skye ran

her finger down Wally's jaw, enjoying the day-old stubble. "But Mom called and talked me into combining the shower and baptismal celebration into one gigantic get-together."

Skye frowned at the flicker of what she thought might be guilt that she saw cross her husband's face, then shrugged off that notion. The other new mothers at her Baby and Me class had warned her about postnatal paranoia.

"How did May get you to go along with her idea?" Wally asked as he began taking off his uniform. "Did she use guilt or bribery?"

"A little of both. She told me it would be easier for her this way and she offered to phone everyone with the change of plans so I wouldn't have to do it."

Skye perched on the end of the bed, the better to appreciate her husband's striptease. Wally might be in his forties, but he had the yummy physique of a man half his age.

Wally stood in his black boxer briefs and asked, "That's good, right?"

"I guess." Skye rested back on her elbows. "It certainly makes more sense. Mom already had a lot of the arrangements in place and only had to adjust the timeline and location. So this Saturday, the twins will be baptized and my mother will hold the shower/baptismal party that same afternoon." Skye was distracted by Wally's muscular chest for a second, but once he went into the bathroom, she raised her voice and continued. "Plus, people won't have to bring us two gifts."

While Wally took one of his super-quick showers, Skye put dinner on the table. A few minutes later, he joined her dressed in tan khakis and a black polo shirt. Before sitting down, he walked into the living room area of the RV, then came back with a long, white box tied with a shiny silver ribbon, and handed the package to Skye.

Skye quickly opened the carton. A dozen stunning white roses in a sparkling crystal vase lay nestled in a cloud of pink tissue. The smell was heavenly.

Wally's sweetness tugged at her insides as Skye smiled and asked, "What are these for?"

"Because I love you more than I ever thought it was possible to love someone." Wally took her in his arms, tucked her cheek against his chest, and rested his chin on the top of her head. "And because you gave me those perfect babies in the bedroom. Being a father was another thing that I never thought possible."

"Aw." Skye was speechless. Her heart melted. The weight of his chin on her head was more reassuring than she could describe. After nearly losing him when an outlaw motorcycle gang kidnapped him last summer, her need for Wally's touch had grown exponentially and she had to fight her tendency to cling to him.

"Married to you, I finally feel like I'm home." He kissed her temple softly. "You gave me that and so much more."

Skye tightened her grip around his waist and sniffed. "You gave me the same things," she assured him, then giggled. "What kind of flowers do you want?"

"How about the lace ones on that new red nightgown I saw in your drawer?"

Wally's baritone voice sent a shiver up Skye's spine. She'd ordered the negligee online, but had been waiting to shed a little more baby weight before wearing it for her husband. Still, Wally always claimed to like her curves, so maybe she'd grant his wish tonight.

"Well, thanks for the amazing flowers." She shot him a flirty, little smile. "And I'll take your request under consideration." Easing out of his embrace, she gestured to the table. "But now we need to eat and clean up before Judy and Anthony get here."

Judy Martin was the town librarian and had been dating Anthony Anserello for over a year. After his recent promotion from part- to full-time police officer, he'd popped the question and she'd accepted. Since the couple wanted to start a family sooner rather than later, they'd offered to babysit the twins for practice.

"I'm still not sure we should leave our babies with them." Wally frowned. "We hardly know this Judy, and Anthony is sort of goofy sometimes. What if there's an emergency and they don't know what to do?"

"Judy is a friend of mine and Anthony is a police officer. If you truly thought he's too goofy, you wouldn't have hired him." Skye overruled his unreasonable objections in her best psychologist voice.

"There's got to be a better option." Wally scowled and glanced around the room as if the perfect babysitter were hiding behind the sofa. "A relative."

"Mom is working. My dad would rather ride through town naked on his lawn mower than change a diaper. And your father wasn't available." Skye put her hands on her hips. "Would you rather I asked Charlie?" She couldn't hold back a snicker at the thought of her cigar-smoking, whiskey-drinking godfather trying to handle the twins.

"No!" Wally wrinkled his forehead for a second, then brightened and asked, "How about Trixie and Owen?"

"Seriously?" Skye snorted. "They are childless by choice. Beyond a few minutes of cuddling, neither one of them is too keen on babies."

"Fine." Wally returned to frowning. "This thing with the priest shouldn't take too long, right? Forty-five minutes, an hour max?"

"Probably longer." Skye took her seat at the table and gestured for Wally to sit down. Bingo, their black cat, was already in his favorite dinnertime position next to her chair. "Father Burns is doing us a huge favor by conducting a private preparation session instead of making us attend the normal class that's held once a month in Joliet."

"Well, we did make a huge contribution to the building fund," Wally muttered, then asked, "What did we do with that teddy bear with the hidden camera Dad bought for us?" Wally's expression conveyed his belief that the bear should magically appear in front of him.

"I returned it." Skye ate a bite of the mac-and-cheeseburger casserole May had given her when she'd picked up the twins. "Did you know that sucker was over five hundred dollars?" She took a swallow of water. "We do not need a nanny cam."

She slipped Bingo a tidbit of ground beef. The vet wouldn't be happy with the cat's weight during his next checkup, but then again, there was an excellent chance that neither would Skye's doctor at hers.

"We need the surveillance if you're going to let virtual strangers watch our children." Wally stabbed a bite of his dinner with a fork and then ate it as if the casserole had personally offended him.

"Strangers?" Skye fought back a giggle. "The librarian that I see at least once a week and a police officer that you see every day?"

"Your point?" Wally stared at her for a second before tucking back into his dinner.

Her husband's overprotectiveness was sort of cute, but they would need to hire someone to watch the twins when Skye went back to work, so she needed to nip his paranoia in the bud right now.

Good gravy! He didn't even have the excuse of postpartum hormones.

Changing the subject, Skye asked, "How are things going at the PD?"

"We're still getting several reports a day about

fraudulent repair companies and other rip-offs." Wally tore off a piece of the warm Italian bread and used it to wipe up the tomato sauce remaining on his plate. "It's like playing whack-a-mole. We shut one down and another pops us."

"I bet." Skye tossed a cherry tomato from her salad into her mouth. After she swallowed, she said, "Homer mentioned his unhappiness with your lack of response to his complaint."

"Godda—!" Wally started to swear, then, with a guilty expression, amended, "I mean for crying out loud. Homer's issue wasn't even with a true scammer. He's upset that his insurance company isn't paying up."

"Hmm." Skye gave Bingo one more morsel of the hamburger, then ate the last few bites of her dinner. "Trixie mentioned that a lot of folks who are insured by Homestead are having trouble with their claims."

"Yeah." Wally wiped his lips with his napkin. "We've had to explain to several people that any issue they have with their insurance company is a civil matter."

"Sounds like we both had a stressful day." Skye stood and began clearing off the table. "At least there's always some humor to dealing with Homer."

"Oh, I had some comic relief, too." Wally rose, walked over to the sink, and turned on the hot water. Squirting in dish soap, he continued, "Martinez is all bent out of shape about this woman who recently moved into town and claims to be a fairy godmother."

"Millicent Rose?" Skye's skin crawled. She grabbed a dish towel and dried the plates as Wally washed them.

"You've heard of her?" Wally flicked a sharp glance in Skye's direction as he rinsed a glass and put it in the drainer.

"More than heard of her." Skye grimaced. "I've met her on several occasions."

"From your expression, you don't like her." Wally's voice sharpened and he scrubbed the casserole dish with frenetic vigor.

"I don't exactly dislike her." Skye forced herself to appear nonchalant and leaned a hip against the counter. "But she's really pushy and there's just something unnerving about her."

Wally dried his hands and turned to give Skye a piercing look. "Pushy how?"

"Well…" Skye licked her lips. Wally wouldn't be happy she hadn't mentioned her encounters with Millicent Rose to him sooner. "The first time I ran into her was at Tales and Treats. I had the twins in their stroller and was chatting with Risé as I was checking out. Millicent commented on one of the mysteries I was buying, which is pretty common in a bookstore, then she spotted the babies and asked me if they'd been christened yet."

"So she's religious?"

"That was my initial thought, so I assured her that the baptism was scheduled, but she didn't say anything about God." Skye wrinkled her nose. "Instead, she asked if she could come to the ceremony."

"I hope you told her no." Wally's eyebrows disappeared into his hairline.

"I said that I was sorry, but it was just for family and friends."

"How did she take that?" Wally moved closer, his stance more interrogator than affectionate husband.

"She muttered something and walked away." Skye hugged her arms around her waist. "But I've run into her on two more occasions. Once at the park and once after my Baby and Me group that meets at the church hall. She was in the corridor when the session ended."

"Oh?"

"Each time, she asked to attend the christening." Skye shivered.

Wally leaned into Skye's personal space. "And why didn't you ever mention these encounters to me?"

"I chalked up my discomfort to my overactive hormones." Skye slid her arms around his waist. "And I'm still not convinced it isn't exactly that."

"Don't worry about it." Wally hugged her, then frowned. "You always carry pepper spray in your purse, right?" When Skye nodded, he said, "Anyway, I'll ask Martinez to keep an eye out at the church on Saturday and make sure this Rose woman doesn't get inside." He paused. "Did she ask any of the other mothers?"

Skye shook her head. "But all the other babies have already been baptized."

Before Wally could respond, a loud knock interrupted them. Skye eased out of his arms and went to let Anthony and Judy into the RV. As she waved them to a seat on the couch, she and Wally sat on the chairs facing the sofa. While they got settled, Skye shot her husband a warning look. He'd better not say anything to insult the couple.

Judy Martin was in her midtwenties, young to be running a library on her own, but the salary was too low to attract a more seasoned librarian. Tonight, she wore her light-brown hair in a ponytail, and instead of her usual vintage outfit, she'd opted for jean shorts and a purple T-shirt.

"Thank you guys so much for offering to watch the twins," Skye said, her hand gripping Wally's knee. "Don't be surprised if you find our cat guarding the bassinets. He might hiss a little when you go near him, but he won't bite."

Skye mentally crossed her fingers that she was telling the truth. Bingo had never attacked anyone before, but he was almost as protective of the babies as Wally.

"Animals like me," Judy said, confidence radiating from her smile.

"Yes, we do," Anthony teased, slipping his arm around his fiancée's shoulder.

Anthony was a nice-looking young man with sandy-blond hair, sincere brown eyes, and a shy grin. He was about as far from an animal as Skye could imagine.

"We'll probably be home by nine, but the babies will want to eat around eight thirty," Skye hurriedly interjected, noticing Wally's frown. "Just put the bottles that are in the fridge under warm running water for a few minutes."

"Got it." Judy wrinkled her freckled nose. "How about diapers?"

"There's a stack on their changing table in the bedroom." Skye gestured behind her. "I originally intended using cloth, but with two babies and the less-than-ideal living conditions, I switched to disposable so you shouldn't have any trouble fastening them."

The men had been quiet, but Anthony chuckled. "And it's not like you guys have to worry about the cost." He waggled his brows. "Interesting article in the *Star*, Chief."

"Can it, Anserello," Wally barked.

Skye rolled her eyes, then looked at Judy and said, "We need to get going. The twins should wake up anytime now. Text or call me if you have any questions."

"Will do."

Judy and Anthony walked Skye and Wally to the door. Skye had already started down the steps when she turned and noticed Wally lean close to Anthony and murmur something in his ear.

Once Wally and Skye were in the Hummer heading toward town, Skye asked, "What did you say to Anthony?"

"I told him that if anything happened to my children, he'd never live to see his own."

"Wally!" Skye thwacked her husband's muscled bicep.

"I also told him that under no circumstances was he to allow Millicent Rose anywhere near the twins."

Skye leaned back and sighed. "Now that's an order I can totally agree with."

CHAPTER 5

Baby, Baby

DESPITE EVERYTHING, WALLY AND SKYE ARRIVED for their appointment with the priest ten minutes early. The rectory was in a midcentury brick ranch that was located next to St. Francis Catholic Church. The living room had been converted to Father Burns's office, and the parish secretary's desk was in what had once been the dining room. She worked from ten to two, so had gone home long ago.

Skye and Wally took a seat on a bench in the foyer and waited for Vince and Loretta to show up.

After several seconds of silence, Wally said, "I've been thinking some more about this Millicent Rose woman." His expression was sober. "When Martinez was telling me about the situation, I thought she was exaggerating. But now, my gut says I was wrong."

Skye felt her chest tighten. She'd been able to discount her own wariness about the woman, chalking it up to new mother syndrome, but if Wally's cop instincts were kicking in, she was worried.

"Can you run some kind of background check on her?" Skye leaned forward with her hands clasped on her lap.

"I can ask around." Wally blew out his cheeks. "But since there've been no complaints, I don't have any probable cause to investigate her."

"Which, I gather, is a deal breaker for an honest cop." Skye chuckled. She thought for a moment, then asked, "Could I make a complaint? It almost feels like she's stalking me."

"'Almost' is the problem." Wally rubbed his neck. "Have you seen her following or watching you on at least two different occasions?"

"Not exactly." Skye considered fudging the truth but couldn't bring herself to lie. If Millicent was nothing more than an eccentric busybody, Skye couldn't, in good conscience, sic the law on her.

"Do you feel your safety or well-being is at risk in some way?" Wally questioned.

"No." Skye sighed. "She just asks about attending the christening, and when I tell her it's only for friends and family, she walks away."

"Then she's not considered to be legally stalking you." Wally ran his thumb down Skye's cheek. "But call me immediately if she approaches you again. I can, and will, talk to her as a husband and father rather than as the Scumble River chief of police."

"I will." Skye made a wry face. "Having the twins has made me über-cautious."

"Good." Wally checked his watch. "Vince and Loretta are late."

"While my brother may be late," Skye said, "Loretta's delay is doubtlessly only collateral damage."

Prior to motherhood, Loretta had been an ambitious, detail-oriented, successful criminal attorney in Chicago, while Vince was a laid-back hairstylist and former garage band musician. If anyone was at fault for the couple's tardiness, it was Skye's brother.

Loretta and Skye were both alums of Alpha Sigma Alpha sorority, and when Vince had been accused of murdering an ex-girlfriend several years ago, Skye had contacted Loretta. Once Vince was cleared of the charge, despite Loretta's often-declared aversion to small towns and their citizens, she had fallen in love with Skye's brother, married him, and agreed to live in Scumble River.

When a second pregnancy surprised the couple a few months after their daughter had been born, Loretta had left her Chicago firm and opened her own law practice in Scumble River. Instead of felonies, she now handled everything from wills and estates to divorces.

"Well, whoever's at fault, Vince and Loretta aren't here." Wally looked at his watch. "And we need to get this show on the road."

"Uh-huh." Skye yawned and leaned her head on

Wally's shoulder. She was so tired. Getting up to feed the twins was taking its toll on her.

"You're exhausted." Wally put an arm around Skye. "Maybe we should look into that list of nannies that Dad's HR department put together. I think it's time we got you some help with the twins."

"Probably. But you don't even like leaving them with our friends." Skye laughed softly and nestled closer. "How would you feel about an actual stranger taking care of them? And where would she live?"

"The list of nannies only includes women who live within driving distance of Scumble River."

"Oh. Good." Skye sat up. "That reminds me; where is your dad staying? I never see his truck at the motor court anymore."

"Dad said he found an apartment, but didn't tell me where it's at." Wally stroked his chin. "In fact, he was cagey when I asked."

Before Skye could venture a guess, the front door opened and Loretta hurried toward them, with Vince trailing at her heels. Well, "hurried" might be a charitable description. At nearly eight months pregnant, "waddled" was a better word, but not one any of them would dare utter in Loretta's presence.

Skye leaped to her feet and hugged her sister-in-law, then said, "How come I never looked this good when I was pregnant?" She stepped back. "You're gorgeous."

Loretta wore a stunning tangerine linen maternity business suit and her dark-brown skin glowed with health. At six feet tall, the only change to her lean-muscled body was her baby bump. As usual, her coal-black hair was impeccably coifed in a crown of braids.

"She sure is." Vince slipped his arm around his wife. His butterscotch-blond locks brushed the collar of his bright-blue polo shirt as he tilted his head. "She could walk any fashion show runway in the world."

Wally stood and nuzzled Skye's neck. "You looked just as beautiful."

Both women snorted at their husbands' flattery and Loretta said, "Right. We'd stay pregnant all the time except for the fact that we can't sleep, can barely get up from a chair without help, and have to pee constantly." Loretta took a breath, then jeered, "But we're sooo glad you think we look pretty during this process."

Clearly, Loretta had not forgiven her husband for his part in her unplanned pregnancy. Their daughter, April, had only been a few months old when the little pink plus sign had appeared on the test stick.

Lucky for Skye's brother, Father Burns chose that moment to open the door of his office and usher them all inside. He was a tall, ascetic-looking man who had been the priest at St. Francis for as long as Skye could remember. He had to be close to seventy, but he had an ageless face that hid his age. His flock dreaded the day when he either retired or was reassigned to another parish.

His desk was against the far wall, bracketed by built-in bookshelves. The other end of the room held a leather sofa, which Skye and Wally chose, leaving the matching chairs for Vince and Loretta. After picking up a folder from his desk, Father Burns sat in the throne-like wingback chair that faced all four of them.

Nodding at the quartet, the priest said, "I know you've had some unusual circumstances, which is why I was happy to conduct a private preparation session for you. But despite the informality, it is important to enter into this as a prayerful meditation on the significance of the sacrament. Try to attain a spirit of awe and reverence and allow it to transform your viewpoint. This is not about being a passive participant, but actively reflecting on the deeper meaning of baptism and seeking a new awareness and passion for this encounter with God's grace."

They all murmured their agreement and settled in for the lesson.

Father Burns flipped open the file and shuffled through the papers inside of it. "First, all the documents you've provided have been found acceptable." He looked at each of them to see if they understood the gravity of the situation. "And although Loretta is not Catholic, she is allowed to serve as a Christian witness to the baptism along with Vince, who is the actual godparent."

"In other words, being a Christian isn't good enough." Loretta narrowed her golden-brown eyes. "I'm not recognized as the twins' godmother?"

"Not in the church." Father Burns's expression was composed. "But that would not prevent you from gaining custody should something happen to Wally and Skye as long as you are a legally named guardian."

"There's nothing to worry about, sweetheart. It's a Catholic thing." Vince stroked Loretta's arm. "Don't you remember? Skye was April's actual godmother and your brother was the Christian witness?"

"Correct." Father Burns smiled. "I'd forgotten you went through this a year or so ago. I don't know when I've seen the church so packed." He winked. "Although I suspect that record might be broken this Saturday."

Shooting her sister-in-law a hushing look, Skye said, "Not to rush you, Father, but we're ready to begin the class when you are."

Father Burns's dark, serious eyes studied them for a long moment before he said, "We will begin with an overview of the theology of the sacrament of baptism, then I'll walk you through the rite itself, and finally, and most importantly, we will discuss the sacrament and how we can live it in our lives and in our children's."

"Sounds like we have a lot of ground to cover," Wally said, then whispered in Skye's ear, "And we have two inexperienced babysitters."

"What is baptism?" Father Burns folded his hands on top of the file folder in his lap and looked them each in the eye. "Baptism is the physical sign of a divine action that leads to inner grace, where we both embrace and are embraced by the redemption won for us by Christ. Through baptism, we enter a life with God.

"We are freed from original sin and all past sins,

reborn as an adopted child of God, initiated into the Church, and united to other Christians. We are fortified against sin and protected from death."

Skye attempted to concentrate as Father Burns's deep voice further explained sin and grace. But between her exhaustion and her uneasiness about Millicent Rose's odd fascination with her babies, Skye missed large chunks of what he said.

She caught something about the Holy Spirit dwelling within them all, and that the divine adoption could never be destroyed, even by sin, before her thoughts drifted off once more. When she tuned in again, Father Burns was speaking about who can and cannot be baptized, where and when baptism happens, and reiterated the reason for the sacrament. Finally, he paused for questions.

"I think you've about covered it," Wally said dryly. "You were very thorough."

"Thank you." Father Burns looked around at the circle of faces. "But the real question is, do you all understand what I said?"

None of them hesitated. In firm voices they all replied, "Yes."

"I'm happy to hear that." Father Burns's smile was gentle. "Does anyone need a break or should we move on to the actual rite?"

"May I use your restroom?" Loretta struggled to her feet.

"Certainly." Father Burns gestured to the door. "It's down the hall to your left."

While they waited, Skye told Vince about May's phone call and informed him that the after-baptism get-together was now also the baby shower and that their mother was having a party tent erected in Skye and Wally's backyard between the RV and the new house under construction.

Vince was still teasing Skye about a big-top-themed baby shower when Loretta returned. Once she was seated, Father Burns began his explanation on how the ritual would proceed.

"In many churches, they now do a group baptism, but we're still small enough to do individual ceremonies." He tipped his head at Skye. "Besides, considering your large extended family and the number of friends you and Wally have in this community, I thought it best not to tax the church's seating capacity with another baby."

"Probably best," Wally muttered, sharing a glance with Loretta. "April's ceremony was standing room only and May's had time to add to her list since then. Her motto is: leave no guest uninvited."

"May is a woman full of…love." A corner of the priest's lip turned up.

"That's one way to look at her." Loretta's expression was skeptical.

"I'm so happy that God has blessed her with grandchildren." Father Burns steepled his fingers. "I understand that she can be overwhelming, but I can say without a doubt that her actions are well intentioned."

Skye and Vince glanced at each other, then nodded. Their mother had a heart of gold, and after becoming parents themselves, they had a little more understanding and tolerance for her need to nurture.

"My wife is worth whatever amount of smothering I have to take from her mom." Wally gave Skye a loving look. "If it makes May happy to invite every last third cousin twice removed, it's fine with me."

"Thank you." Skye caught her breath at the raw emotion in his voice.

"How about you, honey?" Vince reached out a hand to his wife.

"Considering my mother is twice as bad, May doesn't faze me."

They were wrapping things up when an idea flitted across Skye's mind and she asked, "Father, have you baptized many babies since the tornado?"

"If memory serves, there were two." Father Burns rose from his chair and ushered them to the door. "The Yates and Turner infants. Why?"

"Did you notice any attendees that seemed a little odd?" Skye asked.

"That's hard to say," the priest teased gently. "What do you mean by odd?"

"Wearing a light-blue cape with a pointy hood and tied with a big, pink bow."

"Why yes." Father Burns blinked. "I believe there was a woman like that there."

"Did she do anything unusual?" Wally asked, shooting Skye a concerned glance.

"No." Father Burns tapped his chin. "She did speak to both sets of parents afterward and she may have given each baby a small gift."

"Why are you asking about this woman?" Loretta asked, frowning.

Before Skye or Wally could reply, there was a loud boom and the office shook as if there'd been an earthquake. Skye grabbed Wally's arm and locked her knees. She watched in horror as a porcelain statue of the Virgin Mother wobbled, fell over, and rolled from a shelf, shattering on the hardwood floor.

What in the name of heaven had just happened?

CHAPTER 6

Run, Baby, Run

OUTSIDE, A HEAVY CAR DOOR SLAMMED AND A motor whined, but inside the rectory office, it was eerily quiet. Skye, still clinging to Wally, looked around the room, trying to understand what was going on. It felt as if she'd been standing, frozen in the moment, for hours, but it was probably more like a few minutes.

Wally had unclipped his cell phone from his belt and was repeatedly swiping the redial icon. But the buzz of the busy signal remained a steady annoyance. He growled in frustration and punched in another number.

While Skye's mind had been off-line, rosary beads had somehow appeared in Father Burns's hands and Vince had lowered Loretta back into the chair she had vacated seconds before the blast. Vince stood protectively in front of his wife, holding both her hands in his.

Otherwise, nothing much had changed since the

loud boom and the shaking. Or to be more accurate, nothing in the rectory office had changed. Who knew about the rest of the area?

Fear clogged Skye's throat, and before she could pull herself together enough to speak, Loretta let out a loud moan. Whimpering, she hunched her shoulders and clutched her stomach.

Immediately, Vince dropped to his knees, demanding, "What's wrong?"

"It's probably just a Braxton-Hicks contraction, but it hurts like a son of a"—Loretta ground out between clenched teeth—"bucket."

"Sh…sugar!" Vince swiveled his head toward Wally and yelled, "Call 911! She needs to go to the hospital."

Skye had noticed that Vince and Loretta had also begun to curtail their swearing after becoming parents.

"I've been trying to get through to the station." Although Wally's voice was even, the frustrated look in his eyes gave away his true feelings. "But every fricking line is busy. Including 911."

"Use your handheld radio." Vince's voice cracked like a breaking branch. "This is an emergency."

"I don't have it with me. It's in the car." Wally's expression was thunderous. "One of the promises I made my babies when they were born was to delegate more. When I'm away from the station, Quirk is in charge."

"Fu—"

"Honey." Loretta cut off her husband, throwing a

quick look at the priest. "I'm fine." She stood and then paced the room. "I'm probably just dehydrated."

"Let me get you some water." Father Burns finally seemed to come out of his fog and hurried to a small refrigerator against the rear wall. Handing Loretta a bottle, he said, "Here you go, my dear."

They all watched Loretta drink until Wally's cell phone rang. Skye turned to look at her husband. He swiped the screen with his thumb and pressed the device to his ear.

Skye was standing close enough to hear her mother's voice as May said, "There has been an explosion at Bunny Lanes. Sergeant Quirk is en route along with the fire department and paramedics."

May's words struck with the force of a cleaver severing bone from sinew and Skye gasped as she gripped Wally's bicep. The bowling alley was owned by Skye's ex-boyfriend, Simon Reid. His mother, Bunny, managed the business and lived above it. "We're at St. Francis, so I'm only a block and a half away from the scene." Wally muted the phone and looked at Loretta. "Do you need an ambulance?"

"No." Loretta finished her water. "As I thought, it must have been a Braxton-Hicks. Baby Denison is just giving me some practice."

Wally nodded, unmuted the phone, and asked, "Any injuries?" As he waited for a response, he headed out, the door rattling open as he slammed through it.

The priest crossed himself and murmured a hasty

prayer, while Vince and Loretta gaped at her in shock. Unwilling to be left behind, Skye hastily said goodbye and ran after her husband. He was already unlocking the Hummer when she reached him.

She hadn't heard her mother's response to Wally's question, and when she caught up to him, she asked, "What did Mom say about anyone being hurt? Did a gas main blow up?"

"There's no information yet." Wally helped her into the SUV. "Get in. We'll use the SUV to block the road until Quirk gets set up."

Less than a minute later, Wally had angled the vehicle across Basin Street where it intersected Laurel Avenue. The Hummer, which had previously belonged to his father, was an H1 Alpha. The chassis was made of high-strength steel and it had a Duramax diesel engine with a five-speed Allison transmission, as well run-flat tires and a sixteen-inch ground clearance. In addition, it had been equipped with giant searchlights and a heavy-duty grille guard. Nothing short of a tank could plow through the heavily fortified vehicle.

"Stay here," Wally instructed as he thrust open the driver's side door and then ran toward the bowling alley.

Ignoring her husband's order, Skye jumped out of the Hummer. As she followed him, she couldn't see any damage to the building. But when she got closer, her chest tightened when she saw that the windows were shattered and there was smoke billowing out of the openings. If anyone had been inside the bowling alley during the explosion, there was a good chance that he or she was severely injured, if not dead.

A fire engine and ambulance were already in front of the building and firefighters were setting up huge spotlights around the perimeter. Others were connecting hoses to a hydrant while their counterparts hauled them toward the building. Skye watched a ladder truck disappear behind the structure and she prayed Bunny was okay.

When Wally and Skye reached the bowling alley's parking lot, it was empty except for the squad car blocking the entrance. Sergeant Roy Quirk was at the back of the cruiser, pulling equipment from its trunk.

"I've got Basin blocked to the east," Wally shouted as he ran over to the squad. "Get up a barricade west of here at Creek Street."

"Will do." Quirk gave a single, sharp nod. The sergeant was built like Captain America, but he didn't have the superhero's charm. "I told May to call in all available officers. Martinez can handle one of the barriers and Tolman can be stationed at the other end."

Skye gave Roy a mental thumbs-up for calling in officers to manage the crowds rather than try to do it himself. He'd been Wally's right hand at the PD for years, but he wasn't exactly an easygoing man. After a particularly nasty run-in with Skye, Wally had insisted Roy participate in anger-management therapy, which seemed to be helping him control his temper—most of the time. However, dealing with the public wasn't his strength.

"I'll get Martinez and Tolman on that." Wally clapped the brawny sergeant on the back and spoke into the portable radio he'd grabbed from the Hummer.

While Wally issued orders to his officers, Skye walked to the far end of the parking lot and watched a couple of firefighters as they carefully climbed the rear staircase. On a nearby ladder truck, two additional firefighters clambered onto the roof. The building was shaped like a massive cube, with a second story over the rear half of the square. There didn't seem to be any smoke or flames coming out of the back of the building, which gave her hope that Bunny was okay.

In fact, with the artificial lights illuminating the scene, she could almost pretend she was watching a movie being filmed. But all too soon, the background noise of men shouting to each other crashed through her fantasy and reality returned, allowing the worry she'd been attempting to keep at bay to seep through the cracks of her emotional shields.

Skye's throat tightened. Bunny had worked so hard to make the bowling alley a success. She'd been estranged from her son for years, and when he'd bought the business and made her the manager, it had been the first step on the path of recovery for their relationship.

Skye may have chosen to marry Wally instead of Simon, but she still wanted her ex-boyfriend to be happy. And having his mother back in his life in a positive way was a huge part of that happiness.

It had been wonderful to see Bunny turn a run-down bowling alley into a vital business. She had redone it from top to bottom, tearing out decor that had been there for decades and giving the place a modern vibe. She'd expanded the alley's services, offering party packages and special programs for the kids during school breaks.

Recently she'd obtained one of the few available licenses for video gambling. She'd put the machines in the bar, which had been enclosed and expanded during the renovations, and the unused stage area had been converted into a lounge containing half a dozen slot machines.

Skye prayed that Bunny was safe and the bowling alley wasn't too badly damaged. At least there was one blessing—the lanes were closed on Mondays, so there shouldn't have been anyone in the building.

She glanced back at where Wally stood with Fire Chief Eaton. Utility trucks had arrived and the two men were listening to the guys from the electric and gas companies talk. When another squad car pulled into the parking lot, Wally left the fire chief's group and walked over to the cruiser.

Paul Tolman exited the vehicle. During the tornado and most of its immediate aftermath, Paul had been out on medical leave due to an emergency appendectomy and he still seemed a bit under the weather.

His normally olive skin was pasty and his movements seemed stiff and painful.

Although Skye worked as a psychological consultant to the police department, she didn't know the middle-aged officer very well. He was quiet and minded his own business. He did his job but didn't seem to have any ambition to rise in the ranks. Maybe losing his partner while he was a Chicago cop had taught him that it was safer to blend in and reach retirement age than be a dead hero. That was a lesson Skye wouldn't mind her own husband learning.

Paul's wife, June, owned a local insurance agency, and even though it was a different company than the one Trixie had mentioned, June's job had to be extremely difficult right now. Many people didn't understand that the agent who sold them their policy had no control over how quickly claims were handled. Skye watched Paul nod and stroll off, whistling. Clearly, he was happy with his assignment to man the barricades. Skye suspected Zelda's reaction wouldn't be as positive. The young woman often complained that Wally only allowed her to do the boring stuff. And she was dying to dig her teeth into meatier responsibilities.

With everyone else occupied, Skye pulled out her cell phone. She didn't want to leave until she knew if Bunny was okay, but she needed to check with Judy and Anthony and make sure her friends were all right with another hour or two of babysitting.

Judy answered on the first ring and reported, "The twins have been fed and are both asleep."

After Judy's reassurance that the babies were fine, Skye explained the situation, ending with "so we may be here a while."

"No problem," Judy said. "Anthony was called into work, so I heard about the explosion."

"Sheesh!" Skye hit her forehead with her palm. "Of course Anthony would have been called in. I can't believe I didn't think of that. We can give you a ride home if he doesn't make it back."

"Zelda picked him up, so I've got his car. And I have tomorrow off, so don't worry about keeping me up late." Judy seemed to be winding up to ask something, like a batter taking a few practice swings. Finally, after a long pause, almost as if she was afraid of the answer, she asked, "How's it look there? Any word yet on casualties or…"

"Nothing so far. All I can see from the outside is some smoke and broken windows." Skye moved a little farther toward the rear of the building and squinted. "I have no idea what's really happening with the inside of the bowling alley, but the firefighters in the rear are trying to get the apartment door open. It looks as if it's stuck. The explosion must have wedged it shut."

"I hope Bunny's okay." Judy's voice wavered. "She's such a hoot."

Skye opened her mouth to respond, but the words died on her lips when she spotted Simon marching across the parking lot in her direction. She hastily told her friend goodbye and turned to her ex.

Where Wally was tall with a muscular chest tapering to a narrow waist, Simon was lean and elegant. As always, he was wearing an impeccably tailored suit with a crisp shirt, although Skye noticed that his silk tie was loosened and there was a scuff on the toe of his highly polished, black Italian leather shoes.

"Have you seen my mother?" Simon's stylishly cut auburn hair was sticking up in spikes, as if he'd run his fingers through it. "I've been trying to call her, but her cell goes directly to voicemail and she's not responding to any of my messages."

When Skye had first returned to Scumble River, she and Simon had dated on and off for nearly three years. Then Skye caught Simon cheating on her. Actually, he really hadn't been, but he'd been too stubborn to explain what was going on. Shortly afterward, Wally and Skye became an item.

Unfortunately, because Simon owned the local funeral home and was the county coroner, Skye and Wally were often forced to work with him. "Awkward" did not begin to describe those encounters.

"There hasn't been any sign of your mom since we got here," Skye said, then went on to explain about the jammed door. Frowning, she added, "They've been working on it, but it doesn't seem to be budging."

"Son of a pup!" Simon scowled. "I had a

steel-reinforced door put in after I heard about that biker gang burglarizing homes in the area."

"Do you have the key?" Skye grabbed a tissue from her purse and wiped her forehead. The unseasonable heat was starting to wear her down. "Maybe it's locked instead of stuck."

"It's in my office at the funeral home." Simon pulled out his cell. "It'll be faster if I have Xavier find it and bring it over."

Once Simon completed the call to his assistant, Skye tried to inject a note of optimism into her voice as she said, "Maybe your mom's not even home."

"True." Simon's tone was hopeful, but his brow was wrinkled in concern. "This *is* her only full day off. She might be out."

"Jeez!" Simon's golden-hazel eyes widened. "It just occurred to me that they could get into the apartment from inside the bowling alley. I need to go ask if they've tried that door."

"Ooh! I forgot about that other entrance, too." Skye patted his shoulder. "Let's pray if this door is truly stuck, they can get in that way."

Once Simon jogged away from her, Skye made her way over to the sidewalk where Wally was talking to Chief Eaton. The fire chief was a distinguished-looking man in his late fifties. Although his muscles had softened a bit, his spine was militarily straight and his mane of sandy hair mixed with silver was still thick.

Skye stood quietly next to her husband and listened

to the men's conversation. Her mind had drifted when a firefighter trotted up to their group and waited for the chief to acknowledge him.

"Get on with it, Michaelson," Chief Eaton snapped.

"It looks as if the explosion was restricted to the enclosed bar area." Michaelson held his helmet under his arm and wiped the sweat from his face with a bright-red hanky. "The men are putting out a few small fires that were a result of the blast, but should be finished within the hour."

"Good job." The chief waved the man away. "Get back to work."

Wally's grim expression relaxed slightly, and he said, "That's fortunate."

"You have no idea." Chief Eaton shook his head. "This could have been so much worse."

"Chief, do you have any idea what caused the explosion?" Skye asked.

"The utility companies assure me that it isn't a gas leak or anything to do with the wiring." The chief's expression darkened. "Unless there were pressurized tanks or something of that sort being stored in the building, that leaves us with an explosive device."

"You mean like a terrorist attack?" Skye squeaked and grabbed Wally's hand.

"Well…" The chief's lips twitched. "I can't really see an extremist targeting a bowling alley in rural Illinois, so that's doubtful." Before Skye could tell the chief what she thought of his condescending attitude and explain why Scumble River might be on a fanatic's radar, Chief Eaton continued, "We'll continue sweeping the building to make sure there are no additional sparks, but the major destruction seems limited to the lounge. There's minor damage like broken glass and tossed furniture throughout the building, but the walls and ceiling appear intact."

"You'll need a structural engineer to be certain, right?" Wally asked.

"Yeah." Chief Eaton looked toward the bowling alley. "I put in a call to the Illinois Secretary of State Police Bomb Squad, but it will take them a couple of hours to get here and we can't thoroughly examine the scene until we're sure that there won't be any further lesser detonations, because those can result in the release of hot fragments and fire."

"Understood," Wally said, staring over the other man's shoulder at the building. "How about the second-floor apartment in the back? Have your men been able to get in to check the occupant yet?"

Skye held her breath. Crossing her fingers, she hoped for good news.

"The men working on that entry are hearing some sounds from inside." The chief pursed his lips. "But that door must be steel-reinforced because they're having trouble breaking it down."

"It is," Skye said. When both men looked at her in surprise, she added, "Simon just mentioned it to me. He called his assistant to bring the key, then went to ask the firefighters if they were aware of the inside entrance to the apartment."

"Thanks for the info, Mrs. Boyd." Chief Eaton tipped his head at Skye. "The inside staircase has partially collapsed, but I'll let the men know about the steel-reinforced door." He keyed his walkie-talkie and relayed the facts, paused, then said, "Yeah. Wait for the key."

Fifteen minutes later, Skye heard a commotion behind her and turned. Bunny Reid was mincing across the parking lot; her four-inch-high silver heels glittered in the spotlights and the pink marabou feathers edging her negligee danced in the breeze. But the real surprise was the guy trailing behind her as he hastily buttoned his shirt. Skye put her hand to her mouth and glanced at her husband.

What in the world was Wally's father doing with Simon's mother? And why hadn't he and Bunny finished getting dressed during the time the firefighters were trying to get inside the apartment?

CHAPTER 7

(My Baby Does the) Hanky-Panky

WIND WHISPERED THROUGH THE REMAINING leaves of the nearby trees. The breeze was coming from the north, which Skye sincerely hoped meant cooler weather. Summer had ended weeks ago and she longed for a brisk fall day.

The sound of an annoyed exhale dragged Skye's attention back to Wally and she watched as he stared at his father through narrowed eyes. Carson was slowly walking toward them, his shoulders erect, but with an *oh crap* expression on his handsome face.

Wally's gaze moved over the couple, clearly cataloging their respective stages of undress. Skye could hear her husband's teeth grind together as he clenched his jaw, and she ran her palm up and down his forearm, trying to soothe away his irritation.

Putting his hand over hers, Wally pleaded, "Is

there any scenario you can think of where my father was not just having sex with Bunny?"

"Sorry, sweetheart." Skye turned her hand over, squeezed his fingers, then stepped back. "No matter how much you don't want it to be true, those two were definitely doing the horizontal hokey pokey before this all happened."

"Why?" Wally looked up and implored the universe. "Why of all the single women in Scumble River and beyond, did my father have to hook up with Bunny Reid?"

Skye followed her husband's scrutiny skyward. Which of the twinkling stars was he addressing? Or maybe it was the crescent moon that he was pleading with for answers.

Realizing that Wally was now gazing at her and waiting for an answer, Skye said, "Because she's unique. She's exciting and beautiful and she doesn't care what other people think about her." Skye smiled fondly. "Bunny is one of those truly optimistic folks who actually enjoys the scenery on a detour."

Skye knew it wasn't that Wally disliked Bunny, although he probably thought she was too flaky for his father; it was that her son was Simon Reid. And despite Skye's assurance to the contrary, Wally was convinced that Simon was still in love with her.

Then, as if to prove her thoughts, Wally said, "Reid will just use his mother's relationship with my father to come sniffing around you again. It will be the perfect excuse to stay in contact with you." Wally scowled. "Knowing your mother, Reid will be invited to family get-togethers."

Skye was saved from responding by Carson, who approached them and said with a teasing grin, "You seem surprised to see me, Son."

Carson was an older version of Wally—well over six feet tall, slim hips, muscular chest, and intelligent brown eyes that rarely missed a trick.

Wally grunted and shoved his hands into his pockets.

Carson glanced at Skye, who shrugged. He refocused on Wally, gave a little cough, and said, "When I moved out of Up A Lazy River, didn't I mention that Bunny offered to share her apartment with me?" His tone was nonchalant, but his ears were red. "Wasn't that generous of her?"

"No. You didn't mention it," Wally snapped. The look on his face could have melted wax.

Skye dug her nails into his arm and sent him a not-so-subtle nonverbal message to chill.

Wally's expression smoothed and he grudgingly added, "It must've slipped your mind with everything else that's been happening."

"Well…" Carson finished buttoning his shirt and tucked it into his pants. "As you know, with so many folks displaced after the tornado, there's nothing much in the way of housing around here. And living in the motor court was getting mighty wearisome."

"So when I heard Car was unhappy," Bunny piped in, her voice a high-pitched whine reminiscent of a dentist's drill, "I told him that he was welcome to move in with me." She tucked an errant red curl into the cascade of ringlets on top of her head and batted her false lashes. "It seemed greedy to keep that big apartment all for myself."

"Big?" Skye narrowed her eyes. She might have liked Bunny, but she wasn't letting that obviously bogus statement go. "I thought it was a one bedroom."

"It is," Simon said as he walked up and joined the group, stopping near Skye.

Skye stepped slightly away from her ex, more for Wally's peace of mind than because she really thought Simon was coming on to her. The move also took her downwind of Bunny's overpowering perfume, which made it a win-win in Skye's books. The eye-watering scent that reminded her of mothballs, gardenia corsages, and fruitcakes was clogging her sinuses.

"I meant it's real roomy." Bunny examined her sparkly purple nails.

"Actually"—Simon shot his mother a stern look—"it's only five hundred square feet. About average for a one-bedroom rental."

"At least Bunny's place has a kitchen, living room, and dining area." Carson folded his arms. "With nowhere to eat in Scumble River except for fast food, I can finally cook a decent meal."

"Dad." Skye's voice cracked, hurt that Carson felt

that way. "You are always welcome to eat with us. I thought you knew that."

Wally put his arm around Skye and glared at his father. "Despite juggling twins, Skye cooks supper every night and I've heard her invite you over numerous times. Not to mention May's invitations."

"Sorry, sugar." Carson stepped over to Skye, leaned in, and kissed her cheek. "I didn't mean it that way. I know I'm welcome at your table. And your mother's." He peered at Wally. "The truth is that Bunny and I have been courting for the past couple of months."

"Why didn't you just say so?" Wally's posture stiffened. "Mom's been gone a long time and I didn't exactly think you'd been a monk all those years."

"Well…" Carson took a red handkerchief from his jeans pocket, leaned down, and used it to clean off a mark from the toe of his perfectly shined cowboy boot. "I've never rubbed your nose in my personal life before."

Looking between Skye and Simon, Bunny added, "Then there's—"

"There's nothing," Skye said firmly, eager to stop Bunny from finishing whatever embarrassing thought was rolling around in her head. "We're all friends and we're all happy for you two." She elbowed Wally and looked hard at Simon. "Right?"

Skye secretly loved that even after she'd given birth to twins, an act that had caused her already curvy figure to expand, Wally was still a little bit jealous.

However, she didn't want his attitude to ruin things between Carson and Bunny.

"Yeah," Wally answered between clenched teeth. "We're all pals."

He took Skye's hand and played with the enormous engagement ring and diamond-studded wedding band on her finger until they caught the light, then he leaned down to kiss the top of Skye's head. Glancing up, she noticed that her husband was staring at Simon, and the other man had clearly been watching Wally's performance. Stifling a giggle, she wondered if Wally was going to pee on her leg next. Wasn't that how dogs marked their territory?

When Simon remained silent, Bunny tottered over and embraced him, then said, "It's better to have loved and lost than hated and won." Her hazel eyes softened. "And now you have Emmy so we're all good. She's a gorgeous girl, full of fun. Just what you need."

"Uh-huh." Simon's ambiguous response to his mother made Skye worry that his noncommittal attitude would reinforce Wally's suspicions.

Beaming at Skye, Bunny said, "No offense. You're beautiful too, honey. But you and Sonny Boy are too much alike. Way too serious."

"No offense taken." Skye's lips twitched as she tried to hide her grin. When she managed to paste a serious look on her face, she said, "I agree completely. Simon and I weren't a good match for many reasons." She stroked Wally's hand. "Everything worked out the way it was supposed to be. It just took a bit of jiggling for all the pieces to fall into place."

"Right." Simon gave Skye a tight smile. "It was nice while it lasted."

Skye knew that Simon's grudging admission would do nothing to reassure Wally, but she still felt that she had to respond positively and said, "It was what we both needed at the time."

Simon nodded, then squeezed his mother's shoulder and said, "I'm glad you're okay. I was concerned when you didn't answer your cell. What happened in the apartment? Why didn't you unlock the door?"

When Bunny hesitated, Wally turned to Skye and said, "Now that we know everyone is all right, we should probably head home." He pushed a stray curl behind her ear and added, "I bet Judy is more than ready to be relieved from nanny duty, and the twins probably miss us."

"I'm sure that's true." Skye narrowed her eyes. She knew Wally wanted to get her away from Simon, but using their babies as an excuse wasn't playing fair. "We can leave in a second. But first, I want to hear why Bunny and Carson didn't unlock the door. Was it stuck?"

"Not exactly." Bunny pulled her sheer negligee closed, covering up the black silk nightgown that was split down the front and held together with a single red ribbon. "Actually, the shock wave from the explosion must have loosened something and the whole bed just sort of crumpled inward. We were trapped until the firefighters were able to get inside and got it off us." She winked. "Those strapping young men lifted the debris like it was made of feathers rather than solid oak."

"Were either of you hurt?" Skye gasped and stepped toward Bunny and Carson. "Did the paramedics check you out?"

"We're fine," Carson assured her. "The headboard and footboard folded and shoved us and the mattress down, breaking the slats so we were in a sort of protected hollow." He shrugged. "But we were wedged so tight, I couldn't get the leverage to move them."

"Sounds claustrophobic," Wally commented, his lips twitching.

Skye glanced at her husband and saw that he was barely managing to hold back a chuckle. Not that she blamed him. The image of Carson and Bunny trapped like sardines in a can was pretty funny.

"He was so brave. And so strong. He made me feel really safe." Bunny rushed over to Carson and wrapped her arms around him.

Swatting at the mosquitos that were buzzing around her head, Skye marveled at how fast the redhead could walk on sandals that consisted of nothing more than thin soles and a single strap attached to stiletto heels. Taking an amazed breath, Skye noticed that while the smell of smoke lingered in the air, it seemed to have become less intense.

Glancing around, Skye saw that Chief Eaton was standing on the fringes of their group and appeared mesmerized as Bunny flitted from person to person. *Hmm!* Maybe Bunny would get tired of Carson and give Eaton a whirl. Simon's mother wasn't exactly famous for her long-term relationships.

Skye would hate to see Carson hurt, but better sooner than later. Maybe she'd put a bug in May's ear. Her mom wasn't fond of Bunny and could probably come up with a nice single lady who would be more appropriate for Wally's father. One who wasn't related to Skye's ex. It would be so much simpler for everyone concerned if Simon wasn't constantly around to rile up Wally's possessive instincts.

Abruptly, Skye sucked in a rough breath. How could she even think that way? Plotting to steal Carson's happiness because she was afraid of losing her own.

When had she become such a lily-livered coward? Was it because she finally had everything she had always wanted? A husband she loved and needed more than her next breath. A son and daughter she would lay down her life for. And an important job that served her community.

No! She wasn't going to be that kind of woman. She loved Wally and she would just have to make sure that he never had a reason not to trust her. Even if Simon was still interested in her, and she wasn't convinced that was true, she wasn't attracted to him. She'd never give Wally the slightest hint that she was anything but a thousand percent committed to him and their future.

Still it wouldn't hurt to get home. After all, there

was no reason to stay and have the two men continue to rub each other the wrong way.

As she scanned the area to see if Wally's officers had things under control, a movement in the distance caught Skye's attention and her scalp prickled. Although the explosion and subsequent fire and police department activity had drawn a crowd, most of the people were pressed against the barricades trying to get a better view of the action. But it looked as if a single shadowy figure hung back, skulking in the semidarkness, just beyond the taped-off perimeter.

Remembering the fire chief's reaction to her question about terrorists, Skye was reluctant to say anything about the lurker. After a long internal debate, she tugged on Wally's arm until he bent his head down and then she whispered what she'd seen.

"I'll inform Martinez."

While Wally stepped away to radio Skye's observation to Zelda, Skye glanced at Simon. He was listening to his mother, but staring at Wally's retreating figure. And Simon's smile was like a straight razor—sharp and, with one false move, oh so dangerous.

Worried about Simon's chilling expression, Skye nearly missed the commotion at the entrance of the bowling alley. A pair of firefighters burst from the building and ran toward Chief Eaton.

Both men skidded to a stop in front of the chief. The larger one elbowed his buddy out of the way and announced, "We found a body."

As Wally returned from using the squad car's radio, Chief Eaton turned to him and said, "Looks like the police better stick around."

"Shall I get the hearse?" Simon asked, taking a half step away.

"No rush." The fire chief shook his head. "I can't let you go in to retrieve the body yet."

Simon turned to his mother and demanded, "Who was inside? The bowling alley is supposed to be closed on Mondays."

"You took the words right out of my mouth." Wally stared at Bunny.

"Mine too." Chief Eaton joined the other two men glaring at the scantily clad redhead.

Bunny moved so that she was halfway behind Carson, widened her eyes, and said, "I locked the doors last night at nine. The cook, servers, and bartender left about twenty or thirty minutes later. I did a final sweep of the place, then went upstairs to change into something more comfortable." She petted Carson's shoulder. "By then, Car had a couple of steaks going on the grill. We ate outside, then went in and watched TV."

"How about the cleaning service?" Chief Eaton asked. "Do they have a key?"

"No." Bunny twisted a red curl around her finger, her expression virtuous. "Sonny Boy doesn't like me to give out extra keys."

"Maybe whoever it is hid when Bunny closed up,"

Skye suggested. "I doubt she was looking for someone who had deliberately concealed themselves."

"Who would want to spend the night in a deserted bowling alley?" Simon asked, then looked at his mother. "You do lock away the alcohol and cash, right?"

"Of course." Bunny crossed her arms, which caused her robe to gap open.

"I suppose it could be someone who's homeless and just looking for shelter," Skye said slowly. "I think there are more of those folks than we like to believe. Even here in Scumble River."

"That makes sense." Wally scratched his chin. "With so many of the area churches still overwhelmed helping the tornado victims, the people they usually feed and shelter may not be able to get in."

Although everyone nodded, Skye noted that Simon continued to cast suspicious glances at his mother. She'd have to talk to Bunny once her son was gone. People tended to share things with her that they would never tell the cops, which is why she was such a good police psych consultant.

Wally interrupted Skye's thoughts. "Chief, any idea when I can get a look at the crime scene?"

"I put in a call for the county engineer." Chief Eaton rolled his eyes. "But don't hold your breath. He's in Chicago at some convention, so it'll be a couple of hours until he gets here. And even then, he can't start his inspection until the bomb tech arrives."

Wally sighed, then asked, "Have your men

otherwise secured the building and concluded that there are no more unexploded devices?"

"I just received the all clear." Chief Eaton gestured to where the firefighters were packing up. "I'll stick around until the engineer and bomb expert get here, but I ordered the rest of my crew back to the firehouse."

"No use calling in the county forensic techs until the engineer can go in and approve the structure and the bomb expert gets what he needs." Wally rubbed the back of his neck.

Skye tilted her head. Wally's first instinct would be to remain at the scene. She stared appraisingly at Roy Quirk, who was supervising the officers at the barricades. There was nothing Wally could do here and staying would mean precious time away from her and the babies—time there was really no reason he had to waste.

She went up on her tiptoes and spoke quietly into her husband's ear. "I know you probably want to take charge, and that's okay with me. But Roy can take care of this. He can always call if there's a development, but the odds are nothing will happen or be discovered until tomorrow."

Wally's brows drew together, then he sighed and said, "You're right." Looking at his father, he asked, "Do you want to stay with us tonight, Dad? The sofa bed is yours if you want it."

Simon gestured at his mother. "You can stay in my guest room."

"Thanks, boys, but Bunny and I will bunk at the

motor court." Carson smiled wryly. "I kept the room to…uh…store some of my stuff."

"That was a lucky break." Skye heard Carson's unsaid words. He'd kept the room in case things didn't work out with his love life.

Wally caught Quirk's eye and gestured for him to come over. When the sergeant arrived, Wally said, "I'm leaving you in charge. When the county engineer gets here and clears the building for occupancy, contact the crime scene techs." He paused, then, evidently unable to stop himself, added, "But if there's any problem, call me."

"Will do, Chief." Quirk's chest puffed up. "You can count on me."

"I know I can." Wally slipped his arm around Skye and said, "Darlin', are you ready to head home and take care of our babies?"

"Absolutely." Skye kissed his cheek. "There's nothing I would rather do."

CHAPTER 8

Bad Baby

S ORRY, KATHRYN. I STILL HAVEN'T RECEIVED THE ME's report." Wally kept his voice level, but he fidgeted in his chair, anxious to end the conversation. "I promise our public information officer will release a statement as soon as we have anything to share."

Kathryn Steele, the owner and editor of the *Scumble River Star*, had already telephoned the station three times and it wasn't even noon yet. She was more intent on gathering secrets than a locker room full of teenage girls, and twice as vicious.

The local newspaper was a weekly and she was desperate to get something into the edition coming out tomorrow. Wally, on the other hand, would be delighted if none of the particulars of either the explosion or the dead body made it into this week's paper.

"Public information officer my eye," Kathryn sneered, her voice hissing like a swarm of angry wasps.

"You owe me for helping you reveal your family's wealth in a positive way."

"Fine." Wally drew in a deep breath, then released it slowly. "I personally will call you with the official statement as soon as it is available."

"I don't just want the 'official' party line," Kathryn said sharply.

"That's too bad." Wally hung on to his temper by a thread. "Because that's all I'm prepared to offer."

The twins had been extra fussy that morning and it had taken both Wally's and Skye's best efforts to get them fed, changed, and soothed. Consequently, he'd been late getting to work and was still going through the various reports from his officers, the fire department, the bomb expert, and the county engineer. He needed to wrap up this conversation and inform the dispatcher that he was not taking any more calls from the *Star*'s owner.

"If I don't hear from you by three o'clock, I'm printing Bunny Reid's interview by itself." Kathryn paused, then singsonged a warning. "And you do not want her perception of the event to be the only one my readers see."

"Make it four," Wally countered, running his fingers through his short hair. "I promise to have something for you by then."

Disconnecting the line, Wally glanced around his office. It was plain and practical, just how he liked it. He preferred minimal furnishings—a large metal desk, two no-frills chairs for visitors, and a couple of file cabinets. Simplicity and organization, with nothing to clutter either the space or his thinking, soothed his soul. The only nonutilitarian item in the room was his wedding picture.

Wally reached for the framed photo and studied his beautiful bride, still unable to believe that Skye was really his forever. Standing next to her at the altar in his dress uniform, he had realized that he was the luckiest man in the world. He'd gotten a second chance to marry the love of his life and have the family of his dreams. Which reminded him, he needed to get a photograph of the twins for his desk. Maybe he'd have one from the baptism framed.

After placing the picture so that he would see Skye's gorgeous face every time he glanced up from his work, he took a gulp of tepid coffee. He'd poured himself a mug an hour ago and hadn't managed to take more than a couple of sips in between answering the telephone.

If things hadn't been so chaotic at home, he would have stopped at Tales and Treats for a decent cup of java in one of their special to-go cups that kept the liquid piping hot for hours. But the police station's bitter brew was better than nothing, and he needed the hit of caffeine.

At least with May on the afternoon shift yesterday, he knew the PD's coffeemaker had been thoroughly scrubbed out once or twice in the past twenty-four hours. His mother-in-law was nothing if not meticulous.

Giving into his fatigue, Wally closed his eyes and rested his head on the back of his chair. Letting Quirk handle the crime scene last night had been the correct decision. He'd promised Skye and himself to be present in the twins' life, and cutting down on the excessive hours he normally worked was the only way to do that.

There were a lot of people willing to help with the babies, but he wanted to be the one that shared the responsibility with Skye. They were in this together and he refused to be an absentee father. His children would know that they, and their mother, were the most important part of his life.

Last night had been a step in the right direction. The twins were sleeping when he and Skye had gotten home and they'd actually had some couple time. Afterward, instead of falling into an exhausted stupor, he'd held his wife in his arms and they'd narrowed down the list of names for their son and daughter to three possibilities each. One pair was sentimental, the second was Wally's favorite, and the last one was Skye's preference.

As odd as it seemed to other people that they had yet to choose names, Wally agreed with Skye that it was too important to rush. After so many years working with the public, both of them had a lot of names that had bad associations. Also, trying to find a name that none of Skye's enormous extended family had already used was an issue.

Add to that the difficulty of picking names that worked for twins. They didn't want to go cutesy like

Jack and Jill. But they couldn't have a pair that clashed, like Rambo and Edith either.

He and Skye had also had a chance to talk about their new house. Wally had thought that he had a good understanding of what it took to build a custom home. Turned out, he was amazingly wrong.

The major decisions hadn't been too bad. They had a relatively easy time choosing a floor plan. Wally's dad's connections had made hiring a general contractor a snap. And deciding where on the property to locate the structure was a no-brainer.

However, Wally hadn't taken into consideration the little details, and it was those that were killing them. Now he grasped why Skye had the television constantly tuned to HGTV.

The latest problem had been that once the house had been framed, it was clear that the toilet room in the master bath was too small for a regular door. Their options were to completely eliminate the walls or use a pocket door, which should have been a quick pick, but had ended up as a long discussion on claustrophobia versus germs.

The sharp ring of the telephone startled Wally out of his musings, and when he snatched up the receiver, his greeting was terse. "Yes?"

"Chief?" The tone was brisk.

Wally didn't recognize the feminine voice and said, "Yeah. Who is this?"

"Dr. Norris."

The name tugged at Wally's memory, but he couldn't quite place it.

After a paused, the woman added, "The new Stanley County ME."

"Right." Wally rubbed the bridge of his nose. He'd forgotten the old medical examiner had retired a couple of months ago.

"I'll email you the primary report on your bowling alley vic this afternoon, but I figured you'd want the ID sooner than later."

"I appreciate the courtesy call." Wally yanked open his desk drawer, cringing when it gave a loud squeak. He really needed to oil that thing. Grabbing a pen, he flipped open the case file and said, "Not much I can do before the body's identified."

"Lucky for you, her fingerprints were intact." Dr. Norris rustled some paper, cleared her throat, and announced, "Your vic is Paige Myler."

"Paige Myler. Why does that name sound familiar?" Wally pursed his lips and gazed at the ceiling.

"Probably because she's a special investigator for Homestead Insurance, which is why her prints were on file," Dr. Norris answered, then chuckled. "My assistant is from Scumble River and he mentioned that half your citizens were insured by that company and most of them were unhappy with the way their claims were being handled."

"Doggone it!" It was times like these that Wally

was really sorry that he'd promised Skye he would give up swearing.

As soon as the ME had mentioned Homestead Insurance, Wally remembered where he had recently heard the name Paige Myler. It was when Homer Knapik had tried to file a complaint against the woman. The high school principal had been enraged that Ms. Myler had denied him full reimbursement, stating that the age of his roof only entitled him to ten percent of the cost of replacing it.

"Yep. I would say your investigation just expanded by about a hundred percent." Dr. Norris's amused voice broke through Wally's musings.

"At least." The mild headache that Wally had been fighting all morning had turned into a whopper, and as he reached into his drawer for an aspirin, it squeaked again. He scribbled *OIL* in all caps on a sticky note, then attached the yellow square to the offending piece of furniture and asked, "What was the cause of death?"

"Blunt trauma, which resulted in significant cardiac injuries." Dr. Norris paused, then continued, "There was a severe thoracic aortic disruption that triggered the loss of cardiac pump function and brought about cardiogenic shock."

"In English, please." The only words Wally had understood were *blunt*, *trauma*, and *cardiac*.

"A video gambling machine fell on top of her and her chest was crushed." The doctor's crisp tone didn't make the image any less horrific.

Wally swallowed, then said, "Got it." Tapping his pen on the file, he asked, "Any indication if she was the intended target of the blast?"

"Nothing in the forensics." Dr. Norris hesitated, then added, "I can say that if the machine hadn't fallen on her, she would have had some severe injuries, but probably wouldn't have died from the explosion."

"Interesting." Wally twirled the pen in his fingers for a couple of seconds, thinking about the possibilities. "Anything on the tox screen?"

"Nothing significant so far, but all the results won't be in for several days."

"Okay." Wally frowned. "Thanks for the call. Keep me in the loop."

After saying goodbye to the ME, Wally dug into the reports from last night. The figure that Skye had spotted had slipped away before Martinez could get to him or her, but the young officer thought it had to have been Millicent Rose. Martinez suggested that the fairy godmother should be their number one suspect. She was convinced the woman had set off the blast to show the citizens of Scumble River that they needed her services for protection.

While Wally made a note of Martinez's speculation, he wasn't anywhere near ready to believe the young officer's theory.

Sighing, Wally continued to sift through the reports. After the crowd finally dispersed, Quirk had assigned officers to canvas the blocks surrounding the bowling alley, asking about the presence of anyone or anything unusual. Unfortunately, businesses occupied most of the area, and the bank, dry cleaners, real estate office, florist, and two churches had been closed for several hours before the incident.

As he read, Wally created a timeline of the incident. The blast occurred at 8:52 p.m. and the body was extracted by the coroner at 12:47 a.m. In between, the scene had been trampled by firefighters, the structural engineer, and the bomb expert before the crime techs could gather any possible forensics.

Although timing was usually vital in solving a murder case, in this instance, it wouldn't help them all that much. The explosive device could have been planted hours, if not days, prior to its detonation, and the perpetrator could be halfway across the country by now.

Wally sighed and continued to read Quirk's report. The Illinois Secretary of State Police Bomb Squad had collected the remains of the explosive device along with any related debris. Their experts would examine the evidence and send a report in a few days as to how the bomb was detonated—by a timer or someone nearby using a signaling device. Wally chafed at the delay, but he knew that the squad was stretched thin serving communities extending from just past Joliet to the southern tip of Illinois.

With the exception of the enclosed gaming lounge, the structural engineer had signed off on the overall safety of the building, allowing authorized personnel to enter it. But before the bowling alley could reopen for business, the windows, doors, and interior staircase needed to be replaced. In addition, the area directly damaged by the blast would have to be completely demolished and rebuilt to code.

Wally thought about the explosion and the resulting death. Was Paige Myler the target? Or was she collateral damage, and destroying the bowling alley's gambling lounge the real objective?

From what he had gathered, a lot of Scumble Riverites hated Paige and wouldn't cry at her funeral. But there were also a heck of a lot of townsfolk who were unhappy that gambling was allowed in their small community. Individuals who had lost a lot of money on the video gaming machines, or were anti-gambling, or even one of Bunny's competitors would be happy to have the bowling alley lounge closed down. And that didn't even take into account Bunny's former gentlemen friends. Who knew how many bitter exes were in her past?

Turning to his computer, Wally did some research. The minimal destruction done to the building suggested a fairly low-level blast, which made bombing an extremely poor method for murder. Not that perps were known for their common sense and ability to make good decisions.

Before he totally ruled out Paige's death as the goal, he needed to know why she'd been in the bowling alley after hours and how she'd gotten inside.

The search for those answers would have to start with Bunny.

It was frustrating that his key witness was a woman who was about as candid as a CIA agent and about as skillful a liar as Bernie Madoff. Wally would have a better chance of getting the CEO of Coca-Cola to give him the secret recipe for the famous soft drink than he had in getting Bunny to tell him the truth.

Unfortunately, his best bet in getting the shifty redhead to come clean was asking Skye to talk to her. Wally's gut clenched and he scrubbed his eyes with the heels of his hands. His wife had enough to do without dragging her into this investigation.

Pushing aside his instinctual protectiveness where Skye was concerned and his need to spare her any stress, Wally took a moment of self-reflection and shook his head. Yes, Skye was busy with the twins and with the new house being built, but she'd probably appreciate a break from those responsibilities. And she considered Bunny a friend, so she would want to help her get the bowling alley up and running as soon as possible.

Guilt tugged at his insides when he admitted that there was the uncomfortable little fact that he didn't really have the right to decide for her. Skye was a grown woman who could make up her own mind. He certainly didn't want to turn into the kind of husband who, in the name of love, thought he was in charge of his wife's choices.

Wally slowly took his cell phone from his pocket and reluctantly dialed Skye's number. One way or another, he needed to talk to Bunny ASAP.

Skye answered on the first ring. "Hey, sweetie. Everything okay?"

"Yep." Wally smiled. Skye was her mother's daughter all right. Her first impulse on receiving an unexpected call was to think something was wrong. "The body at the bowling alley has been identified as Paige Myler, the woman from Homestead Insurance."

"Oh. That's not good," Skye said slowly. "I've heard some unflattering stuff about her."

"Yeah." Wally rocked back in his chair. "Thing is, I need to question Bunny. I'm not convinced she wasn't aware of Ms. Myler's presence in the building."

"I agree." Skye paused, then asked, "Do you want me to go with you? Bunny will probably share things with me that she won't with you."

"If you're not too busy?" Wally wasn't really sure if he wanted her to answer yes or no. "Do you think your mom can babysit?"

"She·stopped by with a pan of lasagna and she's just leaving. Hold on and I'll ask her." The line went silent.

While he waited, Wally jotted down a few questions he wanted to ask Bunny.

"I'm back." Skye's voice was breathless. "I had to chase her down the driveway, but I caught Mom before she pulled away, and she says since she doesn't have to work this afternoon, she's happy to watch little Antonia and Joseph for as long as we want."

"Who?"

"She's decided we should name the twins after her parents." Skye chuckled.

"No." Wally shook his head even though no one could see him. "Just no."

"Don't worry. I told her that if we used one of her parents' names we'd have to use one of your father's parents' names and she backed off."

"What's wrong with Cornelius and Clementine?" Wally pretended to be offended.

Skye giggled, then said, "Do you want to meet me at the motor court, or maybe you should pick me up since we might have to track down Bunny?"

"When can you be ready?"

"Give me ten minutes," Skye said before disconnecting.

Staring at the mess in front of him, Wally quickly pulled the bowling alley file toward him and inserted the reports he'd been reading along with his own notes. Then he grudgingly placed a call to Kathryn Steele. Since the next of kin hadn't been notified, he couldn't reveal the vic's identity, but he gave the newspaper owner a statement that the bomb was being examined by an expert and the body that had been found suffered a crush injury due to a fallen slot machine.

After promising to give Kathryn Steele the name of the victim as soon as he could, he called Martinez and put her to work locating Paige Myler's next of kin, as well as finding out if the woman had been staying in the area, and if so, where. Once he had the rookie working on the vic's background info, Wally informed Thea that he was going out to interview witnesses, hurried to the garage, and slid behind the wheel of the squad car. Backing out, he headed home to pick up Skye.

As always, the sight of the sheared-off trees and fields still littered with debris saddened him. Eventually, most of the trees would grow back and the rubble would be cleared, but the invisible scars left by the tornado would take a lot longer to heal.

Pulling into his driveway, Wally studied the mammoth RV his father had arranged to be hauled to Scumble River and set up on their property when their old house had been destroyed in the storm. He and Skye were fortunate to have a comfortable motor home to live in, but he couldn't wait for their new place to be completed.

They had chosen to build the new house closer to the river with a deck running the entire length of the rear wall facing the water. Since they had plenty of land, they'd picked a sprawling Prairie-style ranch with a welcoming front porch and a screened-in gazebo in the back, as well as a full basement. Having made it through one tornado, he would never live anywhere without a basement again.

May's white Oldsmobile was in the driveway next to the Mercedes-Benz SUV that Wally had bought for his wife right before the birth of their babies. Skye's old Bel Air and his Thunderbird had been totaled when the garage collapsed under the impact of a downed tree.

He pulled the squad car to a stop and opened the driver-side door. As he got out of the cruiser, he heard what sounded like the tinkling of tiny bells and the hair on the back of Wally's neck rose. He whirled around. There weren't many places left for someone to hide with the trees shorn and the landscape mostly barren, but there still were a few bushes and piles of rubbish.

The RV was parked a good distance from where their new house was being built and Wally peered toward that site. He saw the usual workers' vehicles parked near the construction area but nothing else.

Turning back, he looked toward the front of the property. For a second he thought he caught a glimpse of pink near the road, but when he blinked it was gone. Was the stress finally getting to him, or had someone been watching the motor home?

CHAPTER 9

Bossa Nova Baby

As Skye slid into the squad car, she said, "Since your father and Bunny are probably together"—she ignored Wally's wince and continued—"should I try his cell?"

"Don't you have Bunny's number? Just call her."

Wally put his arm across the top of the seat and turned to get a better sight line as he backed out of the long driveway. He reversed slowly and Skye wondered why. He seemed to be examining the front yard closely.

"Are you looking for something?" Skye finally asked.

"What?" Wally shot her a guilty glance. "No. Just thinking that, come spring, we need to get a landscaper here to plant some trees."

"Right." Skye didn't entirely believe him, but she shook her head and went back to their original conversation. "I already called Bunny, but I got an automated message saying the number was no longer in service." Skye glanced sideways at her husband. "I could text Simon and ask him for his mother's new phone number."

"No." Wally's gaze was glued to the road, but tiny lines appeared around his mouth as he sighed. "Just call Dad."

When Carson didn't pick up, Skye left a message, then said, "Well, that didn't get us anywhere. Guess we'll just have to track them down."

"It's after three o'clock." Wally tapped his fingers on the steering wheel. "We'll try the motor court first, but I doubt they're just sitting around the room, and if they aren't there, where would they be?"

While Skye considered the possibilities, she stared out the windshield. There had been a gentle breeze earlier, but it had picked up and with every gust the long grass by the side of the road was nearly flattened to the ground. The sky was an unusual steel blue and the clouds were swirling like milk as it was added to a latte.

Refocusing, Skye said, "Your dad's been volunteering on the cleanup crews who walk the fields and clear out debris."

Wally rolled his eyes. "Bunny certainly wouldn't be with him doing that. Can you see her tripping along in her stilettos picking up litter among the cornstalks?"

"He also helps at the vet clinic," Skye offered. "A lot of the animals that Linc took in after they were displaced by the tornado are still there. Either the owners can't have them in their temporary housing or they've been abandoned. It's sort of turned into a no-kill shelter at this point."

"I can't imagine Bunny scooping dog poop either." Wally chuckled.

"I suppose not. But I sure hope she finds something to do." Skye twisted a curl around her finger. She'd put her hair into a french braid, but there were always one or two tendrils that escaped. "I'm worried that without the bowling alley to occupy her time, Bunny could have a relapse."

When Bunny had first come to town she had been dealing with an addiction to prescription painkillers. Since then, she'd kicked the habit and had been clean for several years.

Wally glanced at Skye. "Reid would be well advised to put her to work at the funeral home until the bowling alley is ready to reopen."

"Or maybe Bunny could help me out with the twins," Skye teased. "Your father's been offering to pay for a nanny and I could—"

"Skye." Wally's voice was unamused. "No." He opened his mouth as if to elaborate, then shook his head and said, "Just no."

"Party pooper." Skye folded her arms. Then, as Wally turned into the Up A Lazy River motor court, she gestured to the empty parking lot and said, "It doesn't look as if anyone's here. Not even Charlie."

"Let's check anyway." Wally pulled into a spot in front of the office.

Skye hopped out of the squad car, holding down the bottom of her trapeze top so the wind didn't blow it over her head. She met Wally as he was walking around the trunk. The cold front hadn't quite made it through yet and it was still hot and humid. Sweat dripped down her back as they approached the door and when the sun emerged from the clouds, it felt like a curling iron pressed against her spine.

A handwritten sign taped to the window part of the door greeted them: *No Vacancy. Office closed. Slip key under door if checking out.*

Wiping his forehead with his handkerchief, Wally cursed. "Son of a—"

"Want me to call Charlie?" Skye offered, waving her cell phone.

"Nah." Wally smiled. "Thanks, darlin', but I doubt Charlie would know Dad's and Bunny's whereabouts."

"Any better ideas?" Skye asked. "It's too early for cocktails. If the Feed Bag were still open, I'd suggest trying there. Maybe Mickey D's, but your dad seemed fed up, pun intended, with fast food."

"True," Wally agreed. "I guess it's time for good old-fashioned police work."

"And that would entail what exactly?" Skye raised a questioning brow.

"Driving around town until we see Dad's truck," Wally explained.

When Carson had decided to stay in Scumble River for an extended period of time, he'd had his tricked-out F-150 Platinum SuperCrew Cab brought in from Texas. Its distinctive metallic-ruby exterior was pretty easy to spot. The high-end Ford was as luxurious as a Mercedes and stood out among the rest of the more commonplace pickups in use around the area.

Getting back into the squad car, Skye reached over and kicked up the air-conditioning, turning the vent to blow on her overheated face.

As they slowly cruised through the streets of Scumble River, Skye asked, "Did the ME have any details that suggested Paige was the target of the explosion versus the bowling alley itself?"

"At this point, there's no way to tell." Wally slowed when a red truck passed them going in the opposite direction, but he sped up when it was obviously not Carson's vehicle. "I'm leaning toward the alley since it's difficult to guarantee anyone would get killed in a bombing like the one yesterday."

"Unless you didn't care if that person ended up dead or only injured," Skye said thoughtfully. "Maybe the goal was just to get Paige out of commission."

"Okay." Wally turned west on Basin Street. "But in that case, the bomber had to know Ms. Myler would be in the gambling lounge."

"Which brings us back to Bunny," Skye said, then yelled, "Stop!"

The squad car's tires squealed as Wally hit the brakes, and although Skye was wearing her seat belt, he put his arm out to hold her back. She patted his hand, then leaned forward and pointed.

Wally squinted through the windshield, then said, "Tell me my dad's truck isn't in front of your aunt Olive's dance studio."

"I thought we promised not to lie to each other." Skye grinned.

"There's a fine line between fibbing and offering your dear husband the comfort he so badly needs." Wally tapped Skye's nose, then pulled the squad car into a parking spot in front of the school. "Just wait until your family is driving you crazy again."

"You did not just jinx me." Skye shot him an outraged glare.

"If the curse fits." Wally shrugged, exited the vehicle, and went around to Skye's side to escort her. "Let's get this over with."

Olive Leofanti had opened the Scumble River School of Adult Dance a little less than two years ago. When her original partner had been unable to come up with her half of the money for the business, the future of the studio had seemed uncertain until Olive had found another investor.

Her new business partner, Ruby Jones, was from out of state, but she'd sent her daughter Emerald—a.k.a. Emmy, a.k.a. Simon's new girlfriend—to represent her interests in the studio. Agreeing with Emmy's suggestions, Olive had changed the name of the school to Turning Pointe and expanded to include lessons for children. Immediately, business had picked up and now the place was thriving.

Skye had only been to the school twice—once for the grand opening and once to investigate a previous murder. However, her mother's bulletins usually kept her informed. Either May didn't know that Carson was taking lessons or he'd sworn her to secrecy. Skye's mom loved a good gossip session, but she always kept her promises.

Loud music greeted Skye and Wally as they walked through the glass doors and into the lobby. Beyond the entrance were three separate rooms that had been carved from the original large space. The studio had started life as a grocery store, but Skye's aunt Olive had gutted it, then added laid hardwood over the cement floors, mounted track lighting along the high ceiling, and installed mirrors on the walls.

Couples ranging in age from millennials to baby boomers and beyond were practicing line dancing in one room, swing in a second, and ballroom in the third. Although there were walls between them, all three rooms had their double doors wide open and Skye wondered how the students were able to block out the peripheral music that spilled into their space and follow the correct beat.

Emerald Jones, a beautiful woman in her early thirties, stood near the entrance of the middle room. She was teaching a half-dozen teenagers the steps to the Lindy Hop. When she noticed Wally and Skye, she told her group to take a break and approached them.

"Well, if it isn't the proud new parents." The stunning blond, dressed in skintight low-rise boy-cut shorts, a barely there crop top, and thigh-high tights, playfully tapped Wally's arm. "When are you going to bring those babies to the club for us all to admire?"

"Hi, Emmy." Wally smiled warmly. "The twins will have to be a little older before they make their first trip to the shooting range."

"That's a shame," Emmy purred. "We were hoping you'd come out for the Halloween party." She tilted her head. "I saw the cutest little peas in a pod costume that would be perfect for them."

Skye had been taking in the exchange, trying to keep the pangs of jealousy at bay. Silently, she repeated the litany of why she shouldn't be upset. *Wally would never cheat. Emmy was dating Simon. And the gorgeous dancer flirted with everyone.*

However, it was difficult to look at the beautiful woman and not compare herself. On most days, showering was a major accomplishment for Skye. Makeup and hair had been slipping lower and lower in her priorities. Taking one more peek at Emmy's perfectly put together appearance, Skye immediately relocated a thorough beauty regime to the top of her to-do list. From now on, she was treating every evening with her husband as a date.

But that would have to wait until tomorrow. Right

now, it was time to join the conversation. She moved closer to Wally, slipped her hand into his, and took a deep breath. Emmy was so close to them, Skye could smell the other woman's peach-and-vanilla-scented perfume. Skye scowled. The dance instructor needed to back off.

Wally glanced at her with a smile, then frowned and leaned down to whisper, "Everything okay, sugar? Are you getting tired?"

Making an effort to erase any lingering self-doubt, Skye kissed his cheek. "I'm fine." She turned to Emmy and said, "That does sound like a cute costume, but you'll need to get in line behind my mother to outfit the twins for their first major holiday."

"Hmm." Emmy tapped her chin. "I always did like a challenge."

"I wouldn't mess with my mother." Skye examined the tall, lithe woman, unable to tell if she was joking or not.

Emmy tossed her ponytail and looked at Wally with a speculative gleam in her eye. "I guess it would all come down to who was judging the entries."

"Mom would make sure whoever was selecting the best costume was someone who couldn't be swayed by flattery." Skye kept her tone light. "Or any other type of coercion."

"You never can tell what someone might fall for." Emmy's honeyed voice had a twist of acidic tartness. "If I would have known what was at stake earlier, I might have tried a little harder the last time I competed with a Denison."

The low-grade agitation that had been humming through Skye's chest amped up and sizzled just under her skin. Was Emmy talking about Wally? Was she implying that if she'd known he was rich as well as gorgeous, she would have tried to break up their engagement and nab him for herself?

Evidently Wally was thinking the same thing because before Skye could frame a reply, he dropped her hand and slid his arm around her waist. Tucking Skye into to his side, he pinned Emmy with a hard stare.

"What?" The dancer arched a feathery brow.

"The results would have been exactly the same." Wally's tone was unyielding.

"Are you sure?" Emmy pupils dilated and she waited a long beat before adding, "Anyway, I won't give in as easily again."

"On what?" Skye asked, trying to figure out what in the heck they were talking about because she thought the subject of their conversation was no longer Wally. "Or should I ask on whom?"

"Well, there *is* another handsome Boyd man available." Emmy poked Wally's arm again and her voice took on the satiny tone of jazz singer crooning a love song. "And he hasn't put a ring on anyone's finger."

"Carson?" Skye's mouth dropped open. "You're talking about my father-in-law? But isn't he dating the mother of your current boyfriend?"

This was beginning to sound like the Dooziers' twisted family tree. The Dooziers, an inbred clan who ruled a section of riverside property through a combination of cunning and ruthlessness, were known to marry cousins and suspected of getting hitched to even closer relations.

"Simon and I aren't exclusive." Emmy's sapphire-blue eyes gleamed and she wrinkled her cute, little turned-up nose. "According to him, he's not ready to commit yet." She straightened her spine. "If there's one thing I learned living in Las Vegas, it's that a girl has to hedge her bets."

"But…" Skye gasped. She could usually read people pretty well, but something about Emmy nullified Skye's psychologist abilities. Was the blond teasing or was her coldhearted approach to love for real?

"Hey." Emmy shook her finger at Skye. "You don't get to be so morally outraged." She jerked her thumb at Wally. "You played him against Simon for long enough before deciding which guy was the better deal."

"I did not!" Skye gritted her teeth to stop herself from telling Emmy exactly what she thought of that type of woman.

"Of course you did." Emmy crossed her arms. "Not that I blame you."

Skye stepped away from Wally and toward the dancer, ready to slap her if she said another maddening word. "Simon may have continued to pursue me after we broke up, but I told him that I wasn't interested.

I did not 'play' him and Wally off one another." She moved closer to the exasperating woman. "And the only 'better deal' I was looking for was a man who loved me the way I was, not the way he wanted me to be."

"Darlin'." Wally moved in front of Skye. "Emmy's joshing you. She enjoys riling up people." He looked hard at the dancer. "Right?"

"Sure." Emmy's lips twitched as she added, "But your father is seriously hot, and Bunny's attention span is notoriously short."

"Emmy." Wally's tone made it clear he'd had enough of the dancer's mischief. "We're here on official police business, so stop playing around."

Emmy pouted. "Fine. Then what can I do for the Scumble River PD?"

"Actually, we're looking for Bunny." Skye glanced around. The redhead wasn't in the line dancing or the ballroom class. "We saw Carson's truck and thought she might be here with him."

"They're in the private studio with Olive." Emmy tilted her head to the left.

"Thanks." Wally put his arm around Skye. "We'll let you get back to your lesson."

"Sure." Emmy started to walk away, then turned and winked. "But if you arrest Bunny, don't forget to send your father my way."

"Stick to Simon," Skye advised. "Carson might be more of a handful than you realize."

"Shh." Wally hugged Skye. "Saying something like that will only encourage her," he murmured.

"I don't think she was kidding." Skye fiddled with her wedding ring, wishing Simon would marry Emmy and they'd both move back to Las Vegas.

"Maybe so." Wally's expression clouded as if wondering who would be worse as a stepmother—Bunny or Emmy. Shaking his head, he said. "Let's go find Dad."

As they approached the door that Emmy had indicated, it burst open. Before Skye could react, Bunny and Carson bossa-novaed out of the room. They glided across the large room, knees bent and hips swaying. Then, with a flourish, Bunny wound an arm around Carson's neck and gave him a passionate kiss.

"Dang it!" Wally stiffened and rubbed his eyes. "How do I ever unsee that?"

Bunny turned at the sound of Wally's voice, then her gaze flicked to Skye. Her eyes widened and she tried to flee back into the private studio they'd been using. Carson started to follow her, but Wally was quicker.

"Going somewhere?" He blocked the door and crossed his arms. "We need to have a chat. Would you rather talk here or the police station?"

"Neither." Bunny inched backward until she bumped into Carson. Bunny stepped sideways, glaring at Wally. "I don't have to talk to you."

"You really do." Skye touched the older woman's arm. "Please. I promise whatever you're trying to avoid telling us is going to eventually come out."

"You can't know that." Bunny's nose twitched like the animal she was named for, and she scowled at Skye.

"I can, because we've identified the body. And with or without your help, we're going to find out why she was at the bowling alley when no one was supposed to be there." Skye's tone was firm but cajoling. "It would be better to get in front of whatever you're trying to hide."

"Paige must have broken in." Bunny refused to meet Skye's gaze.

"How did you know who it was?" Wally asked.

"I heard it around town?" Bunny's answer came out more like a question.

"Uh-uh." Skye shook her head. "The truth."

"Sonny Boy will kill me," Bunny moaned.

"It'll be fine," Skye assured her. It wasn't as if Simon had any illusions about his mother.

Bunny threw herself into Carson's arms and wailed, "It's my fault Paige is dead."

CHAPTER 10

Baby, Baby, Don't Cry

SKYE WATCHED AS BUNNY SOBBED ON CARSON'S shoulder. She wasn't entirely convinced that the redhead was truly weeping due to her guilt over Paige's death rather than her frustration at being trapped. A part of Skye even thought that it was all an act to keep from answering the questions Wally had for her. It was probably a little of both.

However, it was clear that Carson believed his ladylove's distress was genuine remorse. He dug his handkerchief from his pocket and gave it to her. Then, as he rubbed soothing circles on her back and murmured reassuring words in her ear, he glared at his son. Wally, evidently unaffected by his father's censure, leaned a hip against the wall and waited.

When Bunny's crying finally subsided into the occasional sniffle, Skye and Wally shared a glance. He tipped his head at the embracing couple and Skye nodded her understanding. She moved toward Bunny and Carson and gently drew Bunny from Carson's arms. Taking the hanky, she stroked it over the older woman's cheeks and under her eyes.

"There." Skye dabbed one more time. "That's better. Nothing worse than mascara smudges." Giving Bunny a quick hug, she stepped back and said, "Now let's all go somewhere private and talk."

"But I'm starving." Bunny's period of mourning for Paige was evidently over and she turned to Carson and pouted. "You promised to take me somewhere nice for an early dinner after we finished our lesson."

Skye linked her elbow with the older woman's arm. "Let's get this over with, then Dad can feed you. Where were you all thinking of going?"

In order to keep the redhead distracted, as she led a reluctant Bunny toward the front door, Skye continued to chatter away. They were only a couple of feet from the exit when Skye's stomach let out a loud growl, then two more in quick succession.

Wally and Carson were right behind them, and Carson stopped Skye with a hand on her arm and asked, "When did you eat last, sugar?"

"I had a big breakfast after we fed the twins this morning."

Skye tried to keep moving toward the door, but Carson's grip tightened and he said, "It's close to four o'clock. You mean you haven't had a square meal in eight hours?"

"Square meals just make you round," Skye muttered under her breath.

Wally moved in front of Skye and questioned, "Why didn't you have lunch?"

"I was busy with the babies, then Mom stopped by and I just didn't get to it." Skye freed her arm from Carson's grasp, adding, "A lot of the time when I was working in the schools, I didn't have a chance to eat lunch." She shrugged. "And it's not as if I can't afford to lose a few pounds. The baby weight isn't—"

"Don't." Wally took her hand and drew her away from Carson and Bunny. Lowering his voice, he said, "No more worrying about that. You are beautiful no matter what your dress size is and your doctor said you aren't supposed to try to lose weight until after your next checkup. She said it will come off naturally while you breastfeed."

"Dr. J can't know that for sure," Skye whispered, wishing her hormones would get back to normal so she would stop feeling so insecure. "And Mom brought over her lasagna, which has about a billion calories. I was saving up."

"Do you promise not to do that anymore?" Wally asked. When she nodded, he kissed the top of her head and murmured, "Do you think your mom would be willing to watch the twins for a while longer?"

"Since she doesn't have to work, Mom would be happy if she had them all night." Skye smiled. "And I pumped enough milk for their next two feedings."

"Perfect." Wally turned to Carson and asked, "Where were you planning to go for supper?"

"That Italian restaurant in Clay Center," Carson answered. "I heard the tornado damage was repaired and it's open for business."

"Great. Skye and I love Pesto's food." Wally put his arm around Skye's shoulders and walked toward the door. "How about Bunny tells us what she knows about Paige and her presence at the bowling alley over a plate of pasta?"

"Works for us." Carson held out his elbow for Bunny and the couple followed Skye and Wally outside. "Shall we meet you over there?"

Wally lowered his chin and stared at his father. "You promise that you won't let Bunny talk you into helping her escape?"

"You have my word as a Texan." Carson put his hand over his heart. Then, his eyes twinkling, he said, "Or we could all ride together in my truck."

"Sounds like a plan." Wally helped Skye into the back seat of his father's pickup.

Once they were settled, Skye leaned over to Wally and whispered, "I'm surprised you didn't insist on interviewing Bunny at the station. Going out to eat with a suspect is a little unorthodox."

"If she were truly a suspect and not just a witness that might be true." Wally took Skye's hand and brushed his lips against her knuckles. "But more importantly, I wanted to make sure you had a decent meal." He traced a finger down her jaw. "I vowed when we got married that I wouldn't put my job ahead of you. And the babies just reinforce that decision. I'm trying to delegate more."

"You're the best husband." Skye leaned over and kissed his cheek. "I knew I loved you, but every single day you remind me why."

A pair of headlights sliced through the growing darkness, then after the car sped away, the truck was once again the only vehicle on the road. While everyone seemed lost in his or her own thoughts, Skye dug her phone from her purse and called her mother to check on the twins.

Once May assured her that the babies were fine, Skye told her mother that she and Wally would be gone two or three more hours. May was thrilled to have additional time with her grandchildren, and after thanking her mom, Skye put away the cell and relaxed.

Between the soft music coming from the radio, another song with *baby* in the lyrics, and the motion of the truck, Skye's lids fluttered closed, and the next thing she knew, Wally was gently kissing her forehead.

"We're here," Wally said softly. "Are you ready to have a great dinner and an interesting conversation?"

Skye nodded and they all exited the truck and walked inside Pesto. It was a small restaurant set between a real estate agent and podiatrist office in a strip mall at the edge of Clay Center, Scumble River's nearest neighbor.

The atmosphere was casual and the hostess was dressed in jeans and a T-shirt. She quickly seated them in a corner booth and asked what they wanted to drink. Wally and Carson requested iced teas with lemon and Skye went with her usual Caffeine Free Diet Coke with lime, but Bunny ordered a glass of cabernet.

Although no one commented, Bunny giggled. "A meal without wine is called breakfast."

While they waited for their drinks, they scanned the menus. Once Skye decided on her entrée, she looked around the newly repaired restaurant. It was bright and cheerful with a wall of windows facing the street. The decor was modern but welcoming, and the air smelled of oregano, garlic, and melting mozzarella. Her stomach growled again.

When the server returned with their drinks, Wally said, "Let's start with an appetizer tray. That way we can get our talk over with before we have dinner."

Everyone nodded and he ordered breaded mushrooms, bruschetta, and stuffed potato skins. Skye forced herself not to think about the calories and focused on the here and now. A yummy dinner with her handsome husband without worrying about the babies waking up was a real luxury and she was determined to enjoy it.

Even if they were sharing the meal with her father-in-law and his girlfriend, it still felt a little like a date. There were crisp white linen napkins on a pristine tablecloth, soft music in the background, and dim lights. Once she managed to make Bunny tell them what she knew about Paige, Wally and Skye could relax and enjoy this rare treat.

With that in mind, she looked at Bunny and said, "Let's start with why Paige was in the bowling alley after closing time."

"Do you promise not to tell Sonny Boy?" Bunny fidgeted in her chair, refusing to meet Skye's stare.

"I won't tell him, but in all probability he will eventually find out." Skye tilted her head and quirked her lips. "You do know that Simon realizes you aren't an angel, right?"

"Yeah." Bunny's cheeks turned pink. "But I was kind of hoping to earn that halo someday."

"I'm sure you'll get your wings eventually." Carson winked.

When Wally choked on the sip of water he'd just taken, Skye thumped his back.

"So." Skye paused as the server put a basket of warm bread on the table, then poured olive oil in a small saucer, adding pepper and grated Parmesan on top. After the waitress walked away, Skye looked at Bunny and asked, "What was the deal with Paige?"

"She was bored." Bunny tore off a piece of the loaf. "And lonely."

"I can understand that. Scumble River didn't have a lot of entertainment options before the tornado, and from the brief glance I got of Paige, she didn't seem the type to attend a high school volleyball game or go fishing in the park out by the dam." Skye broke off her own slice. "How long had she been in town?"

"Maybe a month, but she usually went home Friday and didn't come back until Monday morning." Bunny dragged the bread through the dish of olive oil. "At first, she came into the alley in the evening during regular hours. She tried to have something to eat at the grill and relax, but people pounced on her like she was the last cookie in the jar."

"Because of all the claims she disallowing," Skye speculated.

"*Ding! Ding! Ding!* Give the girl a prize." Bunny licked the oil off her fingers. "Any time money is involved, people get nasty."

"Which meant that Paige being out in public was stressful, and I'm sure that the last thing she wanted during her leisure hours was to talk about work."

Skye sure understood that problem. She couldn't even run to the bank or grocery store without a parent cornering her to talk about their child's problems or complain about the way the school was handling said problem. And it was the same for Wally. There was no such thing as being off duty.

Skye thought over what she'd heard about Paige, then turned to Wally and asked, "Do we know if she was staying at Charlie's?"

"Not yet. I have Martinez gathering that kind of information, as well as finding the next of kin." Wally sipped his iced tea. "But her only other option would be driving thirty-five minutes one way from Kankakee to meet with her clients or to inspect damaged properties, and in that case, she might as well commute from Normalton."

"Then let's assume she was renting a cabin at the motor court," Skye said. "It would be easy to grab something to eat while she was out and about, but in the evening, when she was alone and wanted to have a drink, she really wouldn't want to drive any great distance. Especially on dark country roads." Skye zeroed in on Bunny. "Which is where you came into the equation. Am I correct so far?"

"Possibly." Bunny grabbed her wine and chugged half the glass.

Noticing that their server was approaching, Skye paused as the woman placed their appetizer tray on the table. After being assured that they didn't need anything else, she left them to their first course.

Immediately, Skye grabbed a slice of bruschetta and bit into the grilled bread topped with chopped tomato. The salty garlic taste was heavenly. She wasn't sure if the chef was really good or if she was really hungry. Probably a little bit of both.

Wally and Carson went for the stuffed potato skins oozing with melted cheese, sour cream, and/chives, while Bunny sampled the breaded mushrooms. For several minutes, they all concentrated on their food.

Finally, Skye wiped her fingers, took a sip of her soda, and, looking at Bunny, said, "I've been thinking.

The bowling alley isn't open at all on Mondays and closes at nine on the other weekdays, right?"

"Yes," Bunny said after she finished the rest of her wine, then started to tear pieces off of the paper napkin under her drink until she'd built a tiny ski slope. "Sonny Boy thinks that those hours suggest a more family-friendly place."

"Hmm." Skye tilted her head. "In that case, I'm a little surprised that he allowed you to add the video gambling machines."

"He took a lot of convincing. I had to promise to keep them behind closed doors and he still wasn't happy." Bunny's brow puckered. "Which is why he's going to blow a gasket if he finds out about Paige."

"What about her?" Skye asked, reaching for the last mushroom.

"Seriously, you've got to keep this from Sonny Boy or my goose is cooked." Bunny waved over the waitress and asked for another glass of wine.

"I'll do what I can." Skye shook her head. "But like I've said before, the news will probably get out and it would be best to tell him yourself."

Wally polished off the remaining potato skin and said, "Back to Paige."

"How much did she offer you to let her into the alley after closing?" Skye asked, having a pretty good guess as to why Bunny would allow Paige into the alley after hours. The redhead was always looking to make a little cash on the side.

"A hundred bucks a week," Bunny said, then thanked the server as the woman placed a full glass of cabernet in front of her.

The waitress took their dinner orders, and when she left, Skye said, "That doesn't seem like enough to risk upsetting Simon."

"That wasn't all there was to it though, was it?" Wally crossed his arms.

"Not exactly." Bunny sighed. "Paige liked to play the machines."

"Now that makes more sense," Skye said. Bunny was no one's fool.

Carson had been silent up until now, but he leaned forward and, his deep voice rumbling like thunder, said, "It sounds as if you're convinced that Ms. Myler was the intended victim."

"Not at all, Dad." Wally turned to his father. "We are just gathering facts right now, but we'll be considering several possibilities."

"Good. If Bunny could be in danger, we need to know." Carson put his arm around her shoulders. "To get her some protection."

"There are several sound motives for the bowling alley being the bomber's objective." Wally held up a finger. "One, some poor schmuck who put his paycheck into the video gaming machines and ended up with nothing. Two, an individual, or a group, who is anti-gambling. Three, one of Bunny's competitors trying to close down the lounge. And, four, one of

Bunny's gentlemen friends who isn't happy she's with someone new."

"There's that woman, Udelle Calvert," Carson offered. "She's the president of the Stanley County Anti-Gambling League Defense. From the flyers she's been leaving around town, SCALD has been trying to keep video gaming out of the area."

Wally took a pad from his shirt pocket and made a note. "I'll look into that."

"Zeus Hammersmith was complaining the other night that the machines are rigged." Carson glanced at Bunny. "What did he say to you, darlin'?"

"He told me I'd be sorry for stealing his money." Bunny twirled a red curl around her finger. "But he was just blowing off steam."

"Maybe." Wally jotted down the guy's name, then skewered Bunny with a look. "I'll check out your competitors as well, but you need to provide me with a list of your exes."

"I can do that right now." Bunny dug through her enormous purse, took out a dry cleaning receipt, and began writing on the back of the crumpled paper.

As the redhead wrote, Skye thought about what they'd learned. The sound of rapid tapping distracted her and she frowned until she realized that it was her own foot bouncing off the back of the booth. She made herself stop, then began piling the dirty plates on the empty appetizer tray. She knew the server would do it, but a tiny part of her mother's cleanliness obsession had evidently welded itself to her DNA.

As Skye tidied up the table, an idea formed and she asked, "Did Paige play the machines every time she came in after hours?"

Bunny nodded. "It's the main reason she wanted access to the place. That and to have a drink alone without anyone bothering her."

"And if the person who planted the explosive device knew that," Skye mused, then finished her own sentence, "it's a lot more likely that she was the target."

CHAPTER 11

My Baby Must Be a Magician

THE REST OF THE MEAL HAD BEEN PLEASANT, AS they all made an effort to discuss topics other than the bombing. However, by the time they finished and were heading back to Scumble River, they'd run out of small talk and everyone was silent.

It had started pouring and rain hammered against the truck's roof so Carson concentrated on the slick road. Bunny stared out the blurred windshield, occasionally jotting another name on the growing list of her ex-boyfriends, while Wally was busy texting instructions to his officers. Skye's full stomach and constant state of exhaustion had her on the verge of dozing off again.

When Carson dropped Wally and Skye off at the dance studio to pick up the squad car, Bunny held out the crumpled scrap of paper she'd been using and said, "These are guys I dated in the last year or two." She glanced uneasily at Carson. "Is that far enough back?"

"For now." Wally tucked the list into his pocket and tapped his father on the shoulder. "You two be careful." He shook his head. "I never thought I'd say this, but keep your cell on and check in with me a few times a day so I know how to find you."

Bunny giggled and Skye burst out laughing. Taking Wally's hand, she tugged. "Come on, Papa Bear. Time to go see how our real cubs are doing." She waved to the older couple and said, "Later."

Although they ran as fast as they could from Carson's pickup to the squad car parked next to it, both Skye and Wally were drenched. The rain was coming down in sheets and there was no dodging the deluge.

Wiping her cheeks with a tissue, Skye glanced at Wally, who was using his handkerchief to dry his own face. Even soaking wet, after a long day at work, he was still the best-looking man she'd ever met. His wet uniform molded to his muscular chest. The threads of silver in his black hair gleamed and his chocolate-brown eyes were filled with a good-humored tolerance for the situation.

When Wally's cell dinged, he read the message, then turned to Skye and asked, "Think your mother would mind if we made one more stop before we went home?"

"Not at all." Skye reached for her phone. "What's up?"

Wally handed Skye his cell and she read the message from Zelda.

You have to see this. Texts went out all over town. Millicent Rose is performing a purification ceremony in front of her cottage. Just like I thought, she set off the bomb to get people to pay her for protection!

Skye glanced at Wally. He hadn't mentioned that Zelda thought the fairy godmother was behind the bombing, so he must not have thought the young officer's theory held water. Would he change his mind now?

Giving Wally back his phone, Skye used hers to update May on their ETA. Once her mother assured her that the twins were fine, Skye realized that Wally had already driven the six blocks between the dance school and the Enchanted Cottage. She had forgotten that the former Young at Heart Photography studio was kitty-corner across the street from Bunny Lanes and she saw that there was a huge crowd of people pressing against the police tape strung around the bowling alley.

"Why in God's green earth are these fools standing out in the rain to watch a charlatan perform some hocus-pocus?" Wally snarled.

"Actually, we're lucky the weather's bad or there'd probably be even more folks here." Skye twisted in her seat to take in the entire scene.

There was already one squad car parked at the curb in front of the Enchanted Cottage, and as Wally slowly inched his police cruiser in behind it, the throng reluctantly parted to give him space.

Skye looked at the sea of umbrellas and saw people sloshing through the puddles that had already formed. Few Scumble Riverites appeared to own rain boots, and Skye cringed as their athletic shoes suffered the consequences.

The windshield wipers worked to keep up with the torrent and it was difficult to make out any details. Scooting forward, Skye spotted the self-proclaimed fairy godmother standing in the cottage's overgrown front lawn with several large spotlights illuminating the yard.

The photography studio had sat empty since its owner had been sent to prison and the years had not been kind to the landscaping. The thorny limbs of bramble bushes competed with the sycamore seedlings to turn the once-well-kept lawn into chaos.

The crowd formed a semicircle around Millicent, the streetlights painting them in a sulfurous glow. Their shadows lengthened and crept like tentacles toward the woman at whose behest they had all gathered.

Millicent Rose was dressed in a light-blue cloak with a pointy hood that concealed much of her face. But rather than the satin cape Skye had seen her wear previously, this one was waterproof and droplets rolled off of it. Unfortunately, the pink bow at her throat was more vulnerable to the rain and it lay in a soggy mess just below her round chin. She stood behind a half-moon-shaped table with an attached canopy and surrounded by a circle of white stones.

Figuring she was already wet, Skye unfastened her

seat belt and lowered her window so that she could hear whatever Millicent said. Wally followed suit. Stinging droplets pelted Skye's cheeks and she held a hand over her eyes to protect them from the rain and help her see what was happening.

Millicent lifted a metal bowl from the silver-cloth-covered table, passed it through a white pillar candle's flame, and held it out, allowing it to fill with the rainwater, then said, "Imbue this instrument with energy, that it may be a source of righteousness." She placed the bowl on her flattened palm, put her other hand over it, and continued, "Sanctify and favor this instrument for the purposes of good. May it always be used for right and never for wrong. May it assist the community of Scumble River well, as long as its citizens are pure of heart and their goals are virtuous, I do devote you."

Millicent's voice had been hypnotic and Skye startled when the screech of an owl broke the night's eerie silence. Goose bumps blossomed across Skye's skin, and she shivered.

As if Millicent had been waiting for the bird's cry, she slowly faced Bunny Lanes and, holding the bowl to her chest, said, "We cleanse you of all evil influences." She dipped her pudgy fingers in the bowl and sprinkled the drops toward the bowling alley. "Be now an instrument of the light. Help us see what is needed that we may regain blessings. So must it be."

With that, she flung the remaining water, blew

out the candle, and wrapped it and the bowl in the cloth covering the table.

Up until now, the crowd had been silent, but it was as if a spell had been broken and someone yelled, "What was the hocus-pocus all about?"

"The Bunny Lanes's aura was covered in evil soot. Whenever there has been a disturbing occurrence in our physical surroundings, it is necessary to perform a ritual to clean up any residue of wickedness that might remain." Millicent's smile was beatific. "Think of it as a baptism."

"So you're saying a demon blew up the bowling alley?" An onlooker approached her and challenged. "Is it the gateway to hell or something?"

By this point, the rain had lessened to a light mist, and although it was still breezy, Millicent's audience was becoming livelier.

"Not at all." Millicent paused, a thoughtful expression on her face. "At least, not of which I'm currently aware. The miscreant who set off the explosive device was no doubt human. But her malevolence will attract others who aren't and they will feed on her cruelty."

"Her?" The guy asked.

"Or his." Millicent shrugged. "Although in my many years as a fairy godmother, I've found that the troublemaker is usually a villainess rather than a villain."

"Then you don't know who's behind the bombing?" a woman asked.

"I'm afraid not." Millicent extended a chubby finger

tipped in a pink fingernail at the cruiser. "Finding criminals is the police department's job. Mine is making sure that the evildoer's forces do no harm."

"Right," the woman sneered, and Skye wondered if she had been offended that Millicent had said most troublemakers were female.

"The more of you who doubt"—Millicent paused and stared at the woman—"the more difficult it is to cleanse the area."

"Why should we care if it is or isn't?" The woman tossed down the gauntlet.

"You want it cleansed." Millicent threw out her arms and said, "Trust me on that."

The woman said something that Skye missed when the wind stilled and the drizzle stopped. The hair on the back of Skye's neck stood up, and suddenly, the neon lights in the Bunny Lanes sign blinked on.

Skye's heart spasmed like she'd just been jolted by a defibrillator.

Looking at Wally, she fought to keep her voice steady and asked, "Didn't the fire department turn off the bowling alley's electricity?"

"The backup generator must have kicked in." Wally's smile was playful. "You don't believe that Millicent's little act was real, do you?"

"No." Skye glanced at Bunny Lanes again, just in time to see the inside lights flicker on. "But the generator didn't do anything last night."

"It must be on a timer." Wally gestured to the

people who were beginning to wander away. "See, no one thinks the lights mean anything."

"Most of them had their backs to the alley and probably don't realize that the lights came on at the precise moment that they did," Skye pointed out, then shrugged. "Anyway, like you said, it's probably just an odd coincidence." She paused, then added, "Unless Zelda's idea that Ms. Rose is the bomber is true. Do you think Zelda's onto something?"

"I'm keeping her theory in mind, but the Rose woman isn't on the top of my suspect list right now." Wally jerked his chin at the other squad car. "Martinez will keep an eye on things here until everyone disburses. Let's go drop off the cruiser and pick up the Hummer. That's if you're ready to go home?"

"Whenever you are." Skye rolled up the window and refastened her seat belt.

"Interesting display," Wally commented as he pulled away from the curb. "What do you think was her purpose in putting on that little show?"

"Maybe she really believes she can purify the area of evil." Skye glanced uneasily back toward the now brightly lit bowling alley. "I mean, she didn't ask for donations of anything."

"More likely she's priming the pump." Wally drove toward the police station. "Once she's stirred up people, she'll start collecting fees."

"I suppose, which would make Zelda's suspicions about her a bit more believable." Skye nibbled on her bottom lip. Her instinct told her Millicent Rose was something other than a con artist, but she didn't know what that other thing could be. Changing the subject, she asked, "After our conversation with Bunny, and if you aren't moving Ms. Rose to the top of your list, what are your thoughts on the bomber's target?"

"It's hard to say." Wally scraped his hand over the stubble on his jaw.

"Oh?" Skye smiled at the bristly sound. His five o'clock shadow generally started around noon and by this time of night, he had a sexy scruff.

"On one side, there's the fact that Paige made a habit of being in the gambling lounge during off hours, and she's made a lot of enemies in town." He glanced at Skye.

She nodded her understanding and added, "There's also her personal life, which no one around her probably has a clue about." Skye took a comb from her purse and ran it through her wet curls, then used the hair tie from her french braid to put it in a ponytail. "Do you have any background info on her?"

"Martinez emailed me a summary of what she's found so far." Wally turned onto the street leading to the station. "Paige was thirty-eight. Her parents are both dead, and according to the executive vice president at Homestead Insurance, she's recently divorced. She's worked for the company for sixteen years."

"What's her exact job title?" Skye asked, finishing with her ponytail.

"She's the head of their special investigations department." Wally parked the squad car in the police lot.

"I'm surprised she didn't send one of her employees to Scumble River." Skye opened her door and followed Wally to his Hummer.

"I believe there was someone else handling things here for a while. Let me think." Wally helped Skye into the huge SUV, then walked around and slid behind the steering wheel. "Oh, yeah. Everybody liked that guy and he was settling claims left and right."

"Meaning that Homestead was bleeding money and probably putting pressure on Paige to stop the hemorrhage." Skye fastened her seat belt.

"Exactly." Wally curled his lip, indicating his thoughts on the matter. "Then suddenly, Paige took over and the flow of cash has all but stopped. I don't believe I've heard of anyone getting a full payment since she arrived in town."

"Plenty of motive to kill her." Skye aimed the Hummer's heating vent at her chest, trying to dry her wet shirt. "How about the ex-husband?"

"Interestingly enough, he works for Homestead Insurance as well." Wally drove the huge SUV out of the lot and pointed it toward home. "He's the head of the auto claims department."

"I wonder if they met at work." Skye plucked at the damp fabric of her capris. "Of course the real question is, how friendly was the divorce?"

"If we pursue Paige as the intended victim, I'll have

to send someone up to Normalton to nose around and find out more about her personal life, but for now, I think it's more likely the bowling alley and/or Bunny were the bomber's actual target."

"Hmm." Skye didn't agree, but she wasn't sure why she felt that way.

As if reading her mind, Wally argued, "Whoever planted the explosive device couldn't be sure that Paige would even be there, let alone that it would kill her. Bombs are only fatal in certain circumstances."

"So you said before." Skye sighed. She didn't have logic to back up her case, so it was useless to try to convince Wally of it.

"But you don't agree," Wally said. "Tell me why you think I'm wrong."

"I can't explain." Unwilling to end the evening on a sour note, Skye waved off her concern. "It's okay." Smiling, she said, "Did I mention my mother's latest battle with her sister?" When Wally shook his head, Skye continued, "Mom and Aunt Minnie are feuding over the flowers on Grandma and Grandpa Leofanti's grave."

"Seriously?"

"You have to ask?" Skye grinned. "You know both Mom and her sister are as stubborn as a robin trying to pull a worm out of the ground."

"True." Wally snickered. "So what's their beef about the flowers?"

"Because the weather has been so unseasonably

warm, the geraniums and impatiens are still going strong, so Aunt Minnie wants to leave them alone." Skye chuckled. "Mom insists that it's autumn so they need to be replaced with chrysanthemums."

"Which does Dante want?" Wally asked. "After all, they're his parents, too. Doesn't he get a vote in the great flower debate?"

"Uncle Dante couldn't care less." Skye made a face. "As long as he's not required to kick in his share to pay for them or do any of the work maintaining them at the graves, he has no opinion."

"Then who's going to win the argument?" Wally turned into their driveway and parked the Hummer near the motor home's front steps.

"Again, you have to ask?" Skye rolled her eyes. "When Mom stopped by this afternoon, she was on her way to the nursery to buy the fall flowers. She planned to plant them this afternoon and present Minnie with a done deal."

"Then our asking her to babysit might have prevented World War III?"

"Postponed, maybe." Skye unfastened her seat belt. "Prevented, I doubt it."

Wally got out of the SUV, walked around, and helped Skye out, then said, "Let's go see what kind of progress they're making on the new house."

"Sure." Wally leaned past Skye and into the open passenger door. "Best be prepared." He grabbed a flashlight from the Hummer's glove box.

He put his arm around Skye and they crossed the yard toward the new structure. While they'd been gone, the builder had finished wrapping the house in a protective barrier that he'd explained was installed to prevent any mold or rotting, as well as to help save on heating and cooling costs. Wally seemed impressed by the man's sales pitch, but all Skye knew was that it had added to the already skyrocketing costs of the house.

With the windows and doors installed, it seemed increasingly like a real home, and every time Skye crossed the threshold, she was a little more excited. While they strolled through the house, she tried to imagine what the interior would look like once drywall covered the bare bones of the lumber.

They had opted for an open floor plan with the master suite on one side and the other bedrooms in the opposite wing. The kitchen, great room, and dining room occupied the center of the house, and there was a huge bonus room over the three-car garage where Wally could put his workout equipment. And when they got older, the twins could use some of the space as a playroom.

Once Wally and Skye had gone through the entire structure, they headed back to the motor home. As they walked across the lawn, Skye said, "I hope Mrs. Griggs isn't upset that we didn't rebuild her house."

Skye had inherited the original property from Alma Griggs, and her benefactor's spirit had haunted her from the time she'd moved into the house until her wedding night. Once Skye and Wally returned from their honeymoon, the old woman's ghost hadn't made as many appearances. She had still left little gifts, like the occasional vintage baby toy, but nothing destructive.

Since the tornado, Mrs. Griggs had been completely absent. Skye hoped that when her house was destroyed she'd gone toward the white light, but she wasn't counting on it. And a ticked-off ghost was the last thing Skye wanted hanging around their new home.

Wally shrugged. He had never quite believed that a spirit was haunting Skye, but he'd learned to keep his mouth shut about his doubts if he didn't want something to blow up or catch on fire.

A few seconds later, a small cardboard box blew across the yard, stopping at their feet. "I'd better grab that and put it into the recycle bin," Wally said. "Garbage pickup is tomorrow."

When Wally lifted the carton, the label was facing Skye. It read *Naughty Angel* and had a logo of an attractive woman in a 1940s dress holding a martini glass and winking.

The image looked strangely like the wedding pictures that Skye had seen of Alma Griggs.

CHAPTER 12

Baby's Coming Back

WALLY HAD LEFT FOR WORK TWENTY MINUTES ago and Skye was just putting the twins down for their morning nap when her cell phone began to vibrate in her yoga pants pocket. She checked the display, then, not wanting to wake the babies, she walked to the other end of the RV before answering.

"Hey!" Trixie's perky voice hurt Skye's ears. "Can I stop by after work?"

"Absolutely. I'll be here for sure because the party company is coming sometime between two and five to set up the tent for Saturday. When we combined the baptism party with the shower, Mom decided that her garage wasn't big enough," Skye said, wondering what was behind her friend's sudden desire to come visit. They'd just seen each other on Monday. "What's up?"

"Gotta go." Trixie sounded breathless. "See you at threeish."

"But—" The dial tone buzzed in Skye's ear and she disconnected.

Tucking the phone back in her pocket, she thought about the decision she and Wally had made last night. With her maternity leave evaporating at an alarming rate, and despite Wally's worries about a stranger caring for his children, last night, they had decided to begin the process of finding a nanny. The clincher had been when Skye pointed out that it was better to try out someone for a few hours a day while she could still pop back in to check up on the woman than wait until she went back to work and couldn't return for eight hours.

Immediately, Wally had texted his father. Carson had assured them that he had a list of absolutely reliable women who lived within a half hour of Scumble River and wouldn't need accommodations. A few seconds later, fifteen résumés popped up in Skye's email, all with a video of the applicant.

Skye and Wally had studied the candidates and arranged for Skye to meet with six of the best possibilities between nine and three today. All the women seemed eager and willing to drop everything to be considered for the job. The power of Carson's wallet never ceased to amaze Skye.

Glancing at her watch, Skye realized the first nanny would be arriving in less than an hour. After a quick check to make sure the twins were sleeping soundly, Skye hopped into the shower. Once she was clean and dressed in a pair of tan slacks and a black-and-cream trapeze tunic, she hastily applied bronzer, concealer, and a coat of mascara and began to clean up the RV.

The bedroom and kitchen stayed pretty tidy, but the galley-like living room was a different story. It was designed to hold a good-sized couch and two chairs, but the narrow path between the furniture was never intended to accommodate all the gifts that Carson and May showered on the twins. The mobiles, cloth books, and play gyms made navigating the small space tricky. And she didn't want any of the nannies she was interviewing this morning to trip.

The RV was silent as she worked with only the faint humming coming from the baby monitor. After she finished, Skye plopped on the sofa to catch her breath. Instantly, Bingo darted from wherever he'd been hiding, jumped up next to her, and tried to climb onto her lap.

"No." Skye moved the cat to the floor. She didn't want to greet the nannies covered in cat hair.

Bingo stared at her as if asking, "What is this word 'no' that you speak of?" Then he headed for the patch of sunlight that spilled from the RV's windows and turned his back on her.

A few seconds later, the first nanny candidate knocked on the door. Skye asked all six interviewees a set of questions that she and Wally had come up with the night before. She also made sure each woman had some time to interact with the twins. And while the nannies fed, changed, or played with the babies, Skye observed.

By the end of the last appointment, Skye had narrowed her choices to the top two. One had gotten down on the floor and joined the babies as they batted objects hanging from the overhead gym. The other had easily managed to feed one twin as she diapered the second. They both had petted Bingo and asked if he was allowed to have treats.

While Skye waited for Trixie, she texted the four women who hadn't made the cut, thanking them for their time, but telling them they would not be called for a second interview. The remaining two, she asked to see again the next evening when Wally would be available to meet with them.

Skye had just changed back to her comfortable knit pants and T-shirt when she spotted a large spider crawling across the bathroom floor. The ringing of the doorbell and Skye's shriek occurred simultaneously.

Hearing a loud thud, Skye ran into the living room just in time to see Trixie barreling over the threshold. Evidently, she'd forgotten to lock the door.

After Skye explained her scream, Trixie said, "I completely understand. Seeing a spider is always a problem."

Skye shook her head. "Seeing it isn't the issue. Not being able to find it and kill it is."

Once they finished giggling and Trixie had oohed and aahed over the babies, the two women settled themselves on either end of the sofa, each holding a twin.

Trixie stared at Skye and said, "We had a faculty meeting before I called you this morning."

"Did something interesting come up?" Skye asked, her pulse racing. What in the world had Homer done to provoke the staff this time?

"Not during the meeting." Trixie shook her head. "But afterward..."

"Afterward what?" Skye shook a rattle in front of her daughter.

"Several of the teachers have had claims denied by Homestead Insurance." Trixie switched the twin she was holding to her other arm.

"I still think you all need to look into a class action suit," Skye said cautiously. She wasn't sure if Wally had released the information regarding Paige Myler's death yet and Skye didn't want to disclose anything that was still confidential.

"It looks as if we might not have to worry about that anymore." Trixie raised a sandy eyebrow. "I mean with Paige Myler dead and all."

Well, that answered that question. Either Wally had announced the bombing victim's identity or someone else had spilled the beans.

"Who told you that?" Skye asked, settling her daughter in her bouncy seat and taking her son from Trixie. "Was there an announcement?"

"Alana Lowe found out from a pal in the ME's office and told the rest of us." Trixie's innocent expression didn't fool Skye. Her friend had probably

been looking for details for her next book and prodded
Alana into asking her friend for the information. "But
it's almost certainly in today's *Star*. Alana and Kathryn
are good friends."

"I sure hope that the next of kin has been notified.
You know, there's a reason that the police withhold
the names of victims."

"Well, yeah." Trixie's cheeks turned red. "I guess
finding out your wife or daughter was dead via newspaper would really suck."

"You think?" Skye was well aware there were no
secrets in a small town, but since her jobs as a school
psych and the PD psych consultant both required con-
fidentiality, she often resented that fact.

"We were just excited at the possibility of finally
getting our claims settled." Trixie must have noticed
Skye's offended expression and added, "Not that we
wanted Paige to die, especially like that."

"Her replacement might be just as bad or even
worse." Skye placed her son in a bouncy chair. "Like
they say, the devil you know."

"Don't even think that." Trixie's shoulders
drooped. Then she brightened. "The guy before Paige
was a sweetheart. Maybe he'll be assigned here again."

"Maybe." Skye shrugged, then leaned back and
casually asked, "Which of the teachers were having a
hard time with Paige?"

Trixie reeled off half a dozen names, then said,
"But Homer was the one who was nearly dancing with

joy when Alana told us all that it was Paige who died in the explosion."

"Really?" Skye recalled that on Monday, when she'd been leaving his office, the high school principal had been screaming about the insurance investigator being late for their meeting. "I'll have to let Wally know about Homer's reaction to the news."

"Any chance Wally will drag him down to the police station for questioning?" Trixie's brown eyes lit up with mischief. "Can I watch?"

"It's a possibility." Skye wanted to see the principal being grilled at the PD herself. "But I think right now, Wally is pursuing a different motivation for the bombing, so Homer's interrogation will have to wait."

"Shoot!" Trixie made a sad face. "You always rain on my parade."

"But I always make sure you have an umbrella, too," Skye reminded her.

Trixie pointed her finger at Skye. "Touché." She started digging in her purse.

"What are you looking for?"

"Well, I'm really searching for the meaning of life, but I'd settle for my car keys."

Skye laughed and said, "Try the front pocket."

"Thanks." Trixie held the ring triumphantly in front of her. "Anyway, I should probably get going." She stood and moved toward the door. "Is there anything you need help with for Saturday's big doings?"

"I have no idea." Skye followed her friend. "Give

Mom a call. She is officially in charge of the new combo shower and baptismal party."

"Will do." Trixie gave Skye a hug and started down the steps. "See you at the church."

"Terrific." Skye hesitated. There was something niggling at her brain and she yelled, "Wait a second." She hurried to where Trixie stood by her car. "There's something I wanted to ask you."

"What?"

"I can't think of it." Skye closed her eyes, willing the elusive idea to break free from her subconscious. "One more second."

"Listen, call me if you remember." Trixie slid behind the wheel. "I've got to get to the grocery store and pick up something to cook for dinner." She tilted her head. "Isn't that a baby I hear crying?"

"Crap!" Skye waved at her friend as she flew up the front steps.

Intellectually, she knew the twins were perfectly fine in their bouncy seats, but emotionally, she felt like a bad mother for leaving them alone for two seconds. Finding them safe and sound, Skye sank to the floor between them, put a hand on each chair, and soothed them.

Once the twins dozed off, she took out her cell phone and sent Wally two texts. One contained a list of the faculty who had a grudge against Homestead Insurance and the other was the names of the two final nanny candidates along with their appointment times.

Wally's return message was full of sweet nothings

and Skye was still smiling at it when there was a volley
of loud knocks on the door. Expecting it to be the
party rental company with the tent for Saturday, she
hoisted herself off the floor and hurried to greet them.

Flinging open the metal door, Skye was surprised
to see Bunny standing on the other side. The redhead
was dressed in skinny jeans and a tight gray T-shirt with
little rhinestone hearts scattered across her substantial
chest, which, for Bunny, was a conservative outfit.

"You have to help me." Bunny shoved Skye back,
stepped across the threshold, and locked the door. "I
don't have much time."

As Bunny entered the RV, Skye got a whiff of
stale sweat and cheap wine. Probably the scent of the
redhead's fear.

"What's wrong? Is someone after you?" Skye
pulled the older woman farther inside and frantically
tapped 911 into her cell.

Bunny snatched Skye's phone before she could hit
the call button. "Don't do that." Bunny's expression
smoothing, she flapped her hand in front of her face.
"I can't remember the end of October ever being this
hot before."

"Forget about the weather." Skye grabbed her
phone back. "Why are you here?"

"I finally convinced Car that he could go with his
usual crew to clear debris from the fields, but I have
a feeling he'll cut it short." Bunny looked around the
RV. "Wow! This is a nice setup."

"Thanks." Skye twitched her shoulders. "It's a little tight, but better than what a lot of folks are stuck with while they rebuild."

Bunny had what Wally called the "pretty lights" syndrome. She was distracted by shiny or expensive objects. Still, even Bunny would concentrate if she were really in danger, so Skye's heart rate slowed.

"And these little angels must be the twins." Bunny bent from the waist, her legs absolutely straight, and touched each baby's cheek. "They are perfectly darling. I see why Car is so smitten."

"Thank you." Skye beamed, fighting the guilt sitting on her chest for letting things get so distant and awkward between them. Bunny was her friend and just because she and Simon were no longer a couple was no excuse. Resolving to get back to their previous relationship, she said, "Would you like to see the rest of the RV? It's a little crowded, but there's not much I can do about that. Even with the storage shed, there's just not enough room for all the twins' stuff."

"I'd love to." Bunny linked arms with Skye and they started the grand tour.

Once Bunny had seen everything, Skye got them both bottles of water and they settled on the couch.

"Okay. Now, tell me why you needed to get rid of Carson and why you're here," Skye ordered, twisting off the cap of her Dasani.

"I'm telling you this as the police psych consultant, not as Carson's daughter-in-law." The redhead's hazel eyes sharpened and Skye could see the astute businesswoman that Bunny usually hid so well.

"Agreed." Skye waved her hand for Bunny to continue speaking.

"I kind of left off one name on that list of my ex-boyfriends that I gave Wally." Bunny fiddled with a loose rhinestone.

"Why would you do that?" Skye asked, hoping her guess wasn't correct.

"Because I don't want him or Carson to know about this guy." Bunny clutched a throw pillow and lowered her voice. "They wouldn't understand about him."

"Why is that?" Skye couldn't quite figure out where Bunny was going.

"Well, Aiden isn't like them." Bunny picked at the label on her bottle of water.

"In what way?" Skye forced herself to be patient. Bunny was a lot like the teenagers she counseled. She made you work for her trust.

"He's…he's more…" Bunny struggled for the right word. "Intense."

"You are aware that Carson is the CEO of a billion-dollar oil company?" Skye asked, arching a brow. "He has to be pretty intense for that."

"But in a more positive way." Bunny scooted to the edge of the sofa cushion. "Aiden might donate money in order to get a tax break, but he'd never volunteer his time."

"Okay so, this Aiden isn't as nice a guy as Carson,"

Skye said, slowly formulating her next question. "What does he do for a living?"

"He's got his fingers in a lot of different enterprises." Bunny refused to meet Skye's gaze.

"Such as what?" Skye asked, a chill creeping down her spine.

"Aiden said it was best that I didn't know the details." Bunny shrugged. "He told me that he makes sure business owners are safe, lends money to people who can't get a loan from the bank, and helps folks who need an intermediary between them and a public official."

Skye's mouth fell open. "In other words, blackmail, loan sharking, and bribery."

"That's a bit harsh." Bunny tried to look outraged but failed.

"What's his last name?" Skye asked.

"He doesn't like me to tell people about him or that we were dating."

"If a relationship has to be kept a secret, you shouldn't be in it." Skye lasered the redhead with a look she usually reserved for her teenage clients.

"Fine." Bunny scowled. "It's O'Twomey."

"Shi—" Skye glanced toward where babies slept. "Shoot! Are we talking about the Irish mob?"

"Maybe." Bunny tensed. "Probably."

"At least tell me you weren't the one to break up with him."

"No." Bunny wiped the perspiration from her brow. "I didn't."

"So he broke up with you?"

"Not exactly." Bunny twisted the hem of her T-shirt.

Skye didn't like where this was heading.

"So if you didn't break up with him, and he didn't break up with you, that means…"

"Aiden was in Ireland for the last couple of months and I wanted to tell him in person that I wouldn't be able to go out with him anymore," Bunny explained. "But it dawned on me he was due back Sunday and I hadn't heard from him."

"He returned the day before the bombing?" Skye wanted to be clear.

"Uh-huh."

"And he still thought he was your boyfriend," Skye squeaked, tendrils of dread unfurling in her stomach.

"I guess. But I never promised him that we were exclusive."

"Okay," Skye said as calmly as she could. "But still, if he saw Carson going in and out of your apartment, he might be a tiny bit upset?"

"Maybe not." Bunny shrugged, but her attempt to look unconcerned didn't work. "But you see why I can't tell Carson or Wally? Carson will think I'm a cheater and Wally already doesn't like me."

"You have a guy who at best is a criminal and at worst is in the Irish mob mad at you, and your bowling alley was bombed," Skye said through clenched teeth. "So what I see is that you have no choice."

CHAPTER 13

Since I Lost My Baby

WALLY ENTERED THE MAYOR'S OFFICE JUST IN time to hear Dante grumble into the telephone, "I pushed one for English, you moron. Why am I talking to someone in Pakistan?" He paused, then snapped, "No, you are not Garth from Tennessee. Transfer me to someone in America immediately."

Snickering at Hizzoner's frustration, Wally detected the unpleasant odor of cigar along with a layer of room freshener trying to cover up the evidence. There was no smoking allowed in public buildings in Illinois, but the mayor was a firm believer that rules were meant for everyone but him.

As Wally settled into one of the pair of chairs facing the mayor's enormous oak desk, he heard the unusual sound of water running and scanned the room for the source. Near the rear wall, a pedestal held a marble basin containing a pebble-filled metal disc.

Water bubbled over a gazing ball in the center of the bronze saucer.

Evidently, the mayor had recently acquired a Zen fountain. Had he hoped it would lower his sky-high blood pressure? Wally glanced at Dante's flushed face. If so, it wasn't working.

Which was too bad, because in all likelihood, Wally's visit would make Hizzoner's hypertension worse. He was there for clarification about Scumble River's policies regarding video gaming within the city limits and the possible connection of gambling to Monday night's explosion.

Faint music drifted from the receiver Dante was clutching, and Wally assumed the mayor was still on hold. Yawning, Wally eagerly reached for his phone when it vibrated and his usual irritation at being left to cool his heels vanished once he saw a picture of Skye from their honeymoon on the cell's screen, indicating that she had sent him a text.

Skye had no idea that he had this particular photo. But the sight of her luscious curves displayed in that two-piece bathing suit she'd bought for the trip sent a jolt southward every time he looked at it.

He absolutely freaking loved getting texts from his wife throughout his day. He loved that she kept him up-to-date on the twins. And he loved that she always signed her messages with hearts and kisses.

Despite his trepidation at hiring a nanny, spending yesterday afternoon with Skye had opened up his eyes and he'd finally really grasped the extent of her exhaustion. Seeing her barely able to stay awake had forced him to admit that they needed help.

Wally glanced at Hizzoner, noting that Dante was glaring at the telephone. Clearly, the mayor wasn't happy with whatever the caller had to say.

Shrugging, Wally swiped his cell's screen and saw a message with a list of faculty members unhappy with Paige Myler. He forwarded it to his work computer and opened the second text, which gave him a link to the résumés of the final two nanny contenders, as well as Skye's notes on each of them. He clicked on the link and began studying the two women's qualifications.

Dante's phone conversation broke into Wally's concentration and he heard the mayor say in a voice boiling with indignation, "I can't believe there's nothing you can do. We are in desperate need of funds to continue our efforts to rebuild. Many people have lost everything."

Frowning, Wally focused on what the mayor was saying. While it was originally thought that Scumble River had suffered close to three million dollars in damages, after all was said and done, the cost had turned out to be closer to six million. Most people had no idea that there weren't any state disaster recovery funds available. And in order for FEMA to contribute, the state needed to prove that it had over eighteen million in damages. Illinois as a whole had only fifteen million.

"Judas Priest," Dante said under his breath, then

cleared his throat and barked, "Of course we have a long-term recovery committee."

Wally shook his head. The mayor was wasting his time. The state government's finances were in no position to help them and the federal government couldn't care less about a small town in rural Illinois.

"Our volunteers have crawled under houses to repair furnaces and plumbing, they've manually torn down the wreckage of unsafe structures, and they've picked up debris despite the unrelenting heat!" Dante screeched like a rusty hinge. "What more do you want us to do to prove that we're helping ourselves!" Banging the handset into the holder, he scowled at Wally. "The moron in charge of the Rescue Illinois fund refuses to give us a cent until we raise seven hundred and fifty thousand dollars to match their endowment."

"We have to be close to that." Wally scratched head. "Dad has contributed a quarter million all by himself."

"Your father's donations don't count because they were in goods rather than cash." Dante thrust out his chin. "If we'd known about that loophole right away, we could have had Carson give us the money, then bought the stuff from those funds ourselves."

"Well, that sucks." Wally stared at Dante. He rarely saw this side of the mayor—a man trying to do right by his constituents.

Glancing around the mayor's lavish office, the toll of the past few months was obvious. Dante loved his plants and had always shamelessly babied them. But brown leaves drooped from his normally flourishing philodendron and his devil's ivy had overgrown its pot and taken over the file cabinet.

Just as Wally felt a twinge of pity for the mayor, Hizzoner snapped his fingers and said, "Any chance your old man would kick in another quarter mil, but in cash this time?"

Wally crossed his arms. "That would be a lot to ask of one person."

"But for his only son's and grandchildren's home town?" Dante wheedled.

Any sense of sympathy Wally had for Dante immediately evaporated. This was more like the mayor he was used to than the one that had been there a few minutes ago.

"You can ask." Wally threw Dante a warning look. "But leave me and my family out of it."

"Fine." Dante narrowed his eyes. "So what did you want to see me about?"

"Can you run me through the whole video gambling process?" Wally took out his pad and pen.

"What do you want to know?" Dante asked, wariness oozing from every pore.

"How is it decided who gets to have the machines and how many sites are allowed in the city limits?" Wally kept his voice neutral, but noted the mayor's unease.

"According to Illinois law, any place that pours liquor is allowed to have machines, but communities can pass their own ordinance further limiting the

number of machines in the village." Dante straightened a stack of files on his desk, then, not looking up,
said, "Scumble River decided to only permit five such
establishments."

"So if someone wanted to open, say, a video gambling café, one of the current places would have to
give up their machines." Wally stared until Dante
met his gaze.

"Or the city council would have to add an additional permit to expand their maximum." Dante laced
his fingers across his stomach, attempting to appear
relaxed but failing. "Does this have anything to do
with the bombing at Bunny Lanes?"

"It's one of the leads that I'm pursuing." Wally
tapped his pen on his thigh. "This morning when I
was thinking about the case, I remembered meeting a
man at the florist shop Monday afternoon. This guy
said that he runs a chain of video gambling cafés and
had a deal to open several in Stanley County, starting with the flagship in Scumble River. He was really
ticked off that our city council wasn't cooperating."

"And you think that this man blew up the bowling
alley in order to open up a spot on the list?" Dante
snickered, looking strangely relieved. "Seriously?"

"I'd like to talk to him." Wally kept his expression
bland. The mayor loved to get a rise from people. "I'll
have to stop at the florist and see if they have his name
from his credit card purchase."

"No need." Dante puffed up his chest. "You must

mean Yuri Iverson. He's a good friend of mine and I assure you he has no need for explosives."

"Why is that?" Wally narrowed his eyes. "Mr. Iverson seemed more than a little desperate to get this business finished with and leave town."

"Yuri knows that we'll take care of it as soon as the city council has time to meet." Dante fingered the gold chain that stretched across his vest.

"And what would it take for you all to find the time?" Wally drawled.

"If you're suggesting that we're waiting for a bribe…" Dante glowered.

"Why would I think that?" Wally asked, watching the mayor's face redden.

"Because…" Dante squawked. "Because no matter how hard I try, you refuse to believe I have the best interests of the community at heart."

"That's an interesting statement." Wally felt his cell phone vibrate. "Thanks for your time and the information, Mayor."

"Right." The mayor turned away, snatched up the receiver, and began to dial.

"By the way, if you want to talk to my father, he's staying at the motor court. But I wouldn't mention the fact that you don't seem to care that the bowling alley was bombed." Wally walked toward the door. "Seeing as he's dating the alley's manager."

Dante glared but remained silent as Wally stepped over the threshold. Once he was back in his own office, he quickly checked his messages, afraid Skye had been trying to reach him.

When he saw that the missed call was from Thea, he punched in his password and listened to the dispatcher's voicemail. "Paige Myler's ex-husband is here and is extremely anxious to speak to you."

Wally glanced at his watch. It was already 4:50. *Shoot!* He'd been trying to make it home by 5:00 most nights, but there was no way he was delegating this interview. Sighing, he headed downstairs.

When Wally reached the station's lobby, he found a man who appeared to be in his mid to late forties seated on the bench. He was dressed in a dark suit, crisp white shirt, and silk tie and was busy tapping away on his phone.

Spotting Wally, the guy shot to his feet and said, "Chief Boyd?"

"Yes." Wally held out his hand. "And you must be Phillip Myler."

"I am. I just wish I could have gotten here sooner." The man shook Wally's hand. "But I had no idea that Paige was dead until this afternoon when our executive vice president called a meeting and announced that she'd been killed. I wasn't sure how long it would take me to drive down from Normalton, but I left right afterward."

"You've never visited Scumble River before?" Wally watched the man carefully.

"My territory is generally southern Illinois."

Phillip glanced at Thea standing behind the counter and clearly listening to every word. "Can we talk somewhere in private?"

Stepping aside, Wally said, "Come on back. We can use the break room." Which was also the interrogation room, but Wally didn't mention that fact.

"Great." Phillip crossed the threshold and Wally caught a whiff of Phantom, the same pine, cedar leaf, and juniper berry body wash that Skye had bought him duty-free on their honeymoon cruise. The guy had expensive taste.

"Would you like a cup of coffee?"

"That would be terrific. I'm probably already over-caffeinated, but I'll need all the help I can get to keep me awake on the drive back." He scrubbed his eyes with his fist. "We've been so busy since the tornadoes went through Illinois. I never seem to get enough sleep."

"I know what that's like." Wally led the guy down a short hallway and into the break room. He flipped on the switch and the overhead lights sputtered to life. Nodding to the table, he said, "Have a seat."

"Thanks." Phillip settled on one of the chairs and placed his cell on the tabletop in front of him, keeping a finger on it as if he felt the need to be tethered to it at all times.

Wally poured them each a cup of coffee and asked, "Cream or sugar?"

"Black."

Wally nodded and placed the mug in front of Phillip. He sat across from the man and took a sip from his cup, waiting to see what the guy wanted. In his experience, it was unusual for an ex to show up at the police station concerned about a spouse's death.

As the silence lengthened, Phillip squirmed and finally said, "I was shocked to hear about Paige."

"I can imagine." Wally itched to take notes but didn't want to put the guy on guard.

"The VP said the officer who contacted him didn't have any details." Phillip clasped his hands around his mug as if he were cold. "Is there anything new since then?"

"Nothing I can share." Wally scratched the stubble on his jaw and tried to sound nonthreatening. "How long had you and your ex-wife been divorced?"

"We aren't," Phillip said, then quickly added, "At least not quite. We were still waiting for all the i's to be dotted and the t's to be crossed."

"I see." Wally understood. It had taken forever for his own divorce to be finalized. Of course, it hadn't helped that his ex had run off with another man and disappeared into the wilds of Alaska. Shaking off a spark of empathy, Wally said, "Considering you and Paige weren't together anymore, I'm not sure why you're here."

"Me either." Phillip thrust his fingers through his expensively styled blond hair. "I guess it's just so hard to believe."

"You and your wife worked for the same company," Wally said, watching the other man closely. "Was that awkward after your separation?"

"A little." Phillip fiddled with his phone. "Luckily, we weren't in the same department, so it wasn't too bad." He rolled his eyes. "Except for the gossip. But that had pretty much died down."

"I suppose a company is like a small town." Wally sat back. "Rumors fly around here faster than a swarm of bees after a bear that stole their honey."

"Yeah." Phillip sighed. "The divorce was big news for a while."

Wally laced his fingers on the tabletop. "Since you're here, I'd like to try to get a better picture of Paige's life."

"Okay." Phillip tilted his head. "What would you like to know?"

"How did she get along with her colleagues?" Wally knew that she was the head of a department, but not how it was structured.

"I won't lie to you, she was a tough boss." Phillip grimaced. "Paige expected her people to give a hundred and fifty percent."

"I understand that someone else was originally assigned to handle the claims in Scumble River." Wally kept his tone casual. "Do you know why Paige ended up here? Was that her decision or an order from a higher-up?"

"I would assume it was Paige's choice." Phillip

exhaled loudly. "It's not something our company would ever admit, and I'll deny it if you quote me, but the fewer number of claims that are approved, the better her department looks to the bigwigs. And the first adjuster she sent here rubber-stamped just about every single claim."

"Was the guy she replaced upset with her decision to take over?"

"That's hard to say." Phillip shrugged. "He seemed okay with it, but he did put in for a transfer to another department."

Wally made a mental note to look into that guy. "Was there anyone in the company or anyone in her personal life that had a problem with Paige?"

"Not more than the usual type of work things," Phillip said. "And I don't know much about her personal life anymore."

"Were either of you involved in another relationship that caused your divorce?" Wally asked.

"No." Phillip stared over Wally's head. "We just grew apart."

"How long were you and Paige married?" Wally stole a look at his watch. He couldn't rush this, but he really wanted to get home in time to help Skye feed the twins and give them their baths.

"Nearly fifteen years." Phillip took a sip of coffee. "We met when she first came to work for Homestead right after college. I'd already been there for a while and she started off as my intern. There was chemistry between us from the beginning, but we couldn't act on it until the internship was over and she went to work for another department."

Wally asked a few more questions, but Phillip maintained that he didn't know if Paige had any enemies.

Finally, Phillip circled around to his original inquiry and said, "Isn't there anything you can tell me about Paige's death?"

"She was in the bowling alley's video gaming lounge after hours when an explosive device was triggered. She was crushed beneath the debris," Wally said carefully. "But that's all I'm at liberty to release at this point."

"From your questions about her relationships, I'm wondering if you believe that Paige was the target of the bomb." Phillip's gaze was sharp.

"It's one of our working theories." Wally drained his coffee cup. "However, we are also looking into other possibilities."

"What are they?"

"Sorry." Wally shook his head and stood. "I'm afraid we aren't ready to share that information."

"Of course." Phillip nodded, rose from his seat, and joined Wally. "Thank you for taking the time to talk to me, Chief."

"Glad to do it." Wally and Phillip walked to the lobby and Wally said, "I'll be in touch if I think of any more questions."

"Absolutely." Phillip shook Wally's hand and exited the station.

Wally stared at his retreating figure, then whipped out his notepad and jotted down everything he could remember from the interview. The vic's ex—or almost ex—husband had seemed like a nice guy. But then, so had Ted Bundy.

CHAPTER 14

Baby Love

S KYE PUSHED THE DOUBLE STROLLER DOWN THE recently installed faux wooden walkway. The party rental company had set up the path at the same time they'd erected the huge, white tent that now took up a great deal of the yard between the motor home and where the new house was being built.

She stopped to retract the stroller's bright-red canopy so the twins could enjoy the sunshine, and both infants cooed their delight. The long-awaited autumn weather had finally arrived overnight, and Skye and her babies were relishing the cooler, less humid conditions.

Skye gazed around their property. The tornado had knocked down most of their trees and the flowers had been destroyed by high winds. But a few bushes had been spared, including Skye's favorite lilac, which she hoped would still bloom in the spring.

Wally had cut the grass over the weekend, unusual

for this late in the year, but not unheard of for Illinois. Now the lush green lawn's morning dew was gilded by beams of light pouring down from the heavens. It almost looked like a fairy garden.

The building crew had yet to arrive to work on the new house and the road in front of their property didn't see a whole lot of traffic, so for one brief moment, Skye reveled in the silence.

The squawking of a blue jay reminded Skye of the argument that she and Wally had that morning and she frowned. Although she had told him about Bunny's not-quite-ex-boyfriend's possible criminal connections the night before, they hadn't resolved the issue of who had a right to know about Bunny's situation. Wally had insisted his father should be on the list, but Skye had been equally adamant that they had no justification for revealing Bunny's secret to someone not actively involved in the investigation.

During breakfast, Skye and Wally had resumed their disagreement over whether to inform his father about Aiden O'Twomey. Skye maintained that she had been given the facts as an employee of the police department, and sharing that information with Carson was nothing less than gossiping. However, after a prolonged discussion, Wally won Skye over to his side when he pointed out that his dad could be in danger. Still, she had asked that Wally give Bunny a chance to be the one to tell Carson, and Wally had given the older woman until noon today.

Skye had immediately conveyed that deadline to Bunny, who grumbled but agreed. By the time Skye had gotten off the phone with the complaining redhead, it was already past nine, and she'd hurriedly bundled the twins into their stroller and set off to take a look at what the rental company had accomplished yesterday afternoon.

Her mom was due to arrive at nine thirty and Skye wanted to have some time to get an impression of the arrangements before May completely took over the preparations. Not that she had any hope of changing her mother's mind…

As Skye approached the massive tent, she blinked when she saw its sidewalls featured cathedral windows. *What the heck!* St. Francis was only a church. Was May trying to outdo Father Burns?

Shaking her head, Skye wheeled the stroller inside. Lots and lots of round tables were arranged in an arc around a long rectangular table. She did a quick count. Twenty tables, times eight chairs each— *shoot!*—her mother was expecting a hundred and sixty guests. Skye had a large extended family, and between her and Wally, they had a lot of friends, but that was a ridiculous amount of people for a baby shower—even if it was combined with a christening.

Taking it all in, Skye shook her head at the extravagance. No expense had been spared. The setting might be in a tent, but it wouldn't be any casual picnic. The chairs weren't the normal flimsy, plastic folding ones—these were sturdy wood with padded seats and backs adorned in huge pink and blue bows. Matching pink and blue silk cloth had been draped in a swirl pattern behind the head table and twinkle lights had been twisted through the loops.

Skye caught a sparkle and craned her neck. Sunlight shining through the plastic windows illuminated crystal chandeliers hanging from the tent's ceiling. What was next? A grand piano?

Skye brushed her finger across her daughter's cheek and said, "Grandma has gone out of her mind and I don't even want to think about the rest of her decorating plans." Kissing the top of her son's head, she added, "At least with you around, she can't do it all in neon pink."

She narrowed her eyes. Although there was no doubt May was the driving force behind the over-the-top arrangements, she had to have a partner in crime. There was no way that her parents could afford all this. Carson had to be picking up the tab for the party.

Skye squatted in front of the twins and said, "Your daddy is going to have to talk to your grandfather and get him to stop spending so much money on us. I liked it better when we had to be careful that no one found out about your daddy's family money." She paused, then admitted, "Except for the Mercedes. I adore driving the Benz. And the RV. I'd hate to see where we would be living without the motor home." She sighed and added, "Okay, the house, too. I love our new house."

Although Skye knew her father-in-law planned to pay for the nanny, she and Wally could handle the woman's salary themselves and they needed to insist on doing so. They also had to put the brakes on Carson's generosity in other matters as well. She didn't want her children growing up as spoiled brats. She'd seen too many of those kinds of kids in her job as a school psychologist.

Hearing her mother's voice talking to someone, Skye kissed both babies, then straightened from her crouch to see who May had brought with her.

Skye turned just in time to see her mom holding the door as Cora Denison, Skye's grandmother, entered. Skye squealed and ran over to give her grandma a hug. Nearing ninety, Cora had buried a husband, two stillborn babies, and a teenage grandson. Up until a year or so ago, she'd made a batch of her famous Parker House rolls nearly every Sunday.

Cora had always been a big woman, tall, sturdy, and strong as any man, but nowadays she seemed frailer every time Skye visited. And Cora rarely left her house anymore, so Skye was thrilled to see her with May.

Cora leaned heavily on her cane, but used her free arm to return Skye's embrace. Skye breathed in the unique vanilla, cinnamon, and fruit scent of her grandmother. Cora might not bake anymore, but after seventy years of making her famous apple slices, the sweet fragrance had sunk into her pores.

Once she'd kissed Skye, Cora demanded, "Where are my great-grandbabies?"

"Right here." Skye pushed the stroller over to her grandmother and asked, "Would you like to hold them?"

"Maybe later." Cora chuckled. "Never disturb a quiet baby."

"The voice of experience." Skye beamed.

"Too bad," Cora said with a sigh. "Age is such a high price to pay for knowledge."

"I bet you could still whip Dad and Uncle Wiley into shape like you used to in the olden days," Skye reassured her grandmother.

"I don't know." Cora winked. "Nostalgia isn't what it used to be."

Skye giggled, then asked, "Would you like to sit down?" Cora nodded and Skye said, "One chair coming up."

Skye hurried to fetch her grandmother a seat, wondering if Cora really didn't want to wake the babies or if she felt she was just too weak to hold them.

Once Cora was comfortable, May grabbed Skye's hand. Her mother's fingers were cool against hers and Skye shivered, snatching back her hand.

"You know that I'm always cold." May shrugged, then said, "Grandma Denison can keep an eye on the babies while we take a look at what the party company accomplished."

After the tent and its contents had passed May's inspection, they rejoined Cora, and Skye asked, "Do you want to go into the RV? We can have something to drink and visit for a while."

"I wouldn't mind a cup of tea," Cora answered. "But I'm not sure I can make it up the RV's front steps. Let's just sit here."

"Coffee for me," May said. Then she added, "You might as well get that plate of lemon bars from the car, too. We can munch on them while we talk." She pulled the twins' stroller closer and waved Skye away. "I'll watch the babies. You're lucky they're so good. You were colicky and nearly drove me crazy with your constant crying."

"I guess I am." Skye ignored her mother's complaint. She'd heard about how difficult a baby she'd been so many times, she no longer paid any attention to May's grumbles. "The twins usually only cry if they're hungry, need a diaper change, or are overtired."

When Skye returned with the refreshments, she found her mother with a baby in each arm. Cora was shaking a set of plastic keys in front of them both. Happy to see her grandmother interacting with the twins, Skye slid the tray onto the table and took a seat.

After taking a sip of her decaf, Skye looked at her mom and said, "This tent is bigger than the American Legion banquet hall. Just how many people are you expecting to come to this shindig?"

"About a hundred and fifty," May said, settling the dozing twins back into their stroller. "And before you complain, I only invited family. And a few of mine and your father's closest friends." She paused. "And of course our longtime neighbors."

"Seriously?" Skye raised a brow. "There can't be that many relatives."

"How soon they forget," May tsked. "We had this same conversation when we were planning your wedding. Think about how many first, second, and third cousins you have. We can't leave any of them out." She put her hands up with her palms to Skye. "And it's not as if you didn't have folks on your christening list that could have been excluded."

"Like who?" Skye frowned. She'd given her mom the names of about fifty people, but most of them had been the same family members that May was already inviting to the shower. "I only had a few friends and school colleagues on it that you might not have previously thought to include."

"The half a dozen Dooziers for one." May's mouth puckered in distaste. "Why you would want that trashy family in attendance is beyond me."

As her mother continued to complain about the Skye's choice of guests, Skye's thoughts wandered. Her relationship with the Dooziers was hard to explain. They had their own little kingdom on the banks of the Scumble River, and as with so many empires, its rulers could do no wrong. Laws only applied to the peasants, and whoever wasn't a part of the royal family was expected to pay tribute. Their philosophy was the Dooziers were entitled to whatever they could grab.

For some reason, Earl, the king of Doozierland, had adopted Skye. She wasn't sure if it was because he saw her as the ambassador between his domain and the rest of the world—a role she often had to assume within the school system—or because he'd saved her life on more than one occasion. Whatever the reason, he treated Skye like one of his knights, or maybe like one of his faithful hounds.

This association infuriated Skye's mother, and May had not wanted the Dooziers at the baby shower. She'd maintained that they would ruin the event, but Skye had stood firm. They were her friends and they'd be hurt if they didn't receive an invitation. Moreover, Skye figured the family would show up anyway, and it was better they were there as expected guests rather than as party crashers.

Cora's voice broke into Skye's thoughts. "May, honey, Earl and his family will be fine." She patted her daughter-in-law's hand. "I'd be more worried about Carson's date than the Dooziers."

"Do you mean Bunny Reid?" May narrowed her eyes. "You don't think he'd bring that tacky woman, do you? She's not on the list."

"I'm pretty sure that since they're living together and"—Skye slid a sly look in her mother's direction—"Carson's paying for most, if not all, of this little wing-ding, Bunny will be here."

"I… He…" May sputtered, but didn't deny that Carson's black American Express card was involved.

Skye hid her smile by taking another sip of coffee, then asked. "But why should we be worried about Bunny's presence, Grandma?"

Cora turned to Skye. "Well, if whoever blew up the bowling alley was trying to kill Bunny, and that person decides to come after her again…"

Although Cora's expression was sincere, Skye noticed her grandmother snuck a peak at May and there was a twinkle in the elderly woman's eyes.

Skye finished Cora's thought. "A murderer on the loose at the party would cause a lot more trouble than the Dooziers ever could."

"That explosion had nothing to do with Bunny Reid." May's expression was mulish. "At least not personally. It's those cotton-picking slot machines."

"Why do you say that, Mom?" Skye asked. Since when had her mother become anti-gambling? Skye's parents loved going to Las Vegas, not to mention May's visits to the Joliet casinos with her friend Maggie. "Have you heard something around town?"

"Everyone is talking about how tight Bunny has those things set." May's chin had a mutinous set to it.

"Everyone?" Skye glanced at her grandmother, who shook her head and shrugged.

"I worked with the Marthas for Elaine Daly's wake and all the ladies were bellyaching about how much money they lost on the alley's machines."

The Marthas were a group of women from the

Catholic church who coordinated funeral luncheons providing food prep, service, and cleanup.

"Why do you keep playing?" Skye asked. "I mean, if you know the odds are bad."

She didn't see the attraction of pushing a button and watching various wheels spin. Skye was more like her father, who preferred poker or blackjack. At least with those games there was a modicum of something besides pure luck involved.

May scowled. "We all play for a little while before our bowling leagues and no one ever wins. But we're determined to earn back our money."

May's glare dared Skye to state the obvious. The chances of that were slim to none.

"How much do most of you lose each week?" Skye hoped she wouldn't need to perform an intervention with her mother for a gambling addiction.

"Twenty dollars." May's mouth pinched closed, then she added, "But a lot of time we break even. It's just that we never come out ahead."

"I wonder if Bunny will replace the machines," Cora murmured.

"I think she'll want to," Skye said slowly. "But whether Simon agrees is a whole other question. He wasn't too keen on them before the explosion and I can't image a bombing has improved his opinion."

"And how do you know that Simon didn't want his mother to put in video gambling machines?" May demanded, crossing her arms and staring at Skye.

"Because Bunny told me." Skye raised her brows. "How did you think I knew?"

When May's cheeks reddened, Skye snickered. Her mother had done a complete turnaround, jumping from Team Simon to Team Wally in less than a year. Skye would like to think it was because Wally had proved to her mom that he was an amazing person and a wonderful husband. But she suspected it was more that he'd been a participant in producing May's grandchildren.

"While you are only risking twenty bucks a week, I'll bet some of those women are putting a lot more into those one-armed bandits." Cora's eyes were cold. "And how is all this legal gambling affecting the groups like the church and American Legion who count on bingo and King of Diamonds and such to fund their activities?"

"That's a very good question." Skye frowned. She couldn't picture Father Burns planting a bomb to wipe out the competition, but American Legion members might have a little more experience with explosives.

CHAPTER 15

(Baby, You Can) Drive My Car

WITH THE CHRISTENING PARTY/BABY SHOWER IN May's capable, not to mention controlling, hands, and the twins in a cooperative mood, Skye decided to venture into town. First, she'd hit the supermarket, then, if the babies continued to behave nicely, she'd surprise Wally and take him to lunch at McDonald's.

Before her mother and grandmother left, Skye asked them to keep an eye on the twins while she took the dirty dishes from their refreshments into the RV and got ready for her expedition into town. After placing the cups, plates, and spoons in the sink, she evicted Bingo from the diaper bag and packed it with the babies' paraphernalia.

Next, she removed her grocery list from under the magnet on the fridge and stuck it in her purse, then put on a nice pair of jeans and a pink jersey top.

The tornado had taken most of Skye's pre-pregnancy wardrobe and she hadn't had time to get to the mall since the twister, so internet shopping had become her new best friend. She'd ordered the shirt she'd just put on last week, and it had arrived yesterday afternoon. Luckily, with the cooler weather, it had long sleeves. And she loved the boat neck, as well as the tulip-style panels designed for discreet nursing.

A few minutes later, Skye hurriedly returned to the tent. She thanked her mom and grandma for watching the twins and walked with them back to the driveway. Waving, she watched the rear lights of May's white Oldsmobile 88 disappear down the road.

Once they were gone, Skye began the daunting task of getting the babies buckled into the SUV. Thankfully, the stroller that she and Wally had selected was part of a travel system that converted to car seats.

Skye hadn't had much practice—this was her first attempt at a solo trip with the twins. But the seats clicked easily out of the apparatus and into the attached base installed in her Mercedes. With the babies settled into the back of the car, she folded the stroller's frame and hoisted it into the rear of the SUV.

Although the morning had started out bright, with a pleasantly crisp fall breeze, by the time that Skye pulled into the parking lot of the supermarket, clouds had begun to roll in and were covering the sun. It looked as if it could start sprinkling any minute.

The dreary weather sobered Skye's mood, and as she cruised the surprisingly jam-packed lot looking for an open slot, she thought about the bombing. So far, there seemed to be an equal amount of evidence pointing toward Paige and Bunny Lanes as the primary objective of the explosion, but something in her gut had Skye leaning toward the insurance investigator versus the bowling alley as the intended target.

In her perpetually sleep-deprived state, it was difficult to think clearly and figure out what she knew for sure and what was intuition. Skye felt around the corners of her brain, but just as a flash of an idea raced through her mind, she was distracted by the sight of someone putting groceries into a tan Prius parked only three spaces from the door.

Speeding up, Skye zipped around the corner, and stopped almost behind the Toyota. The woman was piling bags into its trunk and Skye put on her turn signal to indicate her intention to claim the spot.

While she waited, she peered into the back seat. Her son was dozing, his little face peaceful, but his sister was grinning and cooing. This seemed to happen a lot—one baby sleeping while the other stayed alert. Almost as if one twin was always in charge of guarding the perimeter. Maybe Wally's police genes had been passed on to his children.

The Prius woman took an eternity to unload her groceries, return her cart to the corral near the doors, and get settled behind the wheel. Finally, her brake lights came on and she began to inch backward. The Toyota was barely out of the parking place when a blue Audi Roadster zipped into the space, narrowly missing Skye's right front bumper.

She hit her horn, but the fiftysomething driver ignored her and as he exited the sports car, all Skye could see was the glowing tip of a long, thin cigarette. He paused at the sidewalk to dispose of his smoke, then entered the supermarket without a backward glance.

Fuming, Skye stifled the urged to swear at the obnoxious jerk. Finally, although it wasn't as if Wally could arrest the creep for stealing her space, she jotted down the license plate number on a paper napkin. At least she'd be able to identify the detestable man if he did break any laws when she was around.

Eventually, she calmed enough to find another empty spot—about a mile and a half from the door— settle the twins' car seats into the stroller frame, and make her way into the store. As the sliding glass door swished open, the enticing smell of chocolate chip cookies and freshly baked bread tickled her nose. Her mouth watered, but she ignored the temptation.

Skye shivered at the sudden coolness of the over air-conditioned store. Goose pimples popped up on the skin on her arms and she rubbed them to get warm. Reaching down, she made sure the babies were covered by their blankets, then blew on her icy fingertips.

She couldn't figure out how to push the stroller along with a grocery cart, so she utilized the basket

under the seats. The store was remarkably busy for a
Thursday morning and Skye had to weave through
crowded aisles to get to the deli counter. People were
stocking up for something, but she had no idea what.
It wasn't as if there was a holiday coming up.

Heck! Yes, there was, too, a holiday. Friday was
Halloween. How in the world had she forgotten that?

Emmy had even mentioned that there was a party
at the shooting range, but Skye had been so annoyed
with the pretty dancer flirting with Wally that the
implication had slipped passed her.

Skye didn't think they'd get any trick-or-treaters out
where they lived. Their house was the only one for miles
along a rural road. Still, she'd better buy a bag of candy
just in case. And if they didn't get any kids, she'd just be
forced to eat the chocolate herself. One tiny sweet treat
a day couldn't hurt, right? Even her doctor told her not
to worry about dieting while she was nursing.

Earlier that morning, before May and Cora's
arrival, Skye had started Italian beef cooking in the
Crock-Pot. That along with a container of coleslaw
from the deli and a bag of Milano French Rolls, and
supper would be ready anytime Wally made it home.

After getting what she needed for dinner, Skye
grabbed an assortment of fruits and vegetables, as well
as some other basics. Next on her list was laundry
detergent. It seemed as if she went through at least a
bottle a week.

Once she'd stowed the huge jug of Woolite in the

bottom of the stroller, she headed to the candy aisle. She had just put her fingers on the last bag of miniature peanut butter cups when a long arm clad in expensive fabric reached above her and snatched it from her grasp.

Skye had heard the heavy footsteps approaching but hadn't paid much attention. As she whirled around, the stench of too much aftershave and stale beer washing over her, making her stomach roil, Skye came face-to-face with the guy who had stolen her parking spot.

He wore a designer suit and a posh tie, but his face looked like a boxer who had lost one too many fights. His nose was mashed to the side and had to have been broken at least once, and there was a scar by the side of his watery brown eyes.

What a jerk! The anger Skye had only partially set aside broke loose and she glared at the man. "Give that back to me right now!" She tried to keep her voice low and firm, but it came out high pitched and pleading.

"Are you out of your mind?" The man snorted. "First come, first served."

Skye bristled. This was one of those cases where she truly hated being a psychologist. She knew intellectually that, in the long run, violence never solved anything, but she also knew that a good punch to the gut, or maybe a shot from the pepper spray in her purse, would shut this guy up and make him give her the candy.

This whole incident reminded her of a run-in she'd had early on when she'd first moved back home and met Simon. He'd taken her parking space and her Diet

Coke at this same store. She should have followed her instincts then and never gone out with him. At least there was no chance she'd end up dating this yahoo.

In a haughty tone, Skye said, "Despite your fancy suit and tie, clearly you are no gentleman. You can pretend otherwise, but you saw me waiting for that parking space and took it anyway. Then, you saw me reaching for the last bag of peanut butter cups and snatched it from my fingers." She narrowed her eyes and let ice drip from her words. "You aren't from around here, are you?"

"What do you mean by that?" The guy clutched the candy to his chest.

"It means small-town folks would rather give you the shirt off their back than even appear to be taking something their neighbors might need." Skye gazed down at the twins, who were staring at her as if they understood every word and were cheering her on, then glanced over his shoulder. "You already made a spectacle of yourself, so hand over those peanut butter cups and choose another candy."

"Or what?" the guy asked, turning his head in the direction she was looking.

The grocery store was small: a bakery, a deli, a refrigerated section, and half a dozen aisles, as well as a frozen foods section. And it appeared as if most of the shoppers in the market had gathered and were watching the exchange. People were frowning and there was a hostile buzz in the air.

Survival instinct must have kicked in, and the guy backed up until he reached the end of the aisle. But before he could escape, a large man with a headful of pure-white hair stepped into his path and said, "Yuri, I see you've met my goddaughter, Skye."

She swallowed a giggle at the man's *oh no* expression. Charlie might be approaching eighty, but at close to six feet and three hundred pounds, he was not easily ignored. And it was best not to underestimate his influence around town. If a robin fell to earth, he knew about it before the feathers hit the ground.

"I… Well, that is…" The man babbled for a second, then sputtered to a stop.

"You were just about to give her that bag of candy, weren't you?" Charlie wore his standard uniform of gray twill pants, a limp white shirt, and red suspenders. His expression implied he'd seen it all—twice— and wasn't interested in a third show.

"I can't," Yuri whined. "My wife wants them. You know she's miserable here in Scumble River. But if I keep her supplied with peanut butter cups, vodka, and gossip magazines, she doesn't complain, at least not quite as much."

As his irritated expression clearly indicated, Charlie wasn't used to people arguing with him and he snapped, "If your wife is so unhappy here, you should take her home to Chicago. Especially since you no longer have a place to stay for the night."

"But the city council is finally meeting tomorrow."

Yuri glared. "And I paid you in advance for that cabin through the weekend."

"Do you have a receipt?" Charlie asked raising a bushy white eyebrow.

"What?" Yuri glanced at the other shoppers who had moved to watch Charlie take on the out-of-towner. "You said cash was a better deal."

"It is." Charlie folded his massive arms, his stare daring the man to continue. "You get a discount and I don't have to deal with the credit card company's paperwork or give them a cut."

"Fine." Yuri threw the bag of peanut butter cups at Skye and scurried away. His voice carried as he hurried out the door. "But most women your size would be eating cottage cheese, not candy."

There were a few unintelligible murmurs from the crowd. Skye's face flamed and she hoped no one was agreeing with Yuri.

But just in case, as she tucked the package into the stroller's basket and walked over to give her godfather a hug, she announced, "The candy is for the trick-or-treaters, not me."

"Everyone knows you always give out peanut butter cups," Charlie said loyally. After kissing her cheek, he bent and gazed at the twins. "Sweetheart, you have two of the most beautiful children I've ever seen. I'm so glad you finally came back to town and settled down."

"Thanks, Uncle Charlie. What a sweet thing to

say." Skye beamed. "Me too. Who knew that being fired from my first job, maxing out my credit cards, and having my fiancé jilt me would turn out so well?"

"I never doubted it for a moment," Charlie said smoothly. "It's nice to see you out and about." He gently patted the babies' heads with his huge hand. "I imagine it's not easy with these two here."

"True." Skye glanced around, happy to see the crowd had dispersed and she and Charlie were out of the spotlight. "And with that in mind, I better check out while the twins are still cooperating."

"Yep." Charlie hugged her goodbye and said, "See you at the baptism on Saturday."

Skye was headed toward the registers at the front of the store when a loud female voice stopped her. "Hey, Skye, wait up."

She turned to find her cousin Gillian Leofanti Tubb hurrying toward her. The overhead fluorescent fixtures cast a harsh light over Gillian, emphasizing every wrinkle, blemish, and scar on her cousin's naked face.

Skye had never seen Gillian without makeup before and also noticed that her cousin was dressed in a stained T-shirt and baggy yoga pants that hung on her tiny frame. Her fine blond hair was scraped back in a greasy ponytail and she wore bright-pink flip-flops.

"Hi!" Skye was surprised to see her cousin anything less than Junior Woman's Club ready.

Gillian gave Skye a perfunctory hug and bent to coo at the twins. "My, my, aren't you chubby, little sweet peas?" She glanced at Skye with a knowing smile. "It must run in the family."

"According to their pediatrician, they weigh exactly what they should." Skye barely kept the annoyance out of her voice.

"Of course they do." Gillian's smile was patronizing. "I guess my children just tend to be more delicate and petite like me." She tugged up her sagging pants. "Have you picked out names yet?"

"Not yet."

Skye could feel the other shoppers observing them and sighed. Their watchfulness had been comforting during the incident with Yuri, but now she could be the one that might come out looking like a creep if she was rude to her cousin. Realizing that there was no graceful way to hurry this encounter along, Skye leaned on the stroller and prayed for patience.

Although she had managed to put aside her animosity toward Gillian and her twin sister, Ginger, they still weren't her favorite relatives. She might have forgiven them for their bullying behavior in high school, but she was still ticked about being kidnapped and threatened by them after their Grandma Leofanti's murder. It would be a cold day in hades before she forgot that greed-fueled incident or trusted either one of them an inch.

"You know, Ginger and I are still hoping one of us will have a set of twins, so you should clear the names you pick with us first," she informed Skye loftily. "That way you don't steal our choices."

"Not happening." Skye folded her arms. "But don't worry. I seriously doubt you and Ginger have the same taste as Wally and I."

"What do you mean by that?" Gillian voice screeched like a rusty garden gate and she narrowed her baby-blue eyes.

"Precisely what it sounded like." Skye didn't blink at her cousin's outraged glare. "We've never liked the same things, which makes it highly improbable that we'd select the same names."

Gillian pouted. "Fine. I'm going to tell you our ideas, but you better not take them. I have dibs on Sonny and Cher and Ginger wants Angelina and Brad."

"You do realize both of those were married couples, not siblings." Skye wondered if her family tree was heading into the same forest as the Dooziers' twisted oak.

"They're divorced," Gillian informed Skye with a bounce of her ponytail.

Attempting to wrap up the conversation sometime this century, Skye said, "I'm surprised to see you here. I thought you worked on Thursdays."

Gillian and Ginger were both tellers at the local bank.

"Kristin is home sick with the flu and we ran out of chicken noodle soup." Gillian looked down at her attire and her mouth pursed. "Irvin is over at Farm and Fleet getting supplies for the farm. He said he'd pick up some soup and bring it home, but Kristin threw a fit when she found out it would take him over an hour to get back."

"She's thirteen, right?" Skye's smile was sympathetic. "Tough age."

"They're all tough." Gillian smirked and glanced at the twins. "You'll see."

"I guess I will." Skye switched the strap of her purse from one shoulder to the other.

"Of course, with a rich father-in-law, it will be a lot easier for you," Gillian sneered. "I hear you're interviewing nannies."

Skye didn't have to ask how her cousin knew about that. Skye had told May, and May must have told her sister, Minnie, who had told her daughter, Gillian.

Ignoring her cousin's dig about Wally's wealthy family, Skye said, "Yes, we have. Sadly, my maternity leave won't last forever."

"Teachers get a lot longer than bank tellers," Gillian sniped.

Skye bit her tongue and didn't correct her cousin. Gillian was hardly the first person who couldn't remember that Skye was a school psychologist, not a teacher. Or to assume the benefits of a public school employee were better than their own.

Figuring that her social obligation was almost fulfilled, Skye turned and took hold of the stroller's handle. "Well, I better let you go. Kristin will be waiting for her chicken noodle soup, and who knows how much longer these two will behave themselves."

Skye started to push the stroller down the first aisle, but Gillian followed. "Any news about the bombing at the bowling alley? We were shocked to hear that annoying woman was a gambling addict."

"To the best of my knowledge, no one has said that Ms. Myler was a compulsive gambler." It always amused Skye how quickly people jumped to conclusions. "Where did you hear that information?"

"Nowhere. It's just obvious since she was so hooked she was playing even after the alley was closed."

"Oh," Skye said noncommittally and kept walking. "See you on Saturday."

Gillian wasn't easily dismissed and she kept pace as Skye quickened her steps. "It's no surprise someone killed that Myler woman."

"Because she was denying everyone's claims?" Skye paused in her escape.

"That, too," Gillian agreed. "But when she was at our house looking at the damage to our screened porch and shed, she took a call and I overheard her side of the conversation." Gillian absently played with a wisp of hair that had escaped from her ponytail. "Paige said to whoever was on the other end of the line that she was determined to become the youngest vice president in her company and that she was willing to lie, cheat, or sleep her way to the top."

"Interesting." Skye smiled. Now she had the perfect excuse to stop at the police station and take her husband to lunch.

CHAPTER 16

'Cause My Baby Says It's So

AFTER LOADING HER GROCERIES AND THE TWINS into the SUV, Skye drove to the police station. The PD shared both a building and a parking lot with the library and city hall, so it wasn't unusual for the area to be full of activity, and today was no exception.

Once she had the babies in their stroller, Skye quickly walked across the lot. The formerly black asphalt had faded to a murky gray, and cracks marred the surface. Since the tornado, people were continually stopping by the city hall and the police department to pick up or drop off paperwork, to lodge a complaint, or to ask for help and the increased traffic had taken its toll on the blacktop.

The odor of gasoline and exhaust was heavy and Skye quickened her pace to get the twins out of the polluted air. She hurried into the police garage and used her key to let herself in through the PD's back entrance.

Once inside, she heard the faint clacking of a computer's keyboard and the murmur of someone on the telephone. As she pushed the twins down the narrow corridor she glanced in the break room's window. It sparkled as if it had just been cleaned and Skye smiled at the image of May wielding her infamous bottle of Windex. Never let it be said that Skye's mother left a pane of glass go unpolished.

Inside the break room, a skinny man with long, stringy hair sat at the table. Wally was standing in the open doorway with a scowl on his handsome face.

Before Skye could greet him, he twisted his head toward the seated guy and said, "I'll be back when your attorney gets here from Chicago."

As Wally closed the break room door, he caught sight of Skye and hurried toward her.

"What's going on?" Skye asked once Wally had kissed the top of his babies' heads and enveloped her in a hug.

"That's Zeus Hammersmith." Wally jerked his jaw at the man who had laid his head down on the tabletop and appeared to be taking a nap. "He's the guy that lost a lot of money in the video gaming machines at the bowling alley and claimed that the machines were rigged."

"He's the one that said Bunny would be sorry for stealing his cash, right?" Skye murmured, mostly to herself, but Wally nodded and she asked, "What does he have to say about the bombing?"

"Good question." Wally rubbed his chin. "Unfortunately, he lawyered up as soon as we asked him to come in to the station and talk to us."

"Shoot!" Skye peered through the window into the break room, attempting to analyze the heavily tattooed man's actions and motives.

"All he would say was that he had nothing to do with the explosion." Wally's voice dripped with cynicism.

"If his attorney is coming from Chicago, that'll take at least ninety minutes, which means you're free for a while." Skye brightened. "How about the twins and I take you to McDonald's for lunch?"

"That sounds like the best offer that I've had all day." Wally grinned. "I'll call Martinez in to babysit the suspect. Hammersmith's lawyer was in court when he phoned him, so he won't be here until three at the earliest."

"Great. While we wait for Zelda, we can feed your son and daughter."

As Skye nursed the babies in Wally's office, he sat with her and brought her up to speed. Paige had been staying at the Up A Lazy River, and Anthony had searched her motel room. He hadn't found anything beyond the normal clothes, toiletries, and business-related items. Paige's laptop was password protected and had been handed over to the county crime techs to unlock. And Wally had walked through the bowling alley but hadn't discovered anything helpful.

Half an hour later, Skye pulled into the McDonald's parking lot with Wally right behind her in his squad car. He'd wanted to drive separately in case he got an emergency call and had to leave quickly.

Walking inside the fast food restaurant, Skye was surprised that the place was so busy. It was well after the lunch rush and this crowd couldn't have anything to do with tomorrow being Halloween.

It took a while to get to the front of the line, then a little longer to order because Nora, the girl behind the counter, was one of Skye's past counselees. Nora was part of a vocational program that allowed students to work in local businesses a few afternoons a week.

Skye had started seeing the girl right after the tornado because Nora had been convinced that it was her fault that her parents had been injured in the storm since she wasn't home at the time it happened. It had turned out that Nora was the one who always alerted the rest of her family to upcoming bad weather, and her guilt had led to panic attacks. Skye had worked with Nora to overcome these attacks and deal with her sense of defeat at her house being destroyed and her grief at the loss of so many of her treasured possessions.

Once Nora finished thanking Skye for helping her, she took her order. A few minutes later, Skye and Wally got their food, grabbed napkins, and headed toward their favorite back corner booth.

Skye parked the stroller at the end of the table and

slid into the bench seat. If she was lucky, with their tummies full and diapers freshly changed, the twins should sleep for the next couple of hours.

As soon as Wally settled across from her, Skye said, "Right now, I'm starving, but don't let me forget to tell you about the visit from my mother and grandmother and my encounters at the supermarket. I have several tidbits of info that might relate to the bombing."

"Will do." Wally grinned and quickly distributed the food from the tray.

"Do you think that Zeus is behind the explosion?" Skye took a bite of her Big Mac and nearly moaned in ecstasy. She'd been trying to avoid greasy food, but there was nothing like a Mickey D's burger.

"Maybe not." Wally took a healthy swallow of his soda. "But he's definitely hiding something if he lawyered up that fast."

"What's your current feeling about the bomb's real target?" Skye ripped open a packet of catsup and squeezed it in the lid of the Big Mac's cardboard box. "I know you were leaning toward something to do with Bunny and the bowling alley. Did the info about the criminal propensities of her not-quite-ex, Aiden O'Twomey, tip you over in that direction?"

"I've been going back and forth." Wally paused and ate a bite of his Quarter Pounder. "Once we get the report on how the explosive was detonated, I think it will be clearer. If it was a timer, it was more likely aimed at the alley. If it was someone nearby,

I'd be more inclined to think Paige Myler was the intended victim."

"When will you find out?" Skye asked selecting a fry from the shiny red carton. "It's been two and a half days since the blast."

"Depends on how busy the state bomb squad is right now." Wally finished his Quarter Pounder in two more bites, then unwrapped his second sandwich. "They're responsible for every incident south of I-80."

"Are there that many bombings?" Skye asked, a fry halfway to her mouth. "I had no idea there was that kind of activity outside of Chicago."

"Yeah." Wally's expression was sheepish. "I didn't realize it either."

Skye wiped her mouth with her napkin. "Speaking of Bunny's sort of ex-boyfriend, have you had time to look into him yet?"

"Uh-huh." Wally crunched into his Chicken Bacon Clubhouse. "While Quirk was searching for Zeus, I talked to a pal in the city."

"And?" Skye glared. She hated it when Wally teased her like this, trickling out information and making her beg for each tidbit.

"According to my buddy"—Wally leaned forward and lowered his voice—"O'Twomey is small time. He exaggerates his connections to organized crime."

"Okay…" Skye drew out the word. "But he's still a bad guy, right?"

"No question about that." Wally drained his soda. "Nowadays he's known as Gentleman A, but when he was younger, he did a nickel in the Joliet Correctional Center before it closed."

"I guess you were right about warning your father." Skye frowned. The guy might be small potatoes criminally speaking, but he still sounded dangerous. "Is O'Twomey on the top of your list of suspects?"

"Let's just say I'd really like to talk to him." Wally crumpled up the wrappers from their food and put them on the tray.

"Hmm." Skye snatched the last of her fries before Wally added the carton to the pile of trash. "Do you have his address?"

"The only one I could find is a post office box." Wally scowled. "There are companies that rent digital PO boxes to people and assign them a U.S. mailing address, which they then use at the DMV."

"Well, heck." Skye paused, then snapped her fingers. "How about requesting his passport records? You could at least see if he really returned from Ireland on the date he told Bunny or if he's still there."

"The request is in." Wally's lips thinned. "But as usual, we aren't a top priority."

"Of course not." Skye leaned over to check on the twins. Her daughter was peacefully asleep, but her son was starting to fuss. Reaching into the diaper bag for a pacifier, she found the napkin where she had written

Yuri's license plate and put it on the table. "It seems as if, at least for now, O'Twomey is a dead end."

"Pretty much." Wally shrugged. "All of my officers and the county deputies who patrol in our area have the guy's latest DMV picture and are on the alert for him entering or leaving the city limits."

"Good thing Scumble River only has a few roads in and out of town."

"There is that." Wally nodded at the napkin she'd retrieved from the diaper bag and asked, "What's that?"

"I'll tell you after you get me a Strawberry & Crème Pie." Skye waved her hand toward the counter, then added, "And a large decaf please."

She had a momentary flash of guilt thinking about the calories. But she'd checked with her ob-gyn yesterday afternoon, and Wally had been right about the doctor's instructions not to attempt to lose weight while breastfeeding in the first few months after giving birth.

When Wally returned with her dessert order, as well as a hot caramel sundae and cup of coffee for himself, he took a pad from his pocket, clicked on his pen, and asked, "Ready to tell me what you've been up to this morning?"

Skye outlined what her grandmother had said about Carson and his date, then ended with, "I hadn't even thought about Bunny coming to the baptism. Not that I don't want her there, but now I'm picturing this O'Twomey guy showing up with a machine gun and killing everyone."

"That's a problem." Wally stroked his jaw. "I know Dad will be hurt if we say she isn't welcome, and you don't want that, right?" He paused, and when Skye nodded her agreement, he continued, "So how about if I hire some off-duty county deputies to provide extra security?"

"That'll work." Skye patted Wally's hand. "Just don't let your father pay for them. He's already given us enough."

"I agree." Wally turned his hand over and threaded his fingers with Skye's. "But one thing to consider is that Dad is one of those rare people who gives without remembering and takes without forgetting."

"True." Skye squeezed Wally's hand and let go. "But I still want to curtail his spending on us."

"Got it. I'm going to call Dad as soon as I get back to the station to make sure Bunny told him about O'Twomey, but I won't mention that I'm hiring security," Wally assured her. "Then I'll put the word out among the county deputies that I'm looking to hire as many as are available and willing to work."

"Terrific." Skye ate a bite of her pie, savoring the strawberry flavor, then said, "Another matter that Grandma mentioned made me think about how now that we have legal gambling machines around here, do they affect the groups like the church and American Legion who count on bingo and King of Diamonds and such to fund their activities?"

"That sure doesn't seem to be the case." Wally

shook his head. "The parking lots at both places are just as packed as they were before."

"Okay." Skye checked that off her mental list. "One last thing from my visit with Grandma, then I'll move on to my thought-provoking and slightly bizarre adventures at the supermarket."

Wally lifted a brow as he spooned caramel-covered ice cream into his mouth and motioned with his other hand for her to continue her stories.

"Do you know if Bunny is going to replace the gambling machines that were destroyed in the blast?" Skye asked, and when Wally shook his head, she said, "If she doesn't, I'm assuming someone else would get her slot because it's my understanding only a certain number of establishments can have video gambling in town."

"That's true." Wally took a sip of his coffee. "Which is why, although Dante assures me it isn't necessary, at some point I need to talk to Yuri Iverson. He owns a chain of video gambling cafés and is anxious to open one in Scumble River."

"Yuri," Skye repeated. "Ah, that's why he was so intent on meeting with the city council tomorrow." After Skye told Wally about her run-in with the gambling entrepreneur, she said, "I took down his license plate number, but since we know who he is, I can throw it away." Wally nodded and she crumpled up the napkin.

Wally crossed his arms. "If this Iverson guy is only sticking around until the meeting tomorrow morning, I

better have Quirk grab him up this afternoon for a chat."
Wally reached for his phone and called the sergeant.
Once he hung up, he said, "I can't see Iverson making a
bomb while living at the motor court, but I'd sure like to
take a look at his room and inside his vehicle."

"You could always talk to the housekeeper that
cleans for Charlie," Skye suggested.

"True."

As Wally made a note, Skye muttered under her
breath, "But Yuri's fancy car seems too small to do
much in."

Wally looked up from his pad and asked, "What?"

"Never mind." Skye finished her pie, licked her
fingers, and took a sip of coffee.

"Anything else?" Wally asked.

"Uh-huh. I saved the best for last. My cousin
Gillian was in the store."

"I thought you weren't too fond of her or her
sister," Wally said, wrinkling his brow in confusion.
"Why is she the best thing?"

"Because she and her husband are insured by
Homestead," Skye said with a little smile. Let Wally
see how it felt to have info dribbled out.

"And you think she killed Paige Myler?" The skin
around Wally's eyes crinkled in amusement. "Let's go
arrest her right now."

"Funny." Skye batted Wally's bicep. "Although it
would be beyond cool to drag Gillian off to jail, it's
what she overheard that's interesting."

"I'll bite." Wally scraped up the last of his sundae. "What did she hear?"

"Paige was making a home visit to inspect Gillian and Irvin's tornado damage when she got a personal call." Skye made a face. "Paige stepped away to take it, but obviously she had no idea how small towns work and Gillian followed her and eavesdropped."

"And?"

"And Gillian heard Paige say she'd do anything to become Homestead Insurance's youngest vice president." Skye paused for effect, then added, "Anything including, lie, cheat, and sleep her way to the top."

Before Wally could respond, there was a loud wail from the stroller. Instantly, a second voice joined in and Skye and Wally each reached for a baby.

Skye checked her son's diaper and found it clean, then bounced him against her shoulder, but he continued to scream. And although their daughter's diaper was dry too, and Wally rubbed soothing circles on her back, she matched her brother's howls shriek for shriek.

Skye shook her head and said, "It doesn't look as if the twins are going to quiet down anytime soon. We better pack it up and get out of here."

Shooting apologetic looks at the other diners, Skye and Wally replaced the twins in their stroller and hurriedly pushed it out of the restaurant.

As Wally and Skye crossed the parking lot, his radio crackled. He unhooked it from his belt, keyed the mic, and said, "Chief Boyd here. Go ahead."

"Your suspect's lawyer has arrived and he's throwing a hissy fit."

"About what?" Wally's eyebrows disappeared into his hairline.

"Not suitable for the radio." The dispatcher's voice held a note of laughter. "But you need to get here sooner rather than later."

"Fine." Wally glanced at Skye and shrugged ruefully. "I'll be there in ten."

"Sorry." Wally helped Skye get the twins loaded into the SUV. "I hate leaving you with two screaming babies."

"No problem." Skye picked up her daughter's and son's chubby little fists and kissed them. "They're already winding down. I wonder what got into them. They never cry without a reason."

"Maybe it was too noisy with all the people there," Wally guessed, then added, "From what you told me it looks like I need to take a road trip to Normalton tomorrow and find out a little more about our vic." He asked with a twinkle in his eye, "Care to join me?"

"I wouldn't miss it." Skye kissed him, slid behind the wheel, and rolled down the window. "And speaking of not missing anything, you better be home by six for the first nanny interview." She shook her finger at him. "I'm not making this decision without you."

Wally grinned and held up his palms in surrender. He leaned in for another kiss, then echoing Skye, said, "Wouldn't miss it."

CHAPTER 17

It's My Own Fault, Baby

SKYE FASTENED HER SEAT BELT AND STARTED TO turn the key. She should go home, put away the groceries, and get ready for that evening's nanny interviews. But the babies were already in the car and once again sleeping peacefully. This was a rare opportunity, and she couldn't resist checking in with Piper.

She'd just zip over to the high school, see how the intern was doing, and make sure Homer had enrolled Mrs. Brodsky's son. If she was quick, she'd get it all done before the twins demanded their next feeding.

Buzzed on a sugar high from her sweet dessert and feeling like for once she had everything under control, Skye pulled out of the McDonald's parking lot and turned toward the school. According to the dashboard clock, it was 2:59. The final bell rang at three, but since staff was required to stay for twenty additional minutes, theoretically, both Piper and the principal should still be around.

A few seconds later, when Skye arrived at the high school, buses idled at the curb as teenagers rushed out of the building and climbed on board. Behind the yellow buses, cars were lined up containing parents impatiently waiting for their sons or daughters to appear. And off to the side, juniors and seniors surged toward the student parking area.

Dodging pedestrians, Skye made her way around back to the faculty lot and went through the process once again of getting the twins in their stroller. At the rear entrance, she fumbled through her purse for her keys, finally digging them out from the bottom of her bag.

Strangely, the metal knob felt icy on her palm, and as she maneuvered herself and the stroller through the rear entrance, she had the strangest urge to turn around and go home. Advancing cautiously, Skye saw that the hallway contained only a few students lingering in front of their lockers—laughing, talking, and flirting with each other.

There was no reason for her unease, and as she walked farther down the corridor, she relaxed. She murmured a greeting to a teacher leaning against a recycle bin. He was probably on hall duty, but his attention was focused on his phone as his thumbs flew over the screen.

Skye headed toward the front office. If she was lucky, Opal, the school secretary, could confirm the

Brodsky boy's enrollment and she wouldn't even have to talk to Homer.

Spotting Opal standing near the front door chatting with someone in her thirties, Skye glanced at the boy next to the two women. She could see at a glance that he wasn't their typical student.

Everything about the young man seemed just a little off. From the strangely stiff way he held himself, as if he were a marionette being held up by an invisible cord, to the quarter-sized depression in the middle of his forehead, to the way his brow pleated over the bridge of his nose.

As Skye got closer, she noticed that his arms and shoulders were heavily muscled and his hands were the diameter of Ping-Pong paddles. His size, combined with the vacant look in his eyes, sent a shudder down Skye's spine. She would bet dollars to doughnuts that his impulse control and social awareness were impaired to some degree, and if he didn't get the appropriate services, there could be a huge problem.

Before she reached the threesome, the woman and boy walked out the door. Opal turned and saw Skye. Squealing in delight, Opal closed the distance between them and dropped to her knees in front of the snoozing babies.

Clapping a hand over her mouth, Opal whispered, "I hope I didn't wake them." Her fingers stretched out as if she wanted to touch the twins, but she fisted them and slowly rose to her feet.

"They're usually pretty heavy sleepers," Skye assured the older woman, crossing her fingers that they wouldn't wake up and have another screaming fit like they'd had at McDonald's.

"Well, they are just adorable," Opal cooed. "I was telling Mother last night that I couldn't wait for you to bring them in for a visit."

"Aw. That's so sweet." Skye smiled, then asked, "How is your mom?"

Mrs. Hill was nearly a hundred and Opal was her only child. During the day while Opal worked, a home health aide stayed with the elderly woman, but all other times, she was her mom's sole caretaker.

"About the same." Opal shrugged. "But Mother's a fighter and is determined to beat her sister. And Aunt Penelope lived to a hundred and two."

"Wow!" Skye's eyes widened. "Your family has really amazing genes."

"Only the women." Opal sighed. "Some say that the men, whether born to or wed into the family, are cursed and die before fifty."

"How awful." Skye wanted to ask if that was why Opal had never married, but the secretary was a private person and had never given Skye the impression she'd welcome questions about her personal life.

"Yes." Opal blinked back a tear. "My father passed on his fortieth birthday."

"That must have been a shock for both you and your mother," Skye said cautiously. She had no idea if Mr. Hill had been a good man or not. When Opal just nodded, Skye changed the subject and asked, "Has a boy by the name of Brodsky been registered for classes?"

"Oh my, yes," Opal tsked. "That was him and his mother just leaving. He had an incident and we had to call her to pick him up. He seems like a sweet child until he gets frustrated, but the teachers are already complaining that he's unable to handle the curriculum. Even the non-core classes seem to be overwhelming for him."

"Because if he were any more stupid, he'd have to be watered twice a week." Homer stomped out of his office and down the short hall, his voice booming as loudly as the entire percussion section of the band. He completely ignored the twins and continued, "I told Poppy that since she was so gung ho on this kid being at our school, she needed to get him tested ASAP."

"Her name is Piper. Piper Townsend," Skye ground out between clenched teeth. Homer's insistence on getting the intern's name wrong was getting on her last nerve. Finally, she loosened her jaw enough to ask, "Does that mean you've already had a referral meeting?" She was certain he hadn't done anything of the sort, but this was her way of reminding the principal that there was a procedure to follow for students who were experiencing difficulties with the academic load. For good measure, she raised a brow and added, "Have interventions been put into place matching instructional resources to educational need?"

"I told you, we aren't doing all that bullpuckey in this school. The feds don't mandate it and I'm not messing with it." Homer rattled the bunch of keys on his belt. "Just test him and get him in special ed ASAP."

Skye rolled her eyes and didn't bother to keep the annoyance from her voice. "In that case, I guess I'd better talk to Piper."

"You do that," Homer thundered. "Tell Puppy to shake a leg."

"Yeah. I'll get right on that," Skye muttered and turned her back on Homer. "Right after I tell her to roll over and play dead."

"Hey! Wait a sec!" Homer yelled before Skye was able to make her escape. "Have you heard anything about that insurance woman?"

"The investigation related to her death is ongoing." Skye didn't believe for a minute that he was concerned about Paige Myler's passing.

"I wonder if she hit the jackpot before the jackpot hit her." Homer snickered. When Skye didn't react, he ran his fingers through his hair, making the wiry mess stand up like a porcupine's quills. "Are they sending someone out to replace her? Maybe someone that will actually write a check?"

"As far as I know, Homestead hasn't contacted the police department since they were notified of Ms. Myler's death."

Skye wrinkled her forehead, trying to recall if Wally had said anything about Paige's employer. It

occurred to Skye that the company's silence seemed a
bit odd. Shouldn't someone have talked to the police,
if for no other reason than to distance the corporation
from liability for Paige's death?

"When are the police letting Bunny open up
again?" Homer asked.

"It'll probably be a while." Skye refocused her
attention. "There are a lot of repairs that need to be
made before the building can pass inspection and
most of the area contractors are still busy with tornado
connected projects."

"I miss my night out with my bowling league,"
Homer griped. Then he brightened. "On the other
hand, things are looking up with that Myler bimbo
gone. Maybe now my claim will be settled."

Skye opened her mouth to comment on Homer's
lack of compassion, but then she walked away before
she was tempted to submit her resignation. Or worse,
tell the offensive principal what she really thought of
him. Right now, the only thing stopping her was that
she didn't want her babies to hear that kind of language.

By the time Skye reached her office, she had
counted to twenty and could speak in a rational tone
of voice. Piper was behind her desk but sprang up
when Skye came through the doorway.

Once the young woman had admired the twins,
Skye leaned a hip against her desk and said, "I understand the Brodsky boy is enrolled and is already having
difficulties."

"Yes." Piper returned to her chair and flipped open a file. "I spoke with Stan's mother about twenty minutes ago and she is anxious to get him help."

"Why hasn't he been evaluated or had services in the past?"

"From what I can gather, six years ago, Mrs. Brodsky's husband emptied their bank account and ran away with another woman, leaving a mountain of debt." Piper shook her head. "Can you believe a man would just abandon his children with no way to support them?"

Skye sighed. "Sadly, I can." Piper was more naive than she'd realized. "What did Mrs. Brodsky do after her husband deserted them?"

"She and her family were homeless for several years, so the kids were in and out of a bunch of schools, but then last spring, she located a church group that had a program to get women and children back on their feet. They found her a job at the Fine Food factory on the edge of town, helped her get into an apartment, and she and the kids were doing pretty well until the tornado."

"Even knowing how bad conditions can get for people, one thing you never get used to in this job is dealing with such a tragic situation." Skye sniffed back a tear. "Especially for someone who has already been through such awful circumstances and fought their way back."

"Luckily, the church group assisted Mrs. Brodsky in securing a temporary place to live." Piper beamed.

"And since Fine Foods wasn't damaged, she still has her job and the healthcare benefits that come with it."

"That is fortunate." Skye moved from her desk to the door. She couldn't stay long and it was best not to get too comfortable. "From what you said, Stan Brodsky and his siblings have had little or inconsistent schooling."

"Mrs. Brodsky has done her best, but yes, there are big gaps." Piper bit her lip and toyed with the folders on her desk. "And I know that usually means ineligibility for special education services, but I'd still like to do a comprehensive initial evaluation."

"That's a team decision," Skye said, knowing full well the team would go along with the eval if for no other reason than to appease Homer.

"I plan to point out to the Student Services Team that the regulations state that if the delay isn't *primarily* the result of environmental or economic disadvantage…et cetera, et cetera." Piper tilted her head. "And I'll emphasize the word 'primarily.'"

"It's too bad Mrs. Brodsky doesn't have the resources to get Stan a neurological exam. We might have to bite the bullet and recommend it, which will make the school district responsible for the charge." Skye sighed, knowing the superintendent would have a fit at the cost.

"I was thinking along those lines, too." Piper screwed up her face. "How much resistance can I expect?"

"A lot, but I'll help you through it." Skye smiled reassuringly. "If you can get any school records from before Stan and his family became homeless, and there's any indication of a prior issue, that will help your case immensely both for evaluation and later placement."

"I have the list of schools he's attended and plan to personally phone each one tomorrow." Piper held up a sheet of paper. "Mrs. Brodsky signed a release of records form, so I'm all set."

"Good job," Skye said, then asked, "Anyone at the other schools mentioning that Stan's two siblings are having any problems?"

"Not so far." Piper consulted her notes. "His brother is nine and his sister is seven." Raising her eyes, she said, "That means their father left their mother with a one-, three-, and six-year-old." Piper's cheeks reddened. "What a…a creepazoid of the genus *Asshat*."

"Don't worry," Skye said. "Karma will come back to bite him on the butt. And all we can do is hope that she has rabies when she does it." Skye rolled the stroller over the threshold, then over her shoulder said, "Call me if you need any advice or suggestions."

"Will do." Piper's voice indicated her zeal, and Skye hoped the intern would be able to retain that enthusiasm throughout her career.

It was nearly four when Skye walked outside pushing the stroller. Behind her, the door slammed shut with a decisive echo. The late-afternoon light was fading and shadows dappled the parking lot. As Skye hurried toward the SUV, a nearby movement caught her eye.

Her heart thudding louder and louder, she glanced

over her shoulder and then quickened her pace. The stroller bumped over uneven patches of asphalt and the twins started to fuss.

Except for the crying babies, the only other sound was the distant bark of a dog. Cold sweat trickled down Skye's sides and she held her breath.

Suddenly, a figure inserted itself between Skye and the Mercedes.

Fear clogged Skye's throat and a taunting litany in her mind of *my fault, my fault, my fault* blamed her for the situation. She had put her children at risk. Why hadn't she gone home after lunch?

A rotund woman dressed in a blue cape with a huge, pink bow at her throat stepped out of the gloom and called out, "Mrs. Boyd!" She advanced toward Skye, and as she fanned her hand in front of her face, she complained, "You are an extremely difficult young woman to get alone."

"Ms. Rose," Skye said. Her heart rate might have returned to normal, but she was still considering a swift retreat back into the school building. "Why would you need to get me alone?"

"Miss." The woman wagged her finger. "As I've told you before, I prefer Miss Rose, or better yet, please call me Millicent."

"What can I do for you, Miss Rose?" Skye kept her body between her babies and the odd, little woman and edged the stroller backward. "My husband's right behind me. He's getting the babies' diaper bag. I forgot it in my office, but he'll be join-ing us in a few seconds."

"Chief Boyd is at the police station dealing with a very annoyed member of the Illinois Gaming Board." Millicent wagged her finger again.

"He is not." Skye frowned. How did the woman know that Wally was at the PD? Besides, he was meeting with an attorney, not someone from the gaming board. "He'll be here any second and won't be happy to see you."

"Stop lying to me." Millicent put her hands on her hips. "I'm trying to help you."

"Help me with what exactly?" Skye felt around behind her for her cell phone in the caddy attached to the stroller's handles, wishing her pepper spray wasn't buried at the bottom of her purse.

"Wickedness continues to lurk around Scumble River." Millicent's expression darkened. "Although I was sent here for you, I wasn't sure at first which mother and baby was the target and I made sure to be there for them all. But now I know it's you and your children who are in danger."

"And how do you know that?" Skye fought to keep her tone civil.

Millicent continued as if Skye hadn't spoken. "This evil is waiting until you and your children are at your most vulnerable and then it will act."

Intellectually, Skye knew the woman was spout-ing nonsense, but her chest tightened and she asked, "Why are my babies and I being targeted?"

"It's not clear." Millicent rubbed her temples. "I feel like you are a means to an end."

"You've said that you're trying to help me, but a vague warning doesn't seem to be much in the way of assistance," Skye retorted.

"Whatever is planned will happen the day of the babies' christening." Millicent inhaled deeply and then, in a voice heavy with importance, declared, "I need to be there to stop it."

"If this is just another way to get an invitation to the baptism—"

Skye's next words were cut off by a loud shriek from the twins. She whirled around to check on her babies. No one and nothing was anywhere near them, but their faces were scrunched up and they were sobbing. She tried to soothe them with pacifiers, but they refused and continued to howl their displeasure.

Turning back to Millicent, Skye attempted to move around the woman. "You'll have to excuse me. I need to get my son and daughter fed."

Millicent opened her mouth to speak, but suddenly, her complexion turned ashen, her eyes rolled back, and she collapsed at Skye's feet.

CHAPTER 18

There Goes My Baby

WHEN WALLY ARRIVED BACK AT THE STATION, Zeus Hammersmith's attorney, Ellis Markey, demanded that his client be immediately released. Wally attempted to explain the need for Zeus to answer a few questions first, but Markey was adamant that Zeus remain silent.

After an hour of escalating threats and demands by Markey, Wally had had enough.

Marching over to the break room door, Wally opened it, then paused at the threshold and warned, "If Zeus doesn't cooperate, he'll be spending the next seventy-eight hours in jail, the maximum length of time I can hold a suspect before charging him."

Instantly, Zeus blurted out, "Mr. Markey isn't really my lawyer." He glared at the man in question and added, "I'm not sitting in any jail cell for you."

Wally allowed the door to click shut behind him

and rejoined Zeus and Markey. Taking a seat across from the two men, he waited for an explanation.

Ellis Markey adjusted his wire-rimmed glasses. "Chief, it is of the utmost importance that you keep what I tell you completely confidential. It can't leave this room."

Wally took a deep breath, the odor of old coffee and burned microwaved meals catching in his gullet. "I guess that will depend on what you say and who, in my opinion, needs to know." He glanced at the old-fashioned tape recorder sitting in front of him. "But for now, I won't turn this on."

Six months ago, the city attorney had decreed that the police had to make an audio record of all official interviews. And since the break room wasn't set up with any kind of modern equipment, and there was no money in the budget to correct that issue, the police had to make do with what they could scrounge up.

"We appreciate your cooperation." Markey fingered his gray mustache.

Wally stared appraisingly at the man's carefully manicured nails. The shine on them definitely looked like a professional job. Did he get a pedicure while he was at it?

The minute that Zeus revealed that Markey wasn't an attorney, Wally figured he was either in law enforcement or from some other government agency. The buffed fingernails implied the latter.

Zeus had to be working as an informant or

undercover for a guy like Markey to drive all the way down from Chicago to save his butt.

When Wally remained silent, Markey straightened his tie and continued, "As you may have guessed, Mr. Hammersmith is not what he appears."

"A poor loser who shouldn't be pissing away his paycheck on slot machines?" Wally asked dryly.

"Hey," Zeus protested. "You ain't got no right to say something like that." He glanced at the older man. "Tell 'em, Mr. Markey."

"I work for the Illinois Gaming Board." Markey handed Wally his identification. "We have received numerous complaints regarding several of the video gambling outlets in Stanley County. And Mr. Hammersmith has been helping me with my investigation into those allegations."

After carefully examining the man's credentials and returning them, Wally asked, "Are the complaints against the establishment owners?"

His gut tightened. He had known from the very beginning that video gambling would be a problem for Scumble River.

"Although they are being looked at as well, we are most interested in the terminal operators. They are the ones that are authorized by the state to purchase, install, and manage the gaming machines. The establishment owners have little to do with the machines other than collecting their percentage of the profits."

"And Zeus does what exactly?" Wally asked. He might not be a fan of Bunny's, but Wally wasn't happy with any man who thought it was okay to abuse a woman verbally. "Besides becoming obnoxious when he loses and threatening women?"

"That's a part of the plan," Zeus protested, fingering a faded scar on his chin that shined pinkly in the harsh fluorescent lights. "I wouldn't hurt anyone." He smiled, revealing nicotine-yellow teeth. "I'm a lover, not a fighter."

"What is this big plan?" Wally tapped his pen on the tabletop, noticing that Markey hadn't answered his original question.

"I'm afraid that's on a need-to-know basis, and there's no reason to share that information with you." Markey voice sounded like grinding metal gears and he shot Zeus a shushing glare.

"I have to disagree. If it has anything to do with a building in my town blowing up, I certainly need to know how the accusations are being investigated." Wally stared at the older man. "Let's not forget that a woman was killed."

"I assure you there is no connection." Markey shook his head. "First of all, the operators have no idea we are investigating them. Second, if you're suggesting the explosion was a cover-up, destroying the machines in a single establishment would be futile."

"Has there been any kind of issue with other

establishments that use the operator you're investigating?" Wally asked, unsatisfied with Markey's glib response. "Machines damaged or stolen?"

"None." Markey reached down and picked up the briefcase sitting next to him on the floor. "And now if you'll release Mr. Hammersmith, I really need to get back to the city."

"Fine." Wally narrowed his eyes. "But before either of you leave, I need a way to contact you should other questions arise."

Markey took out a business card and handed it to Wally. "This has my direct line."

Taking the card, Wally flipped it over and clicked his pen. "Let me get your cell number as well." His smile didn't reach his eyes. "You know, just in case of an emergency with our friend Zeus here."

Grudgingly, Markey recited a string of digits, then stood, gripped Zeus by the elbow, and jerked him to his feet. Markey looked at Wally and said, "I'd like to take Mr. Hammersmith out through the garage so no one sees us."

"This way." Wally led the men out of the break room, down a short hallway, and opened the door to the garage. Staring at Zeus, Wally said, "I have my eye on you."

"Chief." The man raised his hands, palms facing out. "Don't worry. I'm cool."

Wally's scalp prickled. A guy like Zeus had very little allegiance to anyone besides himself. If a better offer came along, his loyalty to Markey would last about as long as powdered sugar on a hot doughnut.

Once Zeus and his handler were gone, Wally looked at his watch. It was past five. He had just enough time to write up his notes and still get home before the first nanny interview was scheduled.

As he climbed the stairs to his office, he checked his cell and saw that Skye had called. Keying in his passcode, he played her message.

"Hi, sweetie. Call me back as soon as you have a chance. Possible info regarding the bombing. Love you." A pause. "See you at six."

After Wally unlocked the door to his office and went inside, he settled behind his desk and listened to the voicemails on his landline. The only interesting communication was from Homestead Insurance's executive vice president asking if there were any updates on Paige Myler's death.

After returning the call and assuring the VP that Wally would let him know if they made any progress on the case, he took out the file, pulled a legal pad toward him, and jotted down the facts from his interview with Hammersmith and Markey. As soon as he finished recording his notes, he unclipped his cell from his belt and dialed Skye.

She answered on the first ring, and he said, "Hi, sugar. What's up?"

His posture became more and more rigid as she related her encounter with Millicent Rose. Wally allowed Skye to finish speaking as he fought back a wave of anger. How dare that woman ambush his wife and children like that? First thing tomorrow morning, he intended to pay the self-styled fairy godmother a visit and warn her to stay away from his family or else he was going to turn Martinez loose on her. He'd let the young officer fully investigate her theory that Millicent Rose was behind the bowling alley bombing.

"Once Miss Rose revived," Skye's sweet voice broke into his thoughts, "I managed to get her to elaborate. She admitted that after seeing someone hanging out near the rectory the night we met with Father Burns, she was even more concerned that the babies were surrounded by evil and felt she needed to redouble her efforts to be allowed to attend the baptism."

"The evening we met with Father Burns was also the night of the bombing," Wally muttered, clicking his pen. "And the church is only a block and a half away from the bowling alley."

"Exactly," Skye said, then added, "Unfortunately, I don't think Miss Rose's testimony would go over very well in a court of law."

"Why is that?" Wally asked, lifting his pen from the legal pad.

"As you know, Miss Rose is a bit eccentric," Skye said slowly. "And according to her, the person she saw was unusually short and bulky and…"

"And what?" Wally scratched his head, trying

to recall if any of the suspects fit the Rose woman's description of the loiterer.

"Silver." Skye giggled. "She said the figure was shiny like tinfoil."

"Son of a—" Wally cut himself off. "So much for our eyewitness."

"True." Skye paused, then said, "But I do think she saw someone, so even if she can't identify the person, it makes me think that Paige Myler was the intended victim and that someone was there ready to set off the explosive device as soon as he or she was sure that Paige was inside the alley playing the machines."

"Or this Millicent Rose is nuts and having visual hallucinations." Wally was already fed up with the woman and her magical crap, and this latest incident didn't help matters.

"Perhaps." Skye's tone told Wally she was unhappy with him. "But since I am a psychologist, you'd think I would be able to figure out if someone is merely eccentric or if she's psychotic."

"Darlin'…" Wally attempted to alleviate the situation before he ended up sleeping on the sofa alone rather than in bed with his wife curled up at his side. "I just want to make sure we follow all the leads and don't get distracted by a witness who may or may not have seen anything useful."

"Right." If anything, Skye sounded more ticked off. "Because I'm not trained to consider all possibilities before coming to a conclusion."

"I'm sorry. That came out all wrong." Wally stared at his phone in concern.

"That's okay," Skye said, clearly indicating it was far from fine.

Wally cringed. *That's okay* was one of the most terrifying statements a woman could make to a man. It meant that she wanted to think carefully before deciding how and when he'd answer for his offense.

"No. Really. I'm sorry." Wally tried to fix things before they got out of hand. "I didn't mean it that way. Of course you consider all the possibilities before making an assessment."

"Look. I'll see you later." Skye's voice was strained. "Just make sure you're home before the nanny candidates arrive for their interviews."

"Wait." Wally didn't want to end their conversation on a sour note. He was well aware that it paid to keep any words he spoke to his wife soft and sweet in case he had to eat them later. "Let's talk about why you're so sure this Rose woman is sincere."

"I don't have time for this right now," Skye muttered. "I've got to get this place straightened up. But first, I need to put on a new top since your son peed on me while I was changing his diaper. Then I have to text the contractor with answers to his latest round of unending questions, which includes, but isn't limited to, selecting the shingles for the roof, the style of gutters and downspouts, and the freaking type of insulation."

"I can take care of that," Wally quickly volunteered. "Forward the GC's text to me, and I'll let him know what we want."

"Fine." Skye sighed and Wally flinched. *Fine* was one of those words that when said by an upset woman meant the opposite. "Now, since the information from Millicent Rose wasn't as important as I thought it was, I need to go."

"It's not that—" Wally stopped talking when he realized she'd hung up on him.

This wasn't like Skye. Although they had their disagreements, they rarely resorted to bickering. Something wasn't right.

CHAPTER 19

Baby, Don't Get Hooked on Me

I'M FINE." SKYE RAISED HER VOICE AS SHE DREW THE curtains in the living room area and headed into the kitchen, Bingo twining around her ankles. "Really."

It was eight o'clock and they'd just finished the second nanny interview. Wally had arrived home seconds before the first applicant arrived and they hadn't had a chance to talk privately.

As soon as the last candidate was out the door, he had disappeared into the bedroom to change out of his uniform. Now he emerged, wearing a pair of navy sweatpants, a plain white T-shirt, and flip-flops.

"You didn't sound like yourself during our earlier phone conversation." Wally's shoulders were tense. His short black hair stood on end, silver strands glinting near his temples, and there was a day's worth of stubble along his jaw. "I really do value your opinion on cases."

"I know you do and I appreciate your apology." Skye

took out plates and silverware. "I think the encounter at the high school with Millicent Rose bothered me more than I thought and you got the brunt of it," Skye admitted, heat creeping up her cheeks.

She hadn't wanted to tell Wally how frightened she'd been being waylaid in the parking lot. She knew he'd want to go after Millicent, and Skye had a hunch that was the worst thing they could do.

"Being accosted like that would shake up anyone." Wally took a beer from the fridge, then sat at the tiny kitchen table. "And I really appreciate how easily you forgive."

"Well let's forget it." Skye's face was still hot and she was anxious to talk about something else.

"Well…" Wally's concerned brown eyes examined her closely. "Are you certain that's all there is to it? I Googled 'postpartum depression' and I have to admit—reading about all those possible symptoms scared the crap out of me."

"I've learned my lesson. I never go to the internet for medical advice." Skye giggled. "Last time I did that, I went from a tiny pimple on my arm to dying in three clicks."

Wally laughed, then said, "Are you sure you feel okay?"

"I'm not back to what I was before I got pregnant, but it's nothing serious. Believe me, I'm hyperaware of what to look for in myself." Skye unplugged the Crock-Pot and brought it to the table along with the basket of Milano French Rolls and a bowl of coleslaw. "My doctor warned me that it can take up to a year for my hormones to return to their normal levels. She also said that my body is already worn-out after giving birth, then you add the fact that new mothers often don't get enough uninterrupted sleep and the constant exercise of pushing a stroller and carrying a baby…"

"You're beat." Wally summed up Skye's explanation as he grabbed a roll, split it open, and heaped it with steaming Italian beef, then added a massive spoonful of slaw to his plate. After taking a swig of his Sam Adams, he added, "Times two."

"Exactly." Skye made her own sandwich and ate a bite. "The problem is that no matter how much I sleep, I still feel tired because I'm aware of every noise the babies make, so I never get to REM sleep. It's almost like having a hangover all the time."

"That brings us back to the nannies we talked with tonight." Wally ate some of his coleslaw, then asked, "Which one did you like?"

"I'm not sure." Skye concentrated on her dinner for a while, then confessed, "I know I need help, but how can we trust a stranger?"

"Now you sound like me." Wally chuckled. "They both have excellent training and impeccable references."

Skye made a face. "Neither of them seemed stupid, so they wouldn't give us the names of someone they didn't want us to contact."

"Their seven-year background checks are spotless."

Wally took another swig of beer before adding, "Dad suggested that one of his security team surveil any nanny we hire for a couple of weeks to see exactly what she does while we're gone."

"So we're back to the nanny cam?" Skye asked, finishing her dinner.

"Probably a little more sophisticated than that," Wally drawled.

"How do we know they wouldn't watch us, too?" Skye cringed at the thought. "Neither one of us can afford to appear in a sex video that blows up the internet."

"None of my father's employees would risk angering him," Wally said, then frowned and added, "In addition, I'll make sure we have a switch to cut off all the cameras."

"So you think it's a good idea?" Skye asked, still uncertain.

"It's pretty much our only option unless we both quit our jobs and stay home with the twins until they're thirty," Wally teased, then got up and cleared the table.

"Tempting." Skye got up to start putting the left-overs away. "Mom did mention taking an unpaid leave from the police department and becoming a granny nanny."

"While we'd know the kids were safe," Wally said as he helped with the cleanup. "Something like that would mean all the independence and space you've fought to create between us and your mother would be gone."

Once the kitchen was tidy, he took Skye's hand and led her to the living room. After flicking on the group of LED candles clustered in the center of the coffee table and turning off the rest of the lights, he sat on the couch and pulled her into his lap.

"In that case," Skye said as she snuggled closer to Wally, enjoying the golden glow of the candles on his handsome face, "I vote for nanny number one."

***

Friday morning after Wally left for work, Skye called the woman they'd selected and she agreed to start work on Monday. Skye had no plans to leave the RV that day, but she would allow the new nanny to take full responsibility for the twins while she did other things around the motor home. If nothing else, she figured she'd have a ton of thank-you notes to write after Saturday's celebration.

Next, Skye phoned Carson, who promised her a member of his security team would be in Scumble River no later than Sunday afternoon to install the surveillance equipment. He guaranteed that someone on his staff in Texas would be watching the live feed anytime the babies were alone with the nanny. And if there was a problem, an app on her and Wally's phones would notify them immediately.

With those details settled, Skye asked her father-in-law if he was free to watch the twins from late morning until dinnertime. Carson was thrilled. He said that Bunny was having a spa day in Joliet, and there was nothing he'd rather do than spend time with his grandchildren.

Having made all the arrangements, Skye texted Wally with the results of her calls, then added she would meet him at the station around ten for their trip to Normalton. With an hour to spare, she played with the twins until Carson arrived.

After making sure her father-in-law had everything he needed for the next several hours, Skye pulled on stretchy black jeans and an asymmetrical, long-sleeved scarlet T-shirt. Once she dusted her face with some bronzer and applied concealer, she headed to the police station.

As soon she turned onto the block that held the combined PD, city hall, and library, she saw a crowd marching in front of the building holding anti-gambling picket signs. She was confused about what they could possibly be protesting until she remembered that the city council meeting was this morning and that jerk from the grocery store was trying to get permission for his video gaming café. It looked as if he might be in for an unpleasant surprise.

The police station lot was packed, and Skye had to drive several blocks before she found a place to park her SUV. Hiking back toward the PD, she noticed the elaborate Halloween decorations on both the houses and businesses.

Skye hadn't bothered putting up any since everything she'd collected over the years had been blown away in the tornado. Evidently, the rest of the town hadn't let any loss from the twister stop them.

She admired the gargantuan spider on the roof of the gas station, the Harley-riding grim reaper in front of the car repair shop, and creepy cemetery in the yard of the high school physics teacher. Each tombstone had a funny epitaph like DIED FROM NOT FORWARDING A TEXT MESSAGE TO TEN PEOPLE and REST IN PIECES.

Smiling, Skye continued her stroll, enjoying the scent of burning leaves in the air and the feel of the sun beating on her face. But as approached the police station she heard a cacophony of angry shouts, then a single sonorous voice rang out.

"No more of the devil's machines!" A regal-looking woman stood in front of the city hall entrance. "Gambling hurts everyone."

At least fifty people were marching, holding placards, and chanting. It was quite a feat getting that many folks together on a Friday morning, especially on Halloween.

Skye stopped in front of the throng to read some of their signs. She nodded to Miss Letitia, the ninety-year-old president of the Scumble River historical society, who held up a poster that read *Gambling: the sure way to get nothing for something.* The saying was carefully credited to Wilson Mizner, and Skye smiled to herself that the elderly woman was making sure that

Mr. Mizner's intellectual property was being suitably acknowledged.

The owner of the dry cleaner's had one that read *Don't Gamble Your Kid's Future Away*. And Skye's aunt Minnie carried a poster with a picture of a slot machine and a toilet, and underneath was written *Do you see the difference? I don't*.

Edging through the protestors, Skye recognized most of them. Several tried to stop her to chat, but she kept moving, intent on reaching the PD's door. When she was a few feet from her goal, the person who appeared to be leading the protest stepped in front of Skye and she was forced to either halt or knock her down.

The woman thrust her hand out to Skye and said, "Udelle Calvert, president of the Stanley County Anti-Gambling League Defense."

Before Skye could respond, Wally pushed open the door and strode outside. "Ms. Calvert." He inserted himself between the woman and Skye. "I assume you're here in response to the numerous messages that I've been leaving you at all of your numbers?"

"Not now, Chief." The woman waved Wally away. "I'm here as the president of SCALD to prevent another den of inequity from opening up in your fair city."

"You mean like the one you bombed earlier in the week?" Wally moved so that the woman was trapped between him and the building.

"SCALD does not condone violence of any sort," Udelle huffed.

"Good to know." Wally grasped the woman's elbow. "Nevertheless, because you have been one of the most vocal in your disapproval of video gaming machines at Bunny Lanes, I need to interview you."

Jerking out of his grip, Udelle straightened her shoulders and said, "I'll speak with you as soon as the city council meeting is over."

Wally checked his watch. "They only have one more item on their agenda, which should be dealt with within an hour. I'll expect you to report to the dispatcher no later than eleven."

"You have my word." Udelle put her hand over her heart and looked him in the eye. "I'll be happy to cooperate."

At that moment, Skye saw Yuri Iverson, wearing a baseball cap and mirrored sunglasses, slinking toward the city hall's door. He was trying to sneak through the crowd unnoticed. Skye nudged Udelle. When the woman looked at her, she jerked her chin at the man.

Udelle smiled her thanks, then turned to her troops and shouted, her voice resonant, "Let Mr. Iverson hear what you think of his iniquitous cafés."

While the protestors surrounded Yuri, Wally took Skye's hand and drew her into the police station. Once they were inside, he continued walking with her until they were in his office.

"Looks as if you and I will have to postpone our fact-finding mission to Normalton." Wally perched on the edge of his desk facing Skye, who had taken a seat in one of the visitor's chairs.

"Most likely that's for the best." Skye crossed her legs. "You do realize today is Halloween. Probably not the best time to try talking to people."

"Adults working in an insurance company shouldn't be too influenced by the holiday." Wally took both of Skye's hands and leaned forward, smiling. "Businesses are not like the school system. No one wears costumes or takes their coworkers from office to office trick-or-treating."

Skye snickered at the image, and as she inhaled, she caught the faint sent of peanut butter. She and Wally had had oatmeal for breakfast. Were there treats in the break room? Had her mother made peanut blossom cookies?

Refocusing, she said, "Fine. Shall we plan to go on Monday?"

"Are you okay with being out of town the first time the nanny is with the babies?" Wally asked, running his thumb over her cheek.

"I'm sure my mother will be willing to stop by, and maybe your father can, too." Skye bit her lip. "It'll never be easy to leave them, so maybe it's best that I'll be miles away and can't pop in."

"Aw, sugar." Wally gave her a sweet kiss, then seemed to realize it was time to change the subject. "I spoke with Millicent Rose this morning and warned her not to approach you anymore."

"And?" Skye quirked a brow.

"She agreed." Wally refused to meet Skye's gaze and quickly continued, "She wasn't able to add much to what she told you about the silver figure loitering near the bowling alley, but she did say that he was near a big, black SUV."

"Are you going to check to see if any of our suspects owns a vehicle like that?" Skye asked.

"I've already got Martinez on it." Wally shrugged. "Unfortunately, a lot of people drive black SUVs."

"True." Skye pursed her lips. "Anything else going on with the case?"

"After I talked to Ms. Rose, I walked through Bunny Lanes. With the explosion, there wasn't much to see, but I wanted to get a picture in my mind of the layout."

"Did it help?"

"Not really." Wally made a face.

She could tell there was more, so she asked, "What else?"

"We've eliminated Zeus Hammersmith and Yuri Iverson as suspects."

"You told me about Zeus, but why Yuri?" Skye wouldn't mind seeing the obnoxious man in jail.

"Turns out that the city council is granting him a special permit, which he knew he was getting, and that means he had no need for Bunny's."

"If the bowling alley was the target, that leaves Udelle and Bunny's not-quite ex." Skye thoughtfully nibbled her thumbnail. "And nearly the whole town, if the perp was after Paige."

"It may come to that." Wally blew out a long breath. "The bomb squad tech emailed me his report and the device wasn't on a timer, so it had to be set off by someone nearby."

"Does that mean Millicent Rose might have really seen the person who detonated the explosive?" Skye asked, her heart racing.

"Probably." Wally sighed. "Now if she could just give us a better description than something resembling a central air-conditioning unit." Skye chuckled and Wally said, "Enough about the case. Are we ready for tomorrow?"

"I think so." Skye ticked items off her fingers. "The twins' christening outfits are ironed. My dress and your suit are hanging in the closet." She paused, then added, "And our shoes are on the shelf."

With almost all their belongings destroyed in the tornado, it was a constant struggle to remember what they'd need to buy for each new occasion. Skye had never realized all the items they both took for granted that had been stored in their closets and drawers.

"How about the party afterward?" Wally asked. "Any last-minute stuff?"

"Mom's got it under control." Skye snickered. "And I do mean *controlled*."

Wally was still chuckling when there was a knock on the door. He walked over and opened it, admitting

Udelle Calvert. The tall, thin woman's black hair was in a sleek french twist and she wore a gray-skirted suit. Spotting the bright-white athletic shoes on her feet, Skye smiled. Evidently Udelle had made a comfort-versus-style decision. Marching a protest line in heels would be painful.

Udelle's dark eyes lit with anticipation when she saw Skye, and she asked, "Are you here to sign up for SCALD? We have another march tomorrow."

"Sorry, no." Skye shook her head. "I'm the police psych consultant."

"Oh." Udelle's patrician nose twitched and her shoulders sagged.

Skye waved the woman to a chair and said, "I understand you've been harassing Bunny Reid about her video gaming machines."

"Not harassing." Udelle scooted her seat away from Skye as if she were contagious. "Attempting to enlighten her as to why children should never be exposed to gambling. It's just disgusting."

"So you'd be happy that her gaming lounge was destroyed." Wally sat behind his desk and stared at the woman. "Do you have any idea how that might have happened?"

"No." Holding up her palms, Udelle used her legs to edge her chair even farther away. "I'm completely nonviolent."

Wally leaned forward and said, "But it does work out well for you."

"Not really." Udelle crossed her arms. "It's not as if Ms. Reid won't just repair the damage and start up again."

"But there will be a delay." Wally quirked a brow. "Maybe enough for you to change Bunny's mind."

"If she had one," Udelle sniffed. "What evidence do you have to accuse me of the bombing?"

"We can clear this up with a simple question," Wally said smoothly. "Where were you Monday night between eight and ten o'clock?"

"I was in Laurel, shopping." Udelle dug through her purse and produced a four-by-six-inch plastic folder. After reaching inside the file, she handed Wally a bundle of receipts and smiled triumphantly. "When you started leaving me messages, I figured you'd want to see these. Look at the time and dates stamped here and see for yourself."

"If you had an alibi, why didn't you call me back?" Wally asked.

"It's not my job to make yours easier." Udelle shrugged. "Besides, I've been busy."

"I can also check the stores' security footage," Wally warned.

"Then you'll realize that I'm telling the truth." Udelle's smile was serene.

After flipping through the slips of paper, Wally stood and opened his office door. "Thank you for your time."

When Udelle had gone, Wally ran his hands

through his hair, looked at Skye, and said, "Well, that leaves O'Twomey, and of course all of Paige Myler's enemies."

"Look at it this way." Skye smiled sympathetically. "At least Bunny's almost-ex isn't a part of the Irish mob like I first thought."

"How comforting."

The sarcasm that dripped from Wally's words made Skye roll her eyes. Evidently, her husband wasn't in a glass half-full sort of mood.

CHAPTER 20

You Must Have Been a Beautiful Baby

So, Aiden is the last suspect we have with a motive for bombing the bowling alley." Skye had explained to Bunny how Udelle, Zeus, and Yuri had been eliminated and was now attempting to get her to take the threat from her almost-ex seriously. "Wally is still waiting to hear from the passport people as to when he returned to Illinois after his trip to Ireland, but you said he was due back the day—"

"Whoa," Bunny broke in, her tone conveying that she was unimpressed with the idea that her ex might be dangerous. "Aiden may have been a little miffed, but it wasn't as if I was his one true love and he was hearing wedding bells."

"Bunny, if you have any idea how the police can find this guy, you need to tell me right now." Skye barely held on to her temper. "For once, make the smart choice."

"Hey," Bunny said sharply. "You could learn a lot from me. My choices reflect my hopes, not my fears."

Skye shook her head. She'd never thought she'd hear Bunny Reid paraphrasing Nelson Mandela. Still, she had a gut feeling that the redhead knew something about O'Twomey that she wasn't telling, which is why she had taken time on the morning of her babies' baptism to phone Bunny and warn her.

Carson tapped Skye on the shoulder and said, "Let me talk to her."

He'd brought the security system technician over to the RV to install the nanny surveillance equipment and stayed to help Skye with anything she needed before going to the church. A comment he'd made about Bunny's recent secretive behavior had niggled Skye into making the call.

Skye handed her cell to Carson and swiped the speaker icon. There was no use pretending to give him any privacy when she fully intended to listen to every word.

"Sweetheart," Carson drawled. "All we want is for you to be safe."

"I've told you and told you that I'm fine." Bunny's voice howled like the wind sweeping down a chimney. "I'm sure that I wasn't the target."

With that, she abruptly disconnected and Carson returned the phone to Skye.

In the silence that followed, the only sound was the refrigerator motor humming.

Finally, Skye asked, "Do you think O'Twomey has been in touch with Bunny?"

"Who knows," Carson grunted. "She is one stubborn little filly. But she has been spending an inordinate amount of time in the bathroom. She says staying at the motor court is driving her nuts and she just needs some space, but Bunny's never been one to want that in the past."

Skye raised her brows and Carson shrugged, but before she could pursue the matter, the phone rang. She glanced at her cell and saw her husband's gorgeous face.

She swiped her thumb across his picture and answered, "Hello, sweetie."

"Just checking to see if you need me to pick up anything before I head home."

Skye glanced around but didn't notice anything they were missing. "I think we're good here. Anything new at the police station?"

"Nope." Wally chuckled. "My guess is that the whole town is home getting ready for the christening/baby shower at our place this afternoon."

"You think you're being funny." Skye shuddered. "But Mom never did let me see the final guest list and she was at over a hundred and fifty on Thursday. She had all of yesterday to invite more people."

"With everything that's happened around here, I've hired a couple of off-duty county deputies to provide security." Wally's voice was grim. "Are you still worried about that Rose woman crashing the party?"

"Not so much," Skye hedged, touching one of the curlers in her hair that was coming loose. Changing the subject, she asked, "We're paying the off-duty deputies, right? It shouldn't come out of the city's budget."

"Of course not," Wally assured her. "Their salaries are on our tab."

"Good." Skye glanced at Carson, who was giving her an odd look.

"What time did you say we needed to be at the church?" Wally asked.

"One thirty." Skye looked at the pile of stuff by the door. "But we should start getting everything into the Mercedes no later than one."

"Wait a second," Wally muttered, and Skye could hear an indistinct voice talking to him. Finally, he came back on the line and said, "I'll leave here as soon as Tolman gets back to the station."

"You need to be here early enough to shower and put on your suit," Skye reminded him. Her stomach tightened. Would he be late for their babies' baptism?

"Tolman is due any second." Wally's tone was reassuring. "I promise to get home in time. I'd never miss the twins' christening."

"I know." Skye forced a cheerful note into her voice. "Mom is coming here in about forty-five minutes to keep an eye on the babies while I get dressed."

"I'll probably beat her there. Love you," Wally said before disconnecting.

While Skye and Carson chatted, she fixed an early lunch. She put aside a plate for Wally, then sat across from her father-in-law and passed him the casserole dish containing the leftover Italian beef and a basket of Milano French Rolls.

While they both made their sandwiches, Skye said, "I just wanted to thank you again for having your security team keep an eye on the nanny."

Peering at Skye, Carson seemed to debate his response, but he finally said, "With the news about our family's wealth coming out, the babies may become targets for kidnappers." He cleared his throat, then said, "I think it's a good idea to keep some sort of security in place for the indefinite future."

"Oh my!" Skye gasped. "I supposed that I should have thought of that possibility, but it never crossed my mind."

"Which is fine." Carson smiled. "It's one of those things that probably will never happen, but we'd all kick ourselves if the kids were abducted and we hadn't taken precautions."

Skye took a bite of her sandwich, chewed, and swallowed as she considered Carson's words, then asked, "Have you discussed this with Wally?"

"Somewhat." Carson was silent as he ate. When his plate was empty, he said, "Wally agrees we need to take measures to keep the babies safe. He just doesn't agree on the method or who should foot the bill."

Before Skye could respond, Carson got up and

headed for the door. Pausing with his hand on the knob, he said, "I'll see you at the church."

"Two o'clock sharp. Don't let Bunny make you late," Skye admonished. "Father Burns waits for no man—or woman for that matter."

"I told her we had to be there at one." Carson chuckled. "Just to be safe."

A few minutes after Skye finished feeding the twins, May arrived, and Skye disappeared into the bathroom to get ready. Bingo was lying in the sink and Skye placed a stack of folded towels in the bathtub before relocating him to his new throne.

With her mother watching the babies, Skye took extra time with her appearance. She coaxed her natural curls into a cascade of ringlets down her back, leaving a few tendrils surrounding her face. Then after applying foundation, concealer, and bronzer, she emphasized her green eyes with a smoky plum shadow and black liner. There would be a million pictures taken of her with the babies, so she might as well look as good as she could.

It was nearly twelve forty-five by the time she was coiffed, made up, and had slipped on her dress. The bodice was black jersey knit and the skirt was a box-pleated, floral-printed jacquard. She wore it with metallic pumps and the necklace that Wally had given her for their wedding. The two swirling ribbons—one lined with shimmering, baguette-cut diamonds, the other with glittering, round diamonds—formed an X and were the perfect length for the dress's neckline.

When she emerged from the bathroom, Skye and her mom shared a teary embrace, and May sobbed, "I can't believe my baby has her own babies. I've dreamed of this forever."

"I know." A mixture of emotions slammed into her chest and Skye patted her mother's arm. Then she stepped back and said, "I see you decided on the navy-and-wine lace sheath. As always, you look fantastic."

Skye continued inspecting May's appearance and narrowed her eyes. Her mom's fingernails gleamed with perfectly applied pink polish. Had May gone for a manicure? She'd always told Skye she was silly to spend money on mani-pedis. Evidently, her mother had changed her mind.

"Thanks, honey." May blinked back tears. "You too." She sniffed, then said, "We'd better get the twins in their outfits."

"Give me one second."

There was still no sign of Wally, and Skye wondered what was keeping him. She stealthily grabbed her cell from the dresser and hid it in the folds of her skirt. Her mother would have a fit if she thought Wally might miss the baptism.

"For what?" May's head snapped up and swiveled in her daughter's direction.

"Uh…" Skye stalled, then fibbed, "I think my bra strap just broke."

May narrowed her eyes, clearly suspicious, but she waved Skye into the bathroom.

Once she was behind closed doors, Skye saw that she had a message and played it.

Wally's voice sounded stressed. "Martinez found Tolman in his squad car near the highway entrance ramp. It looks as if someone hit him over the head with a blunt object and he was out of it for a while. He seems better now, but he's being transported to the hospital. I'm sending Quirk with Tolman. I'll be on my way home to change in a few minutes. See you soon."

Skye debated keeping Wally's message from her mother but decided against it. If even a part of what happened had gone out over the police radio, everyone with a scanner would be talking about it.

Reentering the bedroom, Skye quickly summarized the information about Officer Tolman for May, who clutched her chest and said, "Poor Paul. I hope he's okay."

"Confusion after a head injury is never a good sign." Skye wrung her hands. "What I can't understand is how someone got close enough to attack him."

"Not to speak ill of the wounded, but he was probably napping," May tsked.

"Seriously?" Skye tried to imagine Wally or Roy or Zelda or Anthony sleeping on duty.

"He's not a bad cop," May said quickly. "But he also doesn't have a lot of ambition. For a long time now, I've suspected that Paul goes on patrol, finds an out-of-the-way spot, and parks there for much of his shift."

"I'm guessing that Wally has no idea about Paul's

siestas." Skye frowned. "But wouldn't someone notice that he wasn't putting on the amount of mileage you would expect on the squad car?"

"There's a gadget you can use to adjust the odometer. Paul likes to tinker with cars in his spare time, so he probably has one of those," May answered.

"Okay, then." Skye blinked. Having worked with teens for so many years, she should have known that someone determined to beat the system would manage to do it.

May grimaced. "Maybe I should have mentioned my suspicions to Wally. This might never have happened if Paul had stopped taking his little naps."

"Paul is responsible for leaving himself exposed to attack. And whoever hit him is to blame for him being hurt, not you." Skye hugged her mom, then said, "I know Wally would want to be with his injured officer. Do you think that I should encourage him to go to the hospital and postpone the baptism?"

"It sounds as if Paul will be fine." May took Skye by the shoulders. "And to quote my wise daughter, Wally is responsible for his own actions." She raised her brows. "Not to mention, how in the heck would we be able to contact everyone and call this all off?"

"You're right." Skye glanced at her babies, who were quietly batting at the mobiles over their bassinets. "Let's get the twins ready."

Wally arrived home while Skye was still carefully draping the christening outfits on the bed. He kissed her cheek, assured her and May that he had no further information about Paul, and headed into the bathroom to shower.

By one thirty, Skye, Wally, and the babies were settled in the Mercedes and on their way. May had left in her own car a few seconds earlier.

The church parking lot was already packed when they arrived, and Skye smiled in relief when she saw Vince's Jeep. He tended to have a laissez-faire attitude about time and it wouldn't do to have the godmother and godfather walk in late. She and Wally, each carrying a baby in their car seat, slipped in through the side entrance.

When the door thudded shut behind them, Skye's breath whooshed out of her. This was it. She inhaled and nearly choked at the smell of incense hovering thickly in the air.

Vince and Loretta were waiting and escorted them up to the baptismal font. Skye noticed the beautiful basket of flowers decorating the altar. One of the reasons that she loved St. Francis was its simple interior, with plain wooden pews. To her, it was the ideal place to worship.

Once they were in place, Father Burns turned to the congregation and said, "We are here today to welcome two new members to our church family. In the same way that Skye and Walter joyfully welcomed these beautiful children as a gift from God, so do we."

Skye's heart expanded until her chest felt tight. How had her very ordinary life turned into such a fairy-tale-like story full of love?

Wally's expression matched hers and he squeezed Skye's hand. She knew he would give his life to protect her and their children.

Father Burns turned to them and asked, "What names do you give your children?"

Together, Skye and Wally said, "Carson Jedidiah and Evangeline May."

They had finally decided to name the babies after their parents—Carson and Evangeline for Wally's, Jedidiah and May for Skye's. At first, Skye had been worried that the names wouldn't be acceptable to the church, but Father Burns had cleared up the matter when he'd told her that, since 1983, it was no longer necessary to choose a saint's name.

"What do you ask of God's church for Carson Jedidiah and Evangeline May?"

"Baptism."

Father Burns nodded, then intoned, "You have asked to have your children baptized. In doing so, you are accepting the responsibility of training them in the practice of the faith. It will be your duty to bring them up to keep God's commandments as Christ taught us, by loving God and our neighbor. Do you clearly understand what you are undertaking?"

Skye and Wally answered, "We do."

Turning to Vince and Loretta, Father Burns

asked, "Are you ready to help the parents of this child in their duty as Christian parents?"

They answered, "We are."

"Carson Jedidiah and Evangeline May, the Christian community welcomes you with great joy. In his name, I claim you for Christ our Savior. I now trace his cross on your forehead and invite your parents and godparents to do the same."

After the four of them complied with Father Burns's instructions, he indicated that they all could sit and the rest was a blur until the priest invited them to the font and began his questions.

"Is it your will that Carson Jedidiah and Evangeline May be baptized in the faith of the Church, which we have all professed with you?"

Wally and Skye answered, "It is."

Father Burns turned to the babies and said, "Carson Jedidiah and Evangeline May, I baptize you in the name of the Father." He poured water on both babies' foreheads. "And of the Son." He poured water on them again. "And of the Holy Spirit." He poured a third stream of water on them.

Then the babies were anointed with oil, candles were lit, and Father Burns touched the ears and mouth of the babies with his thumb and said, "The Lord Jesus made the deaf hear and the dumb speak. May he soon touch your ears to receive his word, and your mouth to proclaim his faith. To the praise and glory of God the Father."

Next, Father Burns led them to the altar, where the ceremony was concluded with the Lord's Prayer and a blessing. Finally, the priest said, "Go in peace." Then, with a wink, he added, "And remember that a lot of kneeling keeps you in good standing."

The recessional music started to play and as they walked down the aisle, Skye's glance skimmed the pews. She smiled at all of her friends and relatives who had gathered to help them celebrate, but then, out of the corner of her eye, she caught a glimpse of the back of a woman wearing a bright-blue cape. Evidently, Millicent Rose had managed to slip into the church despite the off-duty deputies working security at the door.

Shrugging, Skye let it go. The woman was leaving and nothing had happened. All Skye's worry and aggravation had been for nothing.

Of course, there was still the party…

CHAPTER 21

I Found a Million-Dollar Baby

"YOU KNOW, THIS WILL ONLY BE MY SECOND BABY shower," Wally commented as he and Skye buckled the twins into the back of the Mercedes. Both babies had been amazingly well behaved during the baptism ceremony, barely whimpering when the priest sprinkled them with holy water, and now they were happily batting the mobiles that hung from their car seats. "What should I expect at this thing?"

"With my mother in charge?" Skye powered down the window. It had been stifling inside the church and she needed to cool down. "I can't even begin to guess. We'll be lucky if she didn't manage to arrange for a star of Bethlehem to appear over the party tent and three wise men to visit bearing gifts of gold, frankincense, and myrrh."

"Huh?" Wally gave her a startled look.

"You know," Skye teased. "Because the Magi are the most famous trio to ever attend a baby shower."

Wally barked out a laugh. "May's not that bad."

"If you say so," Skye murmured, unwilling to burst his optimistic bubble.

"Loretta and Vince's baby shower wasn't too over-the-top," Wally said. "Won't she do something similar for us?"

"In that we'll eat, play a couple of silly games, and then our guests will watch us open gift after gift," Skye said, "yes."

"That doesn't sound too bad," Wally said, turning onto their road.

"And it wouldn't be if my mother wasn't determined to outshine her sister and put on the most elaborate shower anyone around here has ever attended." Skye flipped down the visor and used the vanity mirror to repair her makeup and reapply her lipstick.

"What a surprise." Wally's lips quirked. "Imagine May trying to one-up her sister."

"Aunt Minnie is crying foul since Mom has access to your father's deep pockets." Skye turned to check on the twins, whose eyelids were drooping.

"It looks like a lot of people beat us here." Wally pulled into the already packed driveway. "Do you need to go into the RV before we head over to the tent?"

"I used the restroom, and we changed and fed the twins before we left the church, so all of us should be good to go for a while."

"Then let's get this rodeo started." Wally got out of the SUV, walked around to open Skye's door, and then they each picked up a baby.

As they navigated the faux wooden walkway, a slight breeze cooling her skin, Skye listened to the excited chatter and cheerful laughter coming from inside the tent. It was nice to hear everyone having a good time, and no matter how extravagant her mother had been, she was determined to enjoy the party.

An off-duty county deputy was stationed at the tent's entrance, as well as around the side, and Skye noticed a third man at the exit. The guy at the front had a list of invitees and checked them off as they arrived. Not airtight security, but more than most baby showers required.

When Skye and Wally stepped inside, the first thing she saw was a giant banner that read *Welcome to the Family, Baby CJ and Eva*. The names had been added at the last minute in Magic Marker.

Although unhappy that Skye had refused to tell her the babies' names earlier, after the ceremony, May had hugged Skye and Wally, thrilled at their choices. And Carson had been over the moon that his and his late wife's names had been chosen.

Bracing herself, Skye took her first look at the fully decorated interior of the tent. Had her mother gone with the cloyingly sweet Precious Moments theme? Or the overused Little Prince and Princess idea? At least she knew it wouldn't be the Baby Love concept because May had used that for April, her first granddaughter.

Since Skye's previous visit, the tent had been divided down the middle. Suspended from the ceiling on one side was a canopy of pale-pink tulle pompoms, while the other was hung equally thick with pale-blue ones.

Depending on which side they were on, each guest table was done entirely in blue or entirely in pink from the plates, napkins, cups, and silverware to the life-size cakes shaped as either a frilly dress or cowboy boots with a cowboy hat leaning against them. The latter had to have been Carson's influence.

Skye rose on her tiptoes and whispered in Wally's ear, "Mom's friend Maggie must have been working for weeks to produce all those cakes."

"Maybe your mother ordered them from a bakery," Wally murmured behind his hand. "You said that May broke down and had the food catered."

"No way." Skye shook her head. "Maggie would never speak to Mom again if she did that."

Up until now, no one had noticed their entrance, but suddenly, there was a stampede toward them. May and Carson beat the crowd and each claimed a baby.

Skye had the twins' christening outfits made from the train of her wedding dress, and as Carson cradled his granddaughter, Skye smoothed out the white satin gown and traced the yoke with her finger, finding the W and S she'd had embroidered there. Turning to her son, she brushed the wrinkles from his white satin suit and outlined the same initials stitched into the vest. Kissing each baby, she allowed their grandparents to take them to be shown off.

Wally thumbed away the happy tear that had escaped down Skye's cheek, then squeezed her shoulder and asked, "Do you see your father?"

"He's probably outside with my uncles." Skye giggled. "This whole coed-shower business is way too metrosexual for my older male relatives."

"Their loss." Wally kissed her. "They miss admiring their beautiful wives."

Skye beamed at her sweet husband and tugged his hand. "I want to put the diaper bags and my purse by our chairs, then let's look around."

They made their way to the head table, unloaded, and paused to admire the centerpiece. Several low vases held enough flowers to be an entry in the Rose Bowl parade. Alternating in pink and blue, the containers marched down the center of the table in an unending floral display.

There was a bemused expression on Wally's face when he chuckled and said, "Your mother really goes all out, doesn't she?"

"And then some." Skye adjusted a napkin that she'd knocked askew. "On the other hand, we could have gigantic golden chairs and life-size angels hanging from the ceiling, so this isn't too bad."

"I can think of some fun to have with a throne."

Wally waggled his eyebrows. "I bet you'd enjoy a little ride on your Prince Charming's lap."

"Actually"—Skye tilted her head—"I think I prefer a king. Maturity is so much sexier than youth, and a king isn't still trying to prove himself like a prince."

"Considering our age difference, I'm sure as shootin' glad you feel that way."

"Your gray hairs are just wisdom highlights." Skye brushed the silver strands at his temples. "And the more you get, the wiser you'll become."

"So you don't plan on dyeing your hair when you start to go gray?" Wally drawled, then as Skye smacked his bicep, he glanced toward a commotion at the entrance and begged, "Tell me you didn't invite the Dooziers."

Before Skye could respond, Earl spotted her and yelled, "Miz Skye! Miz Skye!"

Skye smiled and headed toward Earl. Few people were ever as happy to see her as the strange, little man wearing bib overalls, a used-to-be-white T-shirt, and a camo bow tie. At least for once, his wife, Glenda, didn't have her boobs hanging out. Instead, she wore a fake-fur one-shouldered dress that Skye could have sworn she'd stolen from Wilma Flintstone if the cartoon character had been real. The hunter-orange fishnet stockings and tiger-striped high heels were a bit much, but the beehive black wig with the big leopard-pattern velvet bow was the pièce de résistance.

When Skye and Wally reached the Doozier

family, she thought they looked as if they were ready to dance the minuet. Glenda, MeMa, and Bambi were lined up with Earl, Junior, and Cletus facing them.

MeMa, the family's octogenarian—or maybe nonagenarian—matriarch was wearing a black velvet muumuu with Elvis Presley's face painted across her sagging chest and what looked like house slippers made out of beer cartons. Bambi, Earl's fourteen-year-old daughter, had on what Skye thought might be her gym suit and a tutu. The royal-blue bloomers snapped up the front and fit her like a flour sack, but the multicolor tulle skirt was what really made the ensemble.

It seemed as if the Dooziers had tried to put on the dog but ended up looking like something the cat dragged in. That is, except for Junior and Cletus, who wore their normal jeans and heavy metal T-shirts. Not exactly formal attire, but also not as bizarre as the others.

After greeting the family, Skye pointed them toward their table. She wasn't sure who May had put them with, but she hoped that whomever was assigned to the two empty seats at the eight-top had a sense of humor.

As Skye glanced around, trying to locate her children, she saw that the guests had gathered into various clusters. Over in the section of her work friends were several teachers, the secretaries from all three Scumble River schools, and the speech therapist. Skye noted that while the principals of the elementary and junior high were present, there was no sign of Homer, for which she was profoundly grateful.

Still on the lookout for her babies, Skye perused the police department consortium. Zelda Martinez was standing with several of the dispatchers and had somehow nabbed CJ from May. The women were cooing over the infant, who appeared to be enjoying the attention.

Having yet to spot Eva, Skye continued her scan and came to the couples group, where her brother, Vince, and his wife, Loretta, held court with their daughter, April. The three of them made a striking family portrait. Loretta looked like royalty from some exotic African country, a queen wearing a coral silk maternity dress and Louboutin ecru lace peep-toe pumps.

Vince was few inches taller than his wife's six-foot height, and stunning enough to be featured on the cover of a romance novel. His chiseled features, along with the green Leofanti eyes, made most women melt.

Not surprisingly, the couple had produced a beautiful baby. April had a flawless golden complexion, her mother's dark ringlets, and her father's emerald eyes surrounded by lush, black lashes.

Before giving birth to the twins, Skye had been worried that her child would have a difficult time competing with his or her dazzling cousin. But her own babies were nothing less than gorgeous, and anyone who said otherwise could discuss the matter with Skye's fist.

Vince, Loretta, and April were surrounded by Linc Quillen, the local veterinarian, and his date,

Abby Fleming, the school nurse, as well as Trixie and her husband, Owen. Also in that group were Simon and Emmy.

Skye was just close enough to hear Simon discussing his dog, Toby, with Linc. It appeared the Westie had been scratching incessantly and Simon feared it might be something serious, but the vet assured him that it was probably canine seborrhea, suggesting a special shampoo to cleanse and soothe the pooch's skin.

Turning away from the couples' group, Skye finally saw her daughter. Charlie had nabbed the baby from Carson and was showing her off to the guys from his social club, the Grand Union of the Mighty Bulls, a.k.a. the GUMBs. Skye briefly wondered if Simon still belonged, and if so, had he convinced Emmy to join the women's auxiliary as he had Skye?

"You're frowning." Wally nuzzled Skye's neck and asked, "What's up?"

"Just checking on the twins." Skye entwined her fingers with Wally's. "Let's go mingle before Mom starts the games."

"We don't have to play, right?" Wally paled, apparently recalling the Doodie or Die competition from Loretta and Vince's shower.

Each guest had received a tiny diaper made out of a triangular piece of white felt with a miniature gold safety pin closing it up. The guests whose diapers contained a "bonus" inside won. Skye had barely contained her laughter when Wally had nearly vomited after one of the winners ate the candy before Wally figured out the tiny poop was actually an unwrapped Tootsie Roll.

After assuring her big, strong husband that they indeed were exempt from participating in the games, Skye and Wally headed over to where most of the Leofantis were assembled. They chatted with her cousins and her aunts, and Wally asked where the men were. Minnie informed him that her husband, Emmett; her brother, Dante; and his son, Hugo were outside with Jed.

As they moved on to the Denisons, Wally whispered, "Is your dad going to be in trouble with May for having his own party?"

"Nah." Skye hugged Wally's arm to her chest, loving that he was concerned for her father. "Dad has nearly forty years of good saved up his sleeve and will have thought of the perfect excuse by the time Mom gets to him."

They were still a few steps away when Cora Denison spotted them and called out, "Come give Grandma a hug." Skye's grandmother was seated at a table with her daughter-in-law, Kitty, and granddaughter-in-law, Ilene Denison. When she had Skye enfolded in her arms, Cora said, "As usual, you look pretty as a picture and the ceremony was lovely."

"Thank you." Skye kissed her grandmother's cheek. "I was a little nervous, but the twins were amazing. I can't believe they hardly cried."

Wally hugged Cora too and then said, "I wasn't surprised. Our babies are perfect."

"Wally, dear, while I don't disagree, you might live to regret those words," Cora teased with a wicked chuckle. "Wait until they start teething."

Skye and Wally were chatting with Cora, Kitty, and Ilene when Skye heard Cletus Doozier's voice behind her. She turned slightly and saw that the teenager was talking to Iris, her cousin Ginger's daughter.

Cletus, his voice dipping to what Skye was sure he thought was as sexy level, said, "Did you just fart? 'Cause you blow me away."

Stifling a giggle, Skye did a quick round of mental math and realized that both kids were either freshmen or sophomores in high school. She thought Cletus's attempt at flirtation was cute but had a bad feeling that Ginger would be less inclined to see it that way. And although Skye would love to see her cousin's face, she hoped Ginger wouldn't notice and cause a scene that would embarrass Cletus.

Skye was wondering whether she should try to divert her cousin's attention when she heard a ruckus. Not unexpectedly, the Dooziers were in the middle of the hubbub. It appeared Carson and Bunny had drawn the unlucky cards and were the two guests assigned to fill the seventh and eighth chairs. Either that, or Carson being the wonderful man that he was, had volunteered to sit there in order to stop May from whining about the redneck family's presence.

Wally and Skye quickly headed in the Dooziers' direction and as they neared the group, she saw Bunny and Glenda had knocked over their chairs and were standing nose to nose.

Bunny jabbed Glenda in the shoulder and shouted, "Take off my dress!"

Skye blinked. How in the world had Bunny ended up in the same dress as Glenda Doozier? While they both had atrociously bad taste, Bunny's was generally a smidgeon better than Glenda's.

But evidently not in this instance. Bunny had adorned her faux fur Wilma Flintstone-inspired one-shouldered sheath with a fluffy white shrug, black elbow-length gloves, and, of all things, she had an empty cigarette holder between her fingers.

Overcoming her shock, Skye raised her voice above the shouting and said, "Bunny, Glenda has just as much a right to wear that dress as you do."

Skye wasn't sure if Bunny finally noticed that Glenda's relatives could have passed for the cast of *Deliverance* or if she was impressed by Skye's reasoning, but the redhead stopped poking Glenda and turned on Skye. "I ordered this dress special for today so I would look good for Car's family and she's ruining it." Bunny extended a finger and wailed, "She makes the dress look cheap."

While Skye pondered that statement, Glenda's face turned scarlet, but before she could explode, her husband, Earl, bleated, "Make her stop sayin' that,

Miz Skye. It ain't nice to carp at folks. You should tell 'em what is good about theyselfs, not what is bad."

Skye paused. Why did that sound so familiar?

Earl answered her unspoken question. "After all, ain't you been tellin' me and tellin' me that's what I needs to do with the kids?"

Bunny glared at Skye. "Are you taking their side over mine?"

All Doozier eyes swung toward her.

Glenda pointed her orange acrylic fingernail at Skye. "Well, is you or ain't you?"

Skye gulped, "No." When the Doozier family growled, she added quickly, "I mean that I'm not taking anyone's side." She needed to say something quickly to defuse the situation. "You both look lovely in a completely diverse way." She muttered a swift prayer asking forgiveness for her lie.

Both women preened at Skye's compliment and Bunny grudgingly said, "Well, I guess we did accessorize it differently."

Glenda narrowed her rabbit-like brown eyes. "Make her say sorry for callin' my outfit cheap. It cost me thirty-four dollars and forty-eight cents."

"I didn't mean inexpensive." Bunny raised her chin. "I meant tawdry."

Apparently, Skye's mother had snuck up during the discussion, and now with a take-no-prisoners smile, she said with a snicker, "That's like the tramp calling the trollop vulgar."

"Who you callin' a tramp, you old cow?" Glenda's head swiveled until she was staring at May.

Bunny moved until she stood shoulder to shoulder with Glenda and said, "Yeah. Who are you calling a trollop?"

Before Skye could intervene, Wally put an arm around her waist and said, "Your mom got herself into this mess. Let her get herself out. Watch." Wally turned Skye in the direction of the fracas and whispered in her ear, "Remember, the enemy of my enemy is my friend."

"Both of you," May snarled. "If my daughter wasn't so softhearted, neither of you would have ever been invited."

"Say that again." Glenda crowded May on one side.

"Yeah." Bunny joined her new friend. "Say it again."

"I—" May's eyes flicked from Glenda to Bunny and back again.

Evidently, faced with the joined forces of Bunny and Glenda, May realized that she was no longer in a position of strength and mumbled something as she beat a hasty retreat.

Skye opened her mouth to apologize to Glenda and Bunny for her mother's behavior, but Wally put a finger on her lips. "Listen."

"I like your fishnets," Bunny said to Glenda. "Where'd you get them?"

"Walmart." Glenda linked her elbow with Bunny's arm. "That little jacket of yours is real cute. Did you find it around here?"

The two women righted their chairs and sat down while continuing to exchange fashion tips.

Phew! Skye was relieved. Putting her mother and the Dooziers together was like sticking a fork in a microwave. Sparks were going to fly. The only question was whether they'd burn down the whole place or not.

Earl sidled up to Skye and Wally and said, "Fer a minute there, I thought we was fixin' to need to take shelter in one of my new tornado-proof outhouses. They is six by six by seven and made out of rebar and concrete blocks with a steel-reinforced door." He grinned, exhibiting his lone front tooth. "Youse knows that I'm selling them now, right?"

"I had no idea," Skye answered.

Wally put his lips close to Skye's ear and said softly, "The world is Earl's oyster."

"Yeah," Skye whispered back. "Too bad he's allergic to shellfish."

Wally chuckled.

Earl scratched his head and asked, "Why ya laughing?"

Skye, feeling guilty for her mean humor, hastily said, "You know what they say, Earl. Laugh and people laugh with you, but cry and—"

"You have to blow yer nose," Earl finished.

When was she going to learn not to use platitudes in front of Earl?

Clearing her throat, Skye tried to get back to where they were before the conversation had been sidetracked and asked, "When did you start building and selling tornado-proof outhouses?"

"When that insurance lady came to talk about our claim, she suggested it." Earl puffed out his chest. "She said it was innervatif."

Ignoring the last part of his statement, Skye blurted out, "You had insurance?"

"Ah course. On the dog pen." Earl frowned. "But the lady turned us down." His smile returned. "But I'm goin' try again though 'cause I think she was just in a bad mood."

"Oh?" Wally said, his voice mild, but his gaze sharp. "Why is that?"

"She was arguin' something fierce with someone on her cell phone. Yellin' that he had gotten exactly what he deserved and that he better not show up in Scumble River again or she was gettin' a restrain' order."

Skye turned to Wally to ask if Paige's cell had been found among her belongings or if it had been a casualty of the explosion when she heard a scream. Whirling toward the sound, she saw a short, pudgy man with a thatch of fading red hair standing at the tent's entrance.

The guy turned slowly, scanning the tent until he faced the Doozier table, then he shouted, "Bunny Reid, get your arse over here immediately. I have a score to settle with you."

It took Skye less than a nanosecond to figure out this man was the infamous Aiden O'Twomey and even less time to realize that all of Wally's security measures had failed. Fear slammed into her chest. Her babies and everyone else were at the mercy of an enraged criminal.

As she stared in horror, O'Twomey pulled a pistol from his pocket and pointed it at Bunny. The redhead leaped to her feet and backed away from the table, shoving at the people standing between her and the exit.

Suddenly, there was the sound of a gunshot and Wally pushed Skye to the floor.

CHAPTER 22

Baby, Have You Got a Little Love to Spare

WALLY EMBRACED SKYE, COVERING HER BODY with his own as she sobbed, "My babies. My babies."

His wife's eyes were glossy with unspeakable terror and Wally felt a sharp knife of guilt slam into his ribs. He had selected and hired the security team. The men's failures were his own.

He put his lips next to Skye's ear and said softly, "Keep still. The guy shot his gun at the ceiling. No one was hit and the twins are fine. Millicent Rose somehow slipped in behind O'Twomey. As soon as he started yelling, I saw her round up Martinez and Charlie and hustle them and the babies outside."

While Wally had been soothing Skye, O'Twomey had started marching toward them. Bunny immediately kicked off her stilettos and took off running with the infuriated criminal hot on her trail.

Leaping up, Wally looked at Skye and ordered, "Stay here."

Grabbing the gun from his ankle holster, he sprinted after O'Twomey and the fleeing redhead. As he ran, he took a quick look over his shoulder and groaned.

Skye was on her feet and following him, and Carson and Simon were a few steps behind her. Wally swore. Just what he needed. More civilians in the line of fire.

As Wally chased the odd couple, he kept glancing back. Skye's high heels had been slowing her down, but she'd taken Bunny's example and kicked off her shoes. Now she was only a few steps from catching up to him.

Returning his attention to his quarry, Wally saw that the redhead was trying to rip through one of the plastic windows, but her fingernails were no match for the heavy-duty vinyl. After a few futile seconds, Bunny gave up and darted among the few guests who had remained.

The people who had stayed had apparently thought O'Twomey was a part of the entertainment. However, as Bunny careened off a table, and a cowboy boot cake smashed to the floor, they seemed finally to figure out that this was no performance and their panicked screams ripped through the air.

Suddenly, people were running, tipping over tables as they scrambled to get away from the demented woman and the man chasing her. May's elaborate shower was turning into a scene from a disaster movie.

O'Twomey zipped around an elderly couple who clung to each other, frozen in fear. Then as Bunny neared the head table, he closed in on the runaway red-head. At the same time, Carson and Simon, who had taken a different path, came at her from one side while Wally, followed by Skye, approached from the other.

The off-duty deputies that Wally had hired to work security were ushering the remaining guests out of the back exit. And with Martinez busy with Eva, and Quirk at the hospital with Tolman, Wally scanned the area looking for Anthony. His newest officer was his only possible backup, but Anserello was currently AWOL.

A cold sweat glued Wally's shirt to his back and he prayed he could find a way to stop O'Twomey before he killed someone. There had been too many fatal shootings in the news for Wally to ignore the possibility that this could end badly.

With his gun drawn, O'Twomey shouted to Bunny, "Woman, what did you do with me bag?"

Bunny skidded to a stop inches from the head table. Her gaze jerked from O'Twomey to Simon to Carson, and then to Wally and Skye. Clearly realizing she was trapped, she raised her hands.

"It got burned up." Tears streaked mascara down the older woman's cheeks. "I knew you'd be mad and I didn't know how to tell you."

For a long second, the scene seemed frozen, but an instant later, Carson sprang into action. Tackling the much smaller O'Twomey, he knocked the gun from the bad guy's hand. Both teetered for a moment, then, almost in slow motion, toppled backward.

With a giant smack, O'Twomey landed dead center in the line of rose centerpieces. An instant later, Carson followed, taking out the remaining flower arrangements.

Wally cringed as he simultaneously heard the table creak and saw the crystals vases fly into the air like popcorn from a hot skillet. They shattered on the faux wooden floor and glass fragments erupted upward like lava from Mount Vesuvius.

A split second later, Wally grabbed O'Twomey, hauled him to his feet, and recited, "You have the right to remain silent." As Wally finished telling O'Twomey his rights, he handcuffed the man, turned to his father, and said, "Dad, please escort your girl-friend to the station."

Before marching O'Twomey out of the tent, Wally met Skye's gaze. "I'm sorry. I have to take him in."

"Don't worry. You go ahead." She closed her eyes, doubtlessly picturing the messy situation she was being left to deal with alone, then smiled crookedly at him and said, "I'll take care of all this."

Wally's heart filled with admiration for his wife and he mouthed silently to Skye, "Love you."

People were already drifting back inside by the time Wally got O'Twomey out the door. He walked the sub-dued man from the tent to the driveway before realizing that he didn't have a squad car to transport him.

Unwilling to put a dangerous felon in his own vehicle, due to the lack of safety features that a police cruiser possessed, Wally dug out his cell phone to ask for backup. But before he could make the call, Anthony came running over from behind the tent.

Breathlessly, he explained, "I was helping the off-duty deputies with crowd control. Need me to drive you, Chief? I'm on call so I have one of the squads."

"Perfect."

Wally and his officer put O'Twomey in the cruiser's secure rear seat, and as they drove, Wally considered the whole state of affairs. Bunny had arrived in Scumble River a few years ago after a twenty-year absence from her son's life. At the time, she'd been addicted to the painkillers she'd been given when she hurt her back and on probation for trying to forge prescriptions to obtain more of them. To stay out of jail, she'd had to attend Narcotics Anonymous meetings, find work, and establish a permanent address.

Wally thought that she'd been successful at fighting her addiction, but had Bunny fallen off the wagon? Had O'Twomey left her with drugs and she'd taken them rather than just hold on to them for him?

When they arrived at the police station, Anthony escorted O'Twomey through the front entrance with Wally following close behind the handcuffed prisoner.

Lonny, a part-time dispatcher, stood behind the counter and spoke through the intercom. "Chief, I wasn't expecting to see you here today."

His high-pitched voice scraped Wally's nerves like fingernails on a blackboard. Which was doubtlessly why Lonny was called in to work so infrequently.

"Me either." Wally jerked his chin toward the interior door. "Buzz us in."

"Sure." Lonny started to salute, then stared at O'Twomey and asked, "Problem?"

"Not anymore." Wally started to walk toward the doorway where Anthony stood with O'Twomey, but stopped and said, "My father should be here any second with Bunny Reid. Escort them to the interrogation room."

"Uh…" Lonny fingered his mostly nonexistent mustache. "Where is that?"

"It's the break room," Wally explained. The dispatcher worked so rarely that he'd probably never been around when they'd had an active case. "We use it for interrogation when we have a prisoner to interview."

"Got it. I'll keep an eye out for your father." Lonny hit the lock release.

Once the three men were over the threshold, Wally grabbed O'Twomey's elbow and said, "I've got this, Anthony. Call Quirk and get an update on Tolman's condition, then report back to me."

"Yes, sir." The young officer headed for one of the cubicles along the back wall.

Wally walked his prisoner a few more steps, stopped in front of the break/interrogation room at the end, and opened the door. It was a utilitarian space with a counter that ran the length of the sidewall and a long table took up most of the center area. A couple of vending machines occupied the rear.

O'Twomey had been silent up until now, but as Wally pushed him down on a chair and handcuffed him to the table leg, he said, "I want me lawyer."

"Here." Wally gave him the receiver from the wall-mounted telephone. "Go ahead and call him. Tell him we'll be booking you for murder."

"Murder!" O'Twomey screeched. "I shot the ceiling, not the bi—"

"Right. That will be a count of unlawful discharge of a weapon." Wally grabbed the tape recorder from the cabinet and set it up. "But a woman was killed when you detonated the bomb at the bowling alley."

"I had nothing to do with that!" O'Twomey shouted, his face as red as his hair. "Why would I? Me own property might be destroyed!"

Wally was pondering that question when the interrogation room door opened.

Anthony poked his head inside and said, "Paul's doing much better. They're keeping him overnight for observation, but if there are no surprises, they'll release him in the morning. His wife is with him and Quirk is heading back."

"That's terrific news." Wally took a relieved breath. The idea of someone under his command being seriously injured had been sitting heavily on his chest.

Anthony nodded and said, "Oh, and your father and Ms. Reid are here."

"Show them in." Wally waited silently as his dad and Bunny entered the room, then said, "Thanks, Dad." Wally smiled gratefully at his father and asked, "Now can you return to the party and help Skye out with whatever guests stuck around?"

"Certainly." Carson glanced at Bunny. "I'll be back to bring you home."

"I'll take care of her." Wally wasn't entirely sure Bunny wouldn't be sleeping in jail that night rather than at the motor court. It all depended on what was in the bag she was holding for O'Twomey.

"Okay." Carson cleared his throat. "I'll see you later then."

Bunny was surprisingly quiet and obediently took the chair Wally indicated. Evidently, once she realized that this wasn't a situation that fluttering lashes and cute giggles would solve, she'd resorted to silence.

O'Twomey still held the telephone receiver in his nicotine-stained fingers, but he hadn't called his lawyer. Once Bunny and Wally were seated, he said, "If I can prove that I had nothing to do with the bombing, can you forget about the other charge?"

Before Wally answered O'Twomey's question, he went through the spiel needed for the tape recording, announcing the date and time. He had O'Twomey and Bunny state their names and addresses, read them their rights, and made them aware they were being recorded.

Having waded through the formalities, Wally said, "Do you still want your attorney, Mr. O'Twomey?"

"No."

"How about you, Ms. Reid?"

"No. Why would I need one?" Bunny's posture was stiff and her shoulders tense. "I'm the victim."

"Let's start with what was in the bag that Mr. O'Twomey is so anxious to recover from you." Wally looked between Bunny and her ex.

"I have no idea." Bunny refused to meet Wally's eyes, busying herself by dumping her purse on the table and searching the contents until she found a gold compact. She peered into the mirror and used a small brush to fluff her bright-red curls.

"Surely you know, Mr. O'Twomey." Wally lifted a brow at the man.

"Half a mil. Me life savings," O'Twomey said. "I'm between apartments and I didn't have anywhere else to leave it while I visited me sick old mother in Ireland."

"How about a bank?" Wally asked. "If you were worried about the ten-thousand-dollar cash deposit limit you could have used a safe deposit box."

In all probability, the money O'Twomey had stashed with Bunny was a result of some criminal enterprise, but Wally didn't fool himself into thinking he'd ever be able to prove that. Or arrest the man because of it.

"Nah." O'Twomey shook his head. "I don't need those maggots up in me business. And don't pretend you don't know that the feds have cameras watching all of those boxes."

"Okay." Wally refused to get sidetracked. "Was Ms. Reid aware of what was in the bag you left with her?"

He glanced at Bunny who was still fussing with her hair. She appeared to have no idea how much trouble she might be in or at least was pretending she didn't have a clue.

Wally tapped her arm and said, "So, were you aware there was money in the bag?"

"I promised not to look." Bunny waved her hand, still miraculously gripping the empty cigarette holder. She'd taken off the elbow-length gloves and her long, scarlet nails caught the fluorescent light, gleaming like tiny, bloodied daggers. "And I would never break a promise."

Wally stared hard at the redhead. "Cut the crap." Her expression was just too innocent to be real, and Wally was in no mood for Bunny's usual coy behavior.

"Fine." The older woman toyed with the rhinestone bangles on her wrist. "I took a peek right after Aiden left for Ireland."

"Is that when you decided to keep me money for yourself?" O'Twomey demanded.

"No!" Bunny said with a fake catch in her voice. "I'm not a thief." Then the explanation fell from her lips in a rush of words. "I planned to hand it over to you as soon as you got back to Illinois. It really did burn up in the explosion. I can't believe, after all we meant to each other, you'd think so poorly of me."

Wally wasn't buying the poor dumb Bunny routine, and from O'Twomey's expression, neither was her ex.

"The only area damaged was the video gaming lounge," Wally reminded her, watching her reaction carefully.

"That's where I hid the cash." Bunny gave Wally a calculating look. "I couldn't afford to have Car find it in my apartment, so I took it out of the bag, gutted the inside of a couple of the vintage slot machines that I'd bought to decorate the lounge, and hid the money inside them."

"I can't believe five hundred thousand would fit," Wally murmured.

"It was a tight squeeze, but I was motivated." Bunny grinned proudly, as if she'd won the Olympic medal for concealing ill-gotten gains.

"If me money was in a metal slot machine, how did it burn up?" O'Twomey's expression grew darker.

"The explosion knocked them over and the backs came off." Bunny tilted her head seductively. "You know I wouldn't steal from you, sweetheart."

"Then why wasn't there a single damaged bill found by the firefighters, the bomb expert, or the crime scene techs?" Wally asked.

His mouth tightened at the thought that someone might have stolen the cash. Or that Bunny had successfully bribed an official.

"Yeah. Why?" O'Twomey's voice was dangerously calm.

"Well…" Bunny hedged, glancing nervously at Wally.

"You're aware that with your prior record, a judge won't be lenient if I decide to charge you with something," Wally warned.

"You both are so mean." Bunny crossed her arms. "If you must know, that night, when the nice fireman let me go back into my apartment to get a few belongings, I sneaked down the inside staircase."

"I thought those steps had collapsed." Wally frowned. Was this another of the redhead's tall tales?

"Only partially." Bunny puffed out her chest. "Remember, I was a dancer so I can jump and land on my mark without a problem." She inhaled. "As I was saying before you so rudely interrupted me, I gathered up all the burnt hundred-dollar bills that I could find, returned to my apartment, and packed them in my luggage."

"And where is that suitcase now?" O'Twomey demanded.

"It's in the trunk of my car," Bunny answered. "If you weren't so paranoid, and would have just met me in Joliet like I suggested, I was going to hand it over to you." She chewed her lip, then warned, "But there's not much left of the bills."

"Satisfied?" Wally asked. "If Ms. Reid hands over whatever is left of your cash, are you willing to let the matter drop?" When O'Twomey didn't answer, he added, "You know you can turn in mutilated money to the Treasury with an explanation and they might reimburse you."

"Right. The government and I are on such friendly terms," O'Twomey sneered, then looked at Bunny and said, "You give me what you got, and we'll call it square. I can't blame you for a bomb going off."

"That is so sweet of you." Bunny sagged against the back of her seat. "No hard feelings about me dating someone else?"

"Nah." O'Twomey grinned. "It was fun while it lasted."

Wally examined the man's expression and tone of his voice, not entirely convinced of the sincerity of his forgiveness. He'd have to describe the interchange to Skye and get her opinion.

Having committed O'Twomey's demeanor to memory, Wally waited a heartbeat, then asked, "So what about this proof that you couldn't have detonated the explosive?"

CHAPTER 23

Wonder Where My Baby Is Tonight

SKYE GLANCED ACROSS THE HUMMER'S CONSOLE AT Wally's handsome profile as he exited onto I-55 heading south to Normalton. Sighing, she wiggled in her seat until she found a comfortable spot and then turned her thoughts to the last thirty-six hours.

Late Saturday afternoon, once O'Twomey had produced his passport—proof that he'd been out of the country at the time of the bowling alley explosion—Wally had turned him over to the Stanley County State's Attorney, who had charged O'Twomey with reckless discharge of a firearm.

A second, more serious charge of aggravated battery on a police officer would be added, if, after a lineup, Paul Tolman could identify O'Twomey as the man who hit him over the head.

Thankfully, Bunny hadn't been charged with anything. However, she'd had to face Carson. Skye hadn't heard the results of that encounter, but she was pretty darn sure her father-in-law had no idea what he was getting into when he'd begun dating the wild redhead. Skye wouldn't be at all surprised if their relationship ended sooner rather than later.

After O'Twomey had been escorted to the county jail and Bunny had been dropped off at the motor court, Wally had finally been free to go home. But by the time he got there, it was already past 8:00 p.m. While the shower guests were long gone, their unopened gifts were piled in the RV, taking up every available surface.

Although Skye's parents and Carson had helped her get the presents from the tent to the motor home, there had been so many that there hadn't been enough room from them anywhere out of the way.

When Wally had walked into the RV, Skye was attempting to soothe the twins, who had had enough of parties and were sobbing their little hearts out. It had taken both of their parents to get them to sleep. And by then, Skye and Wally were too exhausted to talk about the case.

Sunday hadn't been much better. Luckily, the catering company that May hired included cleanup in their contract, and the rental company had taken down the tent while Skye and Wally were at Mass.

However, after they got home, there had been a continual flow of callers—ostensibly checking to see how Skye and Wally were doing but, in reality, wanting the dirt on the shooting. When their stream of visitors finally dried out, close to 10:00 p.m., she and Wally once again hadn't had a chance to discuss the case before falling asleep.

And this morning, Wally had headed into the police station early so he could put in a couple of hours before they left for Normalton. While Wally was gone, Skye had familiarized the nanny with the twin's routine, showed her where everything was kept, and concentrated on not having a meltdown at the thought of leaving her babies.

It had taken everything she had in her to get into the Hummer when Wally had come to pick her up at ten o'clock. Skye reassured herself that the nanny was under constant surveillance, May would be checking up on things at noon, and Carson was stopping by at two, which was only a couple of hours before Skye and Wally would be home themselves.

Now, Skye finally felt as if she could talk without bursting into tears, so she cleared her throat and asked, "How is Paul doing?"

"Good." Wally kept his eyes on the road. They were passing Dwight, and that could be a busy interchange. "Tolman's doc is satisfied that the mild concussion won't have any lasting effects and released him from the hospital around 8:00 a.m. They initially thought they'd discharge him on Sunday, but his blood pressure was still a little high so they kept him an extra day. He stopped by the county jail on his way home to view a lineup and identified Bunny's ex as the guy who hit him."

"What will that mean for O'Twomey?"

"Aggravated battery to a police officer where the physical contact doesn't result in great bodily harm is a class two felony." Wally's voice was businesslike. "A conviction can put him in state prison for up to seven years."

"So Bunny won't have to worry about him coming after her?" Skye twisted her fingers into a knot of concern.

"Ah." Wally chuckled, raising his brows. "You didn't believe his forgive-and-forget speech either."

Skye shook her head. "From what you describe of his demeanor and expression, not for a second." She relaxed against the back of the seat. "I'm relieved he'll be behind bars for a good long time."

They were both silent for the next few miles, but as they passed the exit for Odell, Wally said, "I've been thinking about the bombing."

"Me too." Skye half turned in her seat, ready to go to work as the PD's psych consultant. "First, are we both in agreement that it is now more likely that Paige Myler was the intended victim of the explosive device rather than Bunny or the bowling alley?"

"Yes." Wally frowned. "Having eliminated all the suspects connected to Bunny, and with the added information of the detonator being separate from the bomb, as well as Millicent Rose's claim that she saw someone hanging around the area, I agree." He paused. "Not that I was able to get a better description of the perp from her. She still insists that the person was about three feet tall, nearly as wide, and had silver skin."

"If we consider Zelda's idea that the fairy godmother was behind the destruction," Skye said slowly, "maybe Miss Rose's description is meant to throw us off her trail."

"Martinez's theory is on the absolute bottom of my list." Wally scowled. "I don't think that Rose woman could put together a jigsaw puzzle let alone a bomb."

Discussing the fairy godmother had reminded Skye of something and she tipped her head. "Speaking of Millicent—"

Wally interrupted, "Let's not get distracted from the murder. We can discuss Millicent's predictions and actions later."

"Okay." Skye nodded, understanding Wally's desire to keep on track. "Earl said something, just before O'Twomey burst into the tent, about overhearing Paige's phone call telling someone not to come back to Scumble River. Who do you think she was talking to?"

"Good question." Wally pursed his lips. "Her cell phone was destroyed in the explosion, but we can ask her carrier for her records." He scowled. "I probably should have done that right away, along with looking into her personal life."

"Quit it!" Skye lightly smacked Wally's thigh. "It will only be a week tonight since the explosion and you have limited resources. You needed to use the manpower you had to look at the most probable scenario first. Not to mention that you didn't know about the remote detonation until a couple of days ago." She whacked his leg again. "You were right to concentrate on Bunny and the bowling alley. They were much more likely targets of the explosion than Paige."

"I could have asked the country sheriff for help." Wally rubbed his eyes. "Or the state police."

"Yes, you could have." Skye watched them fly by the exit for Pontiac. "But do you really believe that either of those agencies would have been able to get the kind of information that you and I have from the people involved?"

"Maybe not." Wally rolled his neck, then nodded and said, "Okay. Pep talk over. Back to the case."

"We should consider the phone call Gillian overheard, too." Skye twisted a curl around her finger as she thought about it. "If Paige was willing to lie, cheat, or sleep her way to the top, there might be someone who she stepped on while she made her way up."

"We'll try to figure out both the identity of the person she threatened with the restraining order and if her unbridled ambition was a problem for anyone while we chat with the vic's coworkers today."

"That's a tall order with people we've never met." Skye raised her eyebrows. "We better hope her colleagues are all gossips."

"I've cleared it with her boss for you to wander around and chat with the employees in her group while I conduct the more formal interviews. And I especially want you to have a conversation with the guy she replaced in Scumble River. He ended up transferring to another department." Wally gripped the steering wheel as a semi darted into his lane, cutting him off, then shot her a grin. "I have every confidence in your suspect-whisperer ability."

"There was something else I wanted to ask you about, but I can't think of it right now." Skye gazed out the window at the meticulously kept houses and recently harvested fields as the question teased at the edge of her mind. Hoping to clear out the cobwebs inhabiting her brain, she rolled down the window a few inches and inhaled. Even with the highway smells, the air was fresh, with only an occasional trace of hog to remind her that around the next bend or just out of sight were working farms. "I know." She snapped her fingers. "You mentioned that Paige's divorce wasn't quite official yet. Do you know the settlement terms?"

"The terms were pretty straightforward." Wally shrugged. "When the divorce became final, everything they owned would be evenly divided."

"Are the couple's assets usually frozen during the procedure?" Skye asked.

"I think that's something that depends on the individual situation and what the couple's lawyers think is necessary."

As they neared the Normalton exit, the scenery changed from farmland to college town. Once Wally made the turn, Skye would never have guessed that crops would be growing less than a mile away.

Wally parked the Hummer in the insurance company lot, and after helping Skye out of the SUV, they hiked across the pristine asphalt toward the entrance. Either it had just been resurfaced or the company hired a really thorough cleaning crew to scrub the blacktop every weekend.

When they approached the row of cars nearest the building, Wally paused and said, "I wonder what business Yuri Iverson has with Homestead Insurance."

"What makes you think the gambling lounge guy is here?" Skye wrinkled her forehead in confusion.

Wally pointed to a black Range Rover with tiger stripes painted down the center of the hood and said, "That's his SUV. The custom paint job is too distinctive for there to be another vehicle around here with the same design."

"This isn't Yuri's car." Skye touched the fender. "He was driving a blue Audi when he stole my parking space at the grocery store."

"Last Monday, when I first met Iverson, he was at the florist. And this Range Rover was parked out front." Wally frowned. "I assumed it was his SUV."

"That's odd." Skye pursed her lips, then said, "You know, Stybr Florist is only a couple doors away from the bowling alley."

"Good point. Let me jot down the license plate number." Wally took the notepad from his shirt pocket and said, "I'll call Thea and have her run it while we're talking to the vic's colleagues."

As they strolled up the sidewalk, Skye examined Homestead's building. It clearly had been built during the 1980s and the repeated modular elements of the concrete design were a stark contrast to the newer structures in the adjacent business parks.

When they reached the entrance, she studied the elaborate double doors. Etched glass and fancy metal scrollwork screamed *Look at me. See how important I am.*

Walking inside, Skye said, "Isn't Normalton where Spencer Drake ended up working?"

"It is." Wally smiled. "Too bad he's head of one of the university's security rather than with the Normalton Police Department."

"Right. We could ask him to help us investigate. Not that the local officers won't cooperate."

"Actually, when I let the NPD chief know we were going to be in town, she offered any assistance we needed."

When Skye reached the elevator, a large woman dressed in a bright-green pantsuit was just getting out. She towered over Skye and had to have at least a hundred pounds on her.

The woman held out her hand to Wally and said, "You must be Chief Boyd. I'm Susie Oldwary, the executive VP's admin."

"Nice to meet you." Wally shook her hand and

said, "And this is my wife, Skye, who acts as the PD's psych consultant."

Susie nodded and led them into the elevator. "I've got you set up in a conference room on the third floor. The claims department occupies the entire level, and, of course, that's where Paige had her office."

When they reached their destination, Wally put his hand on Skye's waist and they exited. Susie ignored Skye but took every opportunity to touch Wally.

Finally, after providing Wally with a list of Paige's coworkers and employees, she gave him two visitor badges and leaned closer. "Why don't you give me your cell number in case I think of something you might find interesting?" She smoothed her hands down her abundant hips. "I understand that a picture is worth a thousand words…"

"No need." Wally took a step back. "I took your statement over the phone. If you have any more information, just call the police station."

"Your loss." With a sniff, the woman left them alone.

Giggling, Skye mimicked Susie's throaty voice and said, "Are you sure I can't help you with anything else, Chief?"

"Right," Wally snorted. "That was odd. I can't understand why she'd come on to me like that with my wife standing right here."

"You seem to attract those types of women." Skye shook her head, glad her recent bouts of paranoia and jealousy seemed to be gone. "Look at Emmy."

"She just likes yanking your chain."

"Uh-huh."

Wisely, Wally didn't pursue the topic and instead called Thea and asked her to run the Range Rover's plate number. And while he did that, Skye checked in with the new nanny. The woman assured her that everything was under control and the babies were sleeping, but glancing at Wally and seeing his face darken, Skye didn't think he'd had as good of news.

Finishing his call, Wally blew out a breath and said, "The system is down. Thea will run the plate as soon as it comes back online."

Skye patted his arm sympathetically. Slow computers and wonky internet service were all part of small-town life and neither of them would trade the benefits for something like a better satellite signal.

Wally kissed her cheek and said, "I've been thinking…" He handed the list to Skye. "If you escort the people we want to talk to here, maybe they'll chat with you while they wait to see me."

"How about we start with Mick Ackerman, the guy who had been in Scumble River before Paige replaced him." She glanced at the paper in her hand. "And once you get going with him, I'll go get Angela Sommer, Paige's administrative assistant. She should know all the dirt."

"Perfect."

Skye quickly located Mick and brought him to Wally. He rejected her attempt at casual conversation, and once he was with Wally, she set off to find Angela.

Angela was a sweet young woman with a ready smile, and once Skye introduced herself as the police psych consultant, she seemed happy to chat with her. Waiting for Wally to finish with Mick, the two women sat in a pair of comfy chairs in an alcove near the conference room and talked about the weather and a movie that Angela had recently seen.

In due course, Skye said, "We haven't been able to find out much about Paige's personal life. I know you'd never share that type of information when she was alive, but it would really help us in trying to find out who murdered her."

"Murdered?" Angela squeaked. "Mr. Myler said that she was just in the wrong place at the wrong time."

"We did think that at first." Skye leaned forward catching the scent of Angela's perfume. She smelled like freshly sliced peaches and vanilla cream. "But we've discovered new evidence that suggests Paige was the intended target."

"It was probably one of those people who were trying to scam us for more money." Angela crossed her arms. "They were so mean."

"I'm not following you." Skye forced herself not to frown. "Do you mean the victims of the tornado who were trying to get their claims settled?"

"Ms. Myler said that they were frauds." Angela shook her head. "She had to remove Mr. Ackerman because he was falling for their sob stories and go down there herself." The young woman scowled. "And it was awful timing for her. She and Mr. Glenn had just gotten engaged."

"Guy Glenn?" Skye asked. "The executive vice president and chief claims officer? No one mentioned that she was in a relationship with him."

"Shoot!" Angela put her hand over her mouth. "It was a secret." She made a face. "They even drove into work separately to keep it quiet."

"They lived together?" Skye asked.

"Since she filed for divorce from her husband." Angela's blue eyes were misty. "It was the most romantic thing. Just like a romance novel. Mr. Glenn had always loved her, but his best friend, Mr. Myler, asked her out first. But Ms. Myler and Mr. Glenn finally couldn't fight their attraction any longer, and she asked Mr. Myler for her freedom."

"Did Paige's ex know about her relationship with Mr. Glenn?"

Skye's mind was racing. Hadn't Wally said that Phillip Myler denied that the divorce was a result of another relationship?

"Yes." Angela twisted a strawberry-blond curl around her finger. "But he was a real sweetheart and never told anyone about Ms. Myler and Mr. Glenn."

Including the police. Skye barely kept the words from escaping her lips.

Keeping her expression sympathetic, she asked,

"Was Mr. Myler very upset about the breakup with his wife? Or was it a mutual kind of thing."

"Although he always kept a brave face, I could tell he was hurt." Angela put her hand over her heart. "But then a few weeks ago when he found out about the money…"

"The money," Skye encouraged.

"What Ms. Myler owed on their joint credit cards and home equity line." Angela paused. "I think that was the day he stopped loving her."

"Was she trying to hide assets because of the divorce settlement?"

"I don't know." Angela suddenly seemed to realize how much she'd revealed, and she toyed with the heart-shaped locket hanging around her neck. "You really should talk to Mr. Myler about all this."

"Oh, we will," Skye assured her. "But he hasn't been very forthcoming in the past."

Skye inspected the young woman's pink cheeks and thought about how her voice had softened when she spoke about Paige's ex. Skye would bet her new Coach purse that Angela had a crush on Phillip Myler and was already regretting everything she'd let slip.

Changing the subject to Paige's work relationships, Skye watched as Angela relaxed. Although, it appeared that while Paige would never be voted Miss Congeniality or Boss of the Year, no one really hated her. Those who couldn't stand her intense type of management transferred to other departments and those that could handle it enjoyed the bonuses and raises Paige's department routinely earned.

At the mention of advancements, Skye recalled the phone conversation Gillian had overheard and said, "I understand that Paige was extremely ambitious and wanted to be the youngest vice president in the company."

"Absolutely." Angela nodded vehemently. "In fact"—she leaned forward and lowered her voice— "Ms. Myler's promotion to second vice president of sales operations was scheduled to be announced as soon as she returned from straightening out the Scumble River mess."

"Was her promotion common knowledge?" Skye sucked in a breath.

"No." Angela's perpetual smile slipped. "But since Mr. Myler was up for the job, they did tell him. Ms. Myler didn't want him to be caught by surprise when they made the announcement and be embarrassed."

"How thoughtful of her." Skye hoped the sarcasm in her voice wasn't too evident.

CHAPTER 24

Baby, Please Don't Go

N OT ONLY DID PAIGE DUMP HER HUSBAND FOR another guy, but she also put him in debt, *and* she got his promotion." Skye walked beside Wally as they made their way to the elevator. "I'd bet the Denison farm that Phillip Myler is the guy who planted the explosives."

"He sure had three good motives." Wally squeezed Skye's hand. "From what everyone I talked to today had to say, Paige's administrative assistant wasn't the only one who didn't realize how bitter he was about the divorce. None of the others noticed Myler arguing with Paige. Even the office busybody said he'd never overheard Myler say anything against her."

"Wow!" Skye wasn't surprised that Angela had been taken in by Phillip since she was pretty sure the young admin was in love with him. But she was a little shocked that none of the others had a clue.

Once they were on the elevator, Wally blew out a disgusted breath, made a face, and said, "Everyone here has an excuse, but my cop instincts should have told me that Myler was playing me when he showed up at the police station and volunteered so much information about his wife."

"That's easy to see now." Skye put her palms on Wally's cheeks and waited until he met her eyes. "But you didn't have all the facts when you originally spoke with him. I hate to see you beating yourself up over this. Some people are talented liars, and it sounds as if Phillip is one of those folks."

Wally shrugged, plainly not convinced.

As they exited the elevator and started walking down the hall toward the executive suite, Skye shivered and rubbed her arms, trying to warm up. This floor was over air-conditioned and it had an eerily deserted feeling. She almost had to force her feet to move forward.

Suddenly, the ringing of Wally's cell phone broke the silence, and Wally grabbed the device from the case clipped to his belt. He glanced at the screen and said, "It's the state's attorney." He glanced around, then whispered, "I called him earlier about getting a warrant to search Paige Myler's residence and I need to bring him up-to-speed about her living in a house as a guest rather than a legal tenant to see if that changes things in any way. I don't see anyone that might be listening, but just in case I'll step into the men's room over there."

"Good idea," Skye said. "I'll meet you at the VP's suite."

Turning, she strolled a few more feet down the corridor and came to a set of double doors with *Guy Glenn Executive Vice President and Chief Claims Officer* painted in gold on the frosted glass. She reached for the wooden handles, then jerked her hand back. She could hear raised voices and an odd muffled sound that she couldn't identify.

Uneasiness prickled at the back of Skye's neck. Should she knock? Wait for Wally? Or…she noticed that the door was slightly ajar, better yet…snoop? She tiptoed, plastered herself against the wall, then leaned forward and peered into the slight gap.

Skye's gaze swept the well-appointed space. She was looking into the office suite's reception area. Susie, the overly amorous admin who had met them earlier, was seated in a chrome chair. Her ankles and wrists were bound to the chair's arms and legs and duct tape covered her mouth. The stifled sounds were her trying to scream around the gag.

Alarm coiled in Skye's stomach and the weight of her fear pressed on her chest until she could barely breathe.

There were two men in the middle of the room. Both were wearing dark suits and subdued ties, but one was standing and waving around a gun, and the other was cowering on his knees. The man on his knees had his hands clasped on top of his head and something that looked like an oversize handcuff around his neck.

Skye immediately fished her cell from her purse, swept her thumb across the video icon, and pressed the device to the small opening between the doors.

The kneeling man looked up and begged, "Phillip, buddy, you don't want to do this." He pleaded, "We've been friends since boot camp."

"Guess you should have gone into Explosive Ordnance Disposal with me instead of the Quartermaster Corps," Phillip taunted.

"But we're still friends."

"Guy. Guy. Guy." Phillip ran the barrel of his gun along the other man's jaw. "You should have thought of that before you started banging my wife."

"I never touched her until she filed for divorce." Guy's face was covered with a thin coat of perspiration and he wiped his forehead with his upraised arm. "Paige said you were okay with us being together."

"News flash," Phillip sneered. "Paige lied almost as well as I do."

"But why are you doing this now?" Guy asked. "She left you six months ago."

"Gee, Guy, I don't know." Phillip's voice sounded like the growl of a rottweiler. "Could it be because you were giving her my promotion?"

"That wasn't solely my decision," Guy whined. "I told you, the CEO had the deciding vote. He was concerned about the mistake you made with that multicar accident a few years ago, and Paige's record was spotless."

"Right," Phillip snorted. He grabbed a chair, spun it

around, and straddled it facing the VP. "I forgot. To err is human but to forgive goes against company policy."

"Well," Guy interjected, "he also thought Paige was more committed to the company."

Skye cringed. The VP should have left well enough alone and kept his mouth shut.

"Did you mention her 'dedication' consisted of her screwing the company's clients out of their rightful claims?" Phillip asked. "Or just screwing you?"

Guy flinched. "Actually, part of the issue they had with you was that the automobile division, your department, handed out too much money too quickly after last summer's tornadoes in Illinois."

Phillip swore, then said, "I suppose the CEO didn't care that Paige had a gambling problem?"

"He had no idea." Guy grimaced. "Hell! I only found out after she died. I can't believe she could keep it a secret with the rumor mill in this building." He looked up when Phillip leaped to his feet and loomed over him. "How long have you known about it?"

"I didn't figure it out until she left me and I started seeing the bills," Phillip snarled. "She always handled the finances so I had no idea she'd maxed out all our credit cards and drained our bank accounts." Suddenly, he whirled around, grabbed a glass paperweight from the reception desk, and smashed it on the marble tiles.

Both hostages recoiled at the sound of the shattering glass and Susie started frantically to scoot the chair she was bound to away from the two men.

"It was then that I realized why she was dragging her heels on signing the final papers for our divorce." Phillip paced up and down the reception area. "I needed to stop her before she pissed away the equity in the house and figured out how to cash in our investments without my signature."

"So you killed her?" Guy's voice broke.

"I didn't mean to." Phillip continued to pace. "The explosion should have just scared her. Maybe caused a few injuries. The slot machine that fell on her wasn't the one she usually played. Her favorite played some stupid German beer song when you hit the bonus."

Evidently noticing that Phillip was distracted, Guy's hands slowly lowered toward the thing around his neck and he tried to lift it off.

Skye swallowed a gasp when Phillip whirled around and pointed his gun at the VP. "Hands in the air."

"Paige and I were together for six months and she's dead." Guy's shoulders slumped in defeat and he asked, "Why kill me now?"

"As long as you do what I say, I won't." Phillip reached down and roughly jerked Guy to his feet. "I just need you to get me out of here, then I'll disarm the device around your neck and let you go."

"What do you need me for?" Guy stumbled as Phillip dragged him across the floor. Gesturing to a duffel bag by the door, he said, "You've got the money from the safe and I can give you my PIN to withdraw more from my bank accounts. Just tie me up and go."

Phillip hit Guy across the face with the gun, and Skye winced. She had to stop Phillip before he got away. She didn't believe for a second he would release Guy. Once he had no more use for him, the executive VP was a dead man. But how could she stop someone with a gun and a bomb?

Halting a few inches from the exit, Phillip snarled, "Don't try to act all innocent. I saw that cop from Scumble River pull into the parking lot." Phillip's voice rose. "Then I heard Angela spill her guts to the woman he has with him. The cop's here to arrest me and you're my ticket to freedom."

"You could just take my car and leave. I have the keys right here and it's gassed up." Guy started to put his hand in his pocket.

But Phillip grabbed him and said, "We're not taking your car. I persuaded Susie here"—he tipped his chin at the bound woman—"to call for the company helicopter. And while *her* IQ is about the same as room temperature, I'm guessing the pilot is a lot smarter and won't fall for the old line that I've always been attracted to him. Which means I need you to convince him to fly me away from here."

"I could write the pilot a note." Guy looked wildly around the room as if expecting a pad of paper and pen to materialize out of thin air.

Phillip stuffed his gun in his waistband, put the

duffel bag's strap across his chest, and took a step toward the door. "Don't make this harder than it has to be. If you behave, I won't use this to detonate that collar bomb you're wearing." He took what looked like a cell phone from his pocket and waggled it in front of Guy's face. "In a couple of hours, you'll be back in your big house, sipping a martini, with an exciting story to tell your grandkids."

Instead of answering, Guy sank to the floor and clutched a nearby column.

Skye jammed her phone in her purse. Phillip would soon pry Guy's grip from the pillar and she needed to be out of sight before they came through the door. She frantically searched the hallway for a place to hide. But before she could move, a palm covered her mouth. She immediately recognized Wally's touch and choked back her scream.

He took his hand from her mouth and put his finger to his lips. When she nodded, he tugged her until they were around a bend in the corridor.

With his mouth to her ear, Wally pointed to a bright-red exit sign and whispered, "The stairs." They slipped through the nearby door and Wally said in a hushed voice, "I heard Myler tell Glenn about the helicopter. If I beat them to the roof, I might be able to get the drop on Myler. You go to the lobby and call for backup."

"No. I'm not leaving you alone." Skye followed Wally as he hustled up the steps. "I'll phone for help once we're on the roof."

"I knew you'd say that," Wally grunted, not slowing down. "But I had to try."

"I suppose," Skye panted right behind him.

She had a brief flicker of guilt about putting herself in danger when she had children depending on her. But that didn't appear to stop Wally, and at the moment, providing backup for their daddy seemed like the right decision.

Luckily, the roof was an alfresco employee lounge and the door was unlocked. Wally and Skye eased through it, both relieved to see that Phillip and his hostage hadn't arrived yet. Spotting a large concrete planter holding a huge evergreen at the edge of the occupied helipad, Skye and Wally darted forward to hide behind it.

While Wally kept an eye on the elevator, Skye dialed 911 and, raising her voice above the noise of the whirling helicopter blades, described the situation. Although the dispatcher tried to keep her on the line, Skye disconnected.

Turning to Wally, she said, "How are we going to do this? What if Phillip detonates the explosive collar around Guy's neck?"

"I'm counting on the fact that Myler won't want to blow up himself," Wally explained. "So I need to take him while he's got Glenn nearby."

"Let's hope Phillip isn't suicidal." Skye crossed her fingers just as the elevator doors slid open.

Chills clawed their way up Skye's spine and she

said a quick prayer that all of them would leave the roof alive and unharmed.

Phillip and Guy strolled toward the helipad. Phillip held the detonator as if it were a cell phone and subtly nudged Guy forward. The pilot waved, but then must have noticed the odd device around Guy's neck. Seconds before the men reached the helicopter, the pilot slammed the open door and started to lift off.

Phillip howled, locked his arm around Guy's chest, and dragged him toward the edge of the roof. "Make that pilot come back right now or I'll kill you."

"How?" Guy asked. "Just tell me how and I will."

When Guy suddenly sagged against Phillip, Skye felt Wally tense. Before she could blink, he burst from behind the planter and tackled Phillip. Guy flung himself away from the pair, but Phillip kept his hold on the other man's wrist even as he and Wally went down in a thrashing pile of limbs.

Wally's larger bulk easily kept Phillip pinned to the ground and he ordered, "Drop the detonator and let go of your hostage."

Skye's heartbeat thudded in her ears so loudly she almost missed Phillip's reply.

His mirthless laugh was like a seal's bark and his voice rose incredulously. "Why should I?"

"Because if you set off that collar bomb, you die too." Wally's voice was steady.

"Like you care what happens to me." Phillip's

demeanor turned belligerent. "Either you let me go, or we all die."

"Turn Glenn loose and I'll let you up," Wally said, his tone deceptively calm. "I won't stop you from getting on that elevator."

Skye held her breath. Would Wally let Phillip leave with his hostage? She dug for the can of pepper spray she always kept in her purse. Her fingers had just curled over the cool metal when Phillip managed to grab his gun from his pocket.

"He's coming with me." Phillip continued to hold on to Guy's arm. "Think I don't know that there'll be cops waiting for me when the elevator opens in the lobby?"

"You're better off going to trial." Wally didn't budge. "Here, you end up dead. With a trial, you have a chance to get off."

Skye realized that Phillip had no intention of letting Guy go and had been squirming his way toward the edge of the roof, clearly hoping to buck Wally over the side. With Phillip's attention on Wally and Guy, Skye eased from behind the planter and sprinted toward the three men.

Surprise was on her side and just before Phillip reached the roof's edge, Skye reached her quarry. Aiming the pepper spray, Skye emptied the contents of the can directly into Phillip's shocked face.

He shrieked in pain, immediately releasing Guy to bring both hands to his burning eyes. Wally pried the gun and detonator from his fingers, gave them to Skye, and reached for his handcuffs.

As Wally secured a screaming Phillip, he winked at Skye and said, "Good thing we got you a new can of pepper spray after the tornado."

EPILOGUE

Cradle of Love

W ITH PAIGE MYLER'S MURDER SOLVED, SKYE and Wally had decided to spend Saturday at the Scumble River Recreation Club. They'd packed a picnic basket, bundled up the twins, and headed out early before the phone could start ringing. Although the weather was too cold to swim at the beach, there were plenty of scenic picnic spots and walking paths that wound around the various lakes.

It had been a busy four days for Wally, and Skye was glad that the case against Phillip Myler was finally in the hands of the Stanley County State's Attorney. Because Phillip had committed crimes in two different counties, there had been quite a bit of discussion as to how his arrest and charges would be handled.

Eventually, it was decided that because the assault and kidnapping of Guy Glenn and his administrative assistant that took place in Bloomer County was a continuation of Phillip's crime in Stanley County, Stanley would take primary jurisdiction on the matter. Phillip's attorney was now in the process of attempting to arrange a plea bargain that would include consolidating the charges and reducing kidnapping to unlawful imprisonment.

However, whatever was negotiated, Phillip Myler would be in prison for a good long time.

As Wally drove the Hummer down one of the rec club's dirt roads, Skye tried not to notice the black SUV following them, but when she couldn't keep it in any longer, she jerked her thumb over her shoulder and said, "Is that really necessary today?"

Wally blew out a resigned breath. "Probably not, but they're just doing their job."

Carson had talked Wally and Skye into allowing him to put a security team on the babies beyond just the nanny surveillance. He'd emphasized that his men were among the best in the country and that Skye wouldn't even be aware of their presence most of the time.

When Skye had expressed her doubts, Carson had pointed out that there had been a team on him since his arrival in Scumble River and that she'd never even known it.

"Why don't you have to have guards?" Skye asked Wally. "Isn't Carson's son just as likely to be abducted as his grandchildren?"

"I did until I graduated from college, then I said no more. It's also why I didn't try to persuade you to have security." Wally took her hand. "But the twins would be a much easier target than an adult."

"I guess." Skye squeezed his fingers, then let go and pointed to a place up ahead of them. "Let's park there. This path leads around Votta Lake and there's a picnic table about halfway."

Skye had worked summers as a lifeguard at the rec club both in high school and later when she first returned home to take the job of the district school psychologist. She had a good map of the club's property in her head and this was her favorite paved trail.

It took them several minutes to settle the twins in their stroller and pack what they needed for their picnic in the basket underneath, but at last they started down the path. They had only gone a few steps when Skye heard a familiar voice.

Fighting to keep a smile on her face—this was supposed to be family time—Skye turned and said, "Trixie, what a surprise."

Skye's friend, dressed in camo and hiking boots, emerged from the surrounding trees, her husband, Owen, a few feet behind her. Both carried bows and other hunting gear.

"We decided to try our luck this morning for a whitetail." Trixie squatted down and said hello to the twins, then jumped back up. "But we didn't get one." Her voice didn't sound all that disappointed.

"This area of the club is posted as no hunting," Skye said, hoping she didn't sound as appalled as she felt. The idea of arrows flying near the walking paths scared the dickens out of her.

"We know that." Owen scowled. "But Trixie wanted to take a shortcut back to the truck."

"Oh. Well, that's good." Skye smiled, then tried to edge away. "We should let you guys go. You're probably tired."

"Not at all." Trixie put down the equipment she was carrying. "Hey." She zeroed in on Wally. "What can you tell me about the Paige Myler case?"

"We've apprehended her husband, and he's been charged with the crime." Wally's answer was succinct, making it clear he didn't want to discuss the matter.

"How did he manage the whole thing?" Trixie wasn't one who took a hint.

"He waited until there wasn't anyone in the gaming lounge Sunday evening, then he planted the explosive," Skye answered for her husband.

Wally had related the details to Skye and told her which ones she could reveal.

"Then he just waited until Monday night to set it off?" Trixie bounced from foot to foot.

"Yep." Skye had to smile at her friend's enthusiasm. "He drove back to Normalton, then returned to Scumble River the next evening. He'd been watching Paige and knew she usually went to the bowling alley to gamble around eight, so he made sure he was there by seven."

"The area near Bunny Lanes is deserted that time of night, so he set up camp and waited until he saw

Paige go inside." Wally, evidently resigned to rehashing the case for Trixie, added, "We found a camping stool and a survival blanket in the back of his Range Rover, which is why our witness thought the guy loitering around the bowling alley was short, squat, and covered with silver scales. Why he had a blanket on when the weather was so warm, I have no idea."

"I know you guys heard him confess down in Normalton," Owen said. "But do you have any other proof?"

Flashing Trixie's husband a look of surprise since Owen wasn't normally interested in this kind of stuff, Skye answered, "Once the police knew where to look and were able to get warrants, there was quite a bit of evidence pointing to him."

Wally added, "Myler claimed he'd never been in Scumble River prior to his visit to the PD after his wife's murder, but it turns out that a very distinctive SUV that I saw parked in front of the florist the Monday afternoon before the blast was his. Also, he was trained to handle explosives when he served in the army."

Skye took over and said, "Plus, there were a ton of calls and texts made from his cell to Paige's phones. The messages were all yelling at her about the debt she'd put on their joint credit cards and threatening to kill her if she didn't return the money she'd drained from their bank accounts before she left him."

Apparently having had enough, Wally jumped in before anyone could ask another question and said,

"We need to get going. We want to reach the picnic area before the twins need to be fed."

"Okay." Trixie rolled her eyes. "I get it. You want to be alone with your wife and kids."

She hugged Skye and the men shook hands. Then the two couples exchanged goodbyes and went their own ways.

Once they were a good distance away, Skye said, "Phew. I love Trixie and Owen, but I didn't want to have to invite them to share our lunch."

Wally slipped his arm around Skye's waist and they pushed the stroller together. "I figured I'd better get us moving before you caved in and asked them to join us."

Taking their time and pausing for frequent pictures of the scenery and the babies, they reached the lake an hour later. Immediately after unpacking the cooler, they sat down to feed the twins, who had started to fuss.

Skye and Wally were just finishing changing the twins' diapers and settling them back in the stroller when a plump figure in a blue cape came marching briskly down the path toward them.

Wally swore and hurriedly stepped in front of Skye and the babies. He glanced at the security team who sat at another picnic table a few feet away and gestured that he had things under control.

Skye moved to her husband's side, tugged at his arm, and said, "Let's just get this over with."

Wally frowned down at her. "Get what over with?"

"I've been wanting to talk to her," Skye patted his bicep. "This is as good a time as any."

"I don't like that she keeps turning up wherever we are." Wally continued to frown.

"Me either." Skye squeezed his arm. "That's one of the matters that I want to clarify with her."

Millicent Rose bustled up to them and said breathlessly, "You two are quite a challenge for an old fairy godmother." She took a pink handkerchief from her pocket and wiped her brow. "It's a good thing my duties to you are nearly over, or I'd have to start going to a health club to build up my stamina."

Wally's stone-like expression didn't crack, but Skye chuckled and said, "I'm sorry we've been so difficult, but I'm glad your assignment is almost finished, too." She reached out and grasped Millicent's hand in both of hers. "But most importantly, I want to thank you for helping get CJ and Eva to safety at the party when Aiden O'Twomey started shooting. If there's anything I can do for you in return, just let me know."

"Thank you, my dear." Millicent beamed. "But my assignment to you was in payment for a good deed you already performed."

"Can we stop all this horse hockey now?" Wally's lip curled. "If your job is done and we don't owe you anything, why are you here?"

"Oh, you are the impatient one." Millicent's laugh sounded like a tinkling bell. "But I still have one more task to complete in regard to your family."

"Look, whatever your con is, I'm not falling for it." Wally crossed his arms. "I'm grateful you assisted in keeping my children safe, but that was simply a matter of right time, right place."

"I know you believe that." Millicent's bright-blue eyes sparkled. "Which is why I was assigned to Skye and not you."

Skye released Millicent's hand and laid her palm on Wally's cheek. "If you're right and Miss Rose is here for some nefarious purpose, we have more than adequate protection, so please let me handle this."

"Fine. But all the lights don't shine in her marquee." Wally stepped back, stared at Millicent, and warned, "I'm watching you."

"Just remember that I have a wand and I'm not afraid to wave it." Millicent's gaze hardened. "You wouldn't like life as a donkey."

Wally mumbled something, but Skye quickly moved to block Millicent's view of Wally. She didn't believe for a minute that the woman would turn him into a mule, but why take chances?

Smiling, Skye waved Millicent to take a seat at the picnic table and offered her a bottle of Dasani. As the chubby, little woman drank, Skye lined up her questions.

When Millicent finished with the water, she tilted her head and said, "Go ahead. I'll answer anything that I can."

"From what I understand, someone requested that

you come to Scumble River and protect Eva and CJ," Skye started, and when Millicent nodded, she continued, "Who asked you to do it?"

"Alma Griggs."

Wally cursed, but Skye ignored him and asked, "You knew Mrs. Griggs? How?"

"Present tense." Millicent smiled. "When Alma's house was destroyed in the tornado, she finally felt as if she could cross over from this mortal coil to the next plane of existence. But she was worried about leaving you before you had the baby, so she sent me."

Skye could hear Wally mumbling about charlatans but concentrated on Millicent. "When you pop up and seem to know things you shouldn't, is Mrs. Griggs guiding you or is it some kind of magic power you have?"

"I don't need any kind of enchantment to find you or know what's going on." Millicent chuckled. "All I have to do is tune into the grapevine. Scumble River has one of the best I've ever seen."

"Did Mrs. Griggs know that the bowling alley would be blown up and O'Twomey would crash the baby shower?" Skye asked.

"No." Millicent sobered. "She just wanted to be sure you and the twins were okay, but when I got here, I sensed the evil swirling around," Millicent tsked. "So many con artists and people trying to take advantage of folks who were already devastated by the tornado. I figured that I'd do what I could to help until your babies were baptized and thus safe."

"So you're leaving now?" Wally's tone was cautious.

"I have one last thing to do for Alma, and then I'll be moving on to my next assignment."

"What do you have to do?" Skye asked.

"These are for CJ and Eva." Millicent fished in the pocket of her cape and came out with two tiny silver medals, which she gave to Skye. "Once they are old enough not to choke on them, they should always wear these. If they're ever in trouble, I'll know and come right away."

"Thank you." Skye examined the discs. One was engraved *godson* and the other *goddaughter*. "Is there anything I can do for you in return?"

"I'd like you to give me your bracelet." Millicent gestured to the bangle on Skye's wrist. "It has a lot of power for good and I can use it."

Skye hesitated. She had gotten the bracelet from her sorority mom during pledging and it meant a lot to her. But something inside of her knew it was time to pass it on. Sliding it over her hand, she laid it in Millicent's palm.

The woman nodded her thanks and turned to leave.

Before Millicent disappeared around the curve of the path, Skye called out, "Tell Mrs. Griggs thank you and we're sorry we couldn't restore her house."

"She understands." Millicent's soft voice floated behind her.

Once she was gone, Wally joined Skye on the

bench and said, "You don't believe all that hooey, do you?"

"I believe there are things in this world we don't comprehend." Skye laid her head on his shoulder. "And since we live in a country where we can be anything we want to be, I choose to be kind."

ACKNOWLEDGMENTS

Thanks to Debbie Purdue for the great line about the Dooziers.